I0583014

UNDER
FALSE
PRETENCES

BILL (GIRLIE) SMITH

Laurence Joseph Murphy

Copyright 2020 Laurence Joseph Murphy

All rights reserved.
This book cannot be reproduced, scanned or distributed in any
printed or electronic form without written permission from the author,
Laurence Joseph Murphy at;-
Laurencemurphy05@gmail.com
or within the sharing guidelines of a Public Library or
Bookseller. Reviewers may quote excerpts in a review.
Do not participate or encourage piracy of copyrighted material
in violation of the author's rights. Purchase only authorised editions.

ISBN 978-0-9923046-5-2

Under False Pretences; Bill (Girlie) Smith
is also available as an Ebook.

Other titles by Laurence Joseph Murphy

Annie Bags; The Lady in Rags
ISBN 978-0-9923046-1-4

Ghost Warrior; Jimmy Morrill
ISBN 978-0-9923046-2-1

The Sound of Liberty
ISBN 978-0-9923046-4-5

Published by
THUNDERBOLT PUBLISHING

Dedication
This book is dedicated to the memory of

Dominic Palmer
(1968 – 2018)

A beautiful man may be an imperfect figure to behold, with a multitude
of physical challenges, but true beauty doesn't always manifest itself on
the outside, sometimes it radiates from deep within, and only makes its
presence known by the gentle tranquillity and calmness of his smile, the
concern for others evident in the troubled gaze that momentarily clouds
the clearness of his eyes, the window to his beautiful soul.
Dominic was such a man.

Contents

Introduction

This book is based on the true-life story of an actual person and many of the events described took place. Some fictional characters have been introduced to provide substance to the narrative as it may have unfolded, but several of these characters have also been created by the author from historical information about real-life individuals who are thought to have played a role and who, subsequently had a major effect on the life of Bill Smith.

The non-fictional characters whose names are mentioned throughout the narrative have been personified, as far as possible, as history has recorded them and their exploits are factual and chronologically correct.

All of the newspaper articles mentioned here are genuine and can be found at *trove.nla.gov.au* in digitised format.

Readers will notice that I have consistently used pounds, shillings and pence in this narrative *(£3/12s/6d)* instead of dollars and cents *($5.50)* and I have also used miles instead of kilometres. Australia changed over to decimal currency in 1966 and most of Bill Smith's story takes place before that date, so I hope I haven't confused anyone, particularly those under the age of fifty. As a guide, there are twelve pence in one shilling and twenty shillings in one pound *(£1)* and one pound is equivalent to two dollars *($2)*. Ten miles is equal to about sixteen kilometres.

The maps provided in the following pages are not comprehensive and do not accurately depict all of the cities and towns in Australia. They are only meant to give readers who are unfamiliar with the Australian Outback an awareness of where the places mentioned in this book are in relation to each other and to the State Capital Cities of Australia.

Foreword by Mary Jane McConnell R.N. (retired)

The City of Cairns, a tropical tourist destination on Australia's north-eastern seaboard looking out over the Coral Sea is more than a thousand miles (sixteen hundred kilometres) north of Brisbane, the capital of Queensland. When my mother, Martha McConnell, was told by the midwife at the Cairns District Hospital in the mid-1940s that she'd just delivered a healthy baby girl, Cairns was a far cry from the modern city of over a hundred and forty thousand people that it is now. It was a working town in that post-war period, with many of its twenty-five thousand involved in the cane growing industry, or the associated trades of harvesting and processing the raw sugar that was then sent from the Port of Cairns to refineries in the south.

The influence of the Great Depression that began with the crash of New York's Wall Street in 1929 was still being felt in North Queensland up until those 1940s. During the Pacific phase of the Second World War, the United States had stationed troops throughout the North Queensland region as a strategic base to supply the Pacific fleet, but public hysteria over the fall of Singapore triggered a mass evacuation of residents to the south. Many homes in Cairns were sold cheaply, and a year later the local population had been reduced to about 15,000 optimistic individuals, around one-tenth of today's tally. Despite the end of the conflict in 1945, many who left never returned, but they were replaced by others who came to the north for various reasons known only to them and perhaps any families they left behind in the southern States. People of all descriptions still came from who-knows-where, soaked up the warmth, lived rough for a while in a makeshift camp in the showgrounds or the surrounding bush, and then moved on. Few questions were asked; a man's business was his alone; if he chose to keep his own company, then so be it, and if he didn't feel like crying on another's shoulder, well then, he was left to carry the burden of his troubles on his own. It was a trend that continued into the 1960s and beyond, and the Hippie movement brought with it a new wave of escapees from southern disappointments and perhaps from reality, - but that's another story that I needn't go into here.

I was duly named Mary Jane McConnell and from the very beginning, I was destined to return to the Cairns Hospital, for nursing and midwifery was a vocation that was deeply entrenched in my family history, and I followed the convention and began my nursing training after I left school. Later, after graduating as a Registered Nurse, I found a placement in a small hospital in the sugar-growing town of Tully and there I gained valuable experience in the particular needs of the people who lived and worked the sugar plantations in the rural districts surrounding the town and whom I held to be some of the greatest assets of our country.

It was an area of nursing that I discovered I loved; apart from caring for the residential patients in the hospital itself I was often called upon to accompany a doctor on a visit to some out of the way station homestead to tend to an elderly person or a sick child who couldn't be moved easily, and the feeling of fulfilment that I received from seeing the absolute relief exhibited in the faces of the people who'd called for help was worth the long and often rough drive to reach them.

I was happy in Tully, as I said, but in 1975, at the ripe old age of thirty, I saw an advertisement for the position of Community Nurse at the hospital in Herberton, a town of just under a thousand people situated almost at the highest elevation of North Queensland's Atherton Tablelands. Simply known as *The Tablelands* by the residents, this is a high plateau with an invigorating climate located atop the mountains of the Great Dividing Range about forty miles inland from Cairns. It is a popular weekend drive away from the heat of the tropical coast and Herberton sits on its south-western edge where it tapers off gradually to the dry western plains of Cape York Peninsula.

I was still single at that stage of my life, - footloose and free, - as they say, so with nothing to hold me back I decided that the change would be a good career move for me. The Herberton Hospital, I'd learned, was a busy little place with general and maternity wards as well as aged care and palliative care facilities, and although about ten years after my arrival the general and maternity sections were moved to the major health hub at the Atherton District Memorial Hospital, at that time it serviced not only the town but also a major part of the surrounding district. I was particularly excited by the primary clause in the position description that stated the successful applicant would be required to undertake regular check-up visits to the many elderly residents of the small settlements in the surrounding district, including the rural communities of Irvinebank, Wondecla, and Innot Hot Springs.

I'd never heard of *any* of those communities and, upon receiving my letter of acceptance from the hospital, I made inquiries with several old-time mining acquaintances of my father who'd worked in the area. I soon confirmed, as I had suspected, that the first two had been productive and prosperous tin mining towns in the late nineteenth and early twentieth century. Most of the tin had already been mined, but a

2

few diehard miners persisted, scratching a living from the earth just as their fathers and grandfathers had done before them.

It wasn't until after I'd commenced my new role that I was able to find out anything about Innot Hot Springs, however, and it turned out to be the most interesting of all of my health check venues for several reasons. The Herbert River, from which the town derives its name, meanders in a generally southern course from its source near Herberton through Millstream and Gunnawarra, and Nettle Creek joins it near its confluence with the Wild River. A geological fault has, for countless millennia, released hot gases and water from deep below the surface creating three hot mineral springs in Nettle Creek and the community of Innot Hot Springs was established around the hot springs in the 1870s.

The other reason for my interest in the community of Innot Hot Springs had nothing to do with geology, however, for it was where I first heard of the pocket-sized, inconspicuous individual whose gentle and unassuming nature would eventually earn him a place close to my heart. His name was Bill Smith. Bill's name had come up several times in exchanges with other residents of Innot Hot Springs who attended my clinic at the community hall and those well-meaning souls expressed their neighbourly concerns about the old recluse who, they said, lived alone in a small ramshackle hut on the banks of Nettle Creek. Their remarks piqued my interest in finding out more about him and, in my early enthusiasm in trying to support *all* of my potential outpatients in the district, I decided that if this enigmatic person wouldn't or couldn't come to my clinic, I would take matters into my own hands and visit him instead, to satisfy myself and his neighbours about the state of his health.

I'd driven along the rutted dirt track that followed Nettle creek to the southernmost fringe of the community and pulled up outside the gate that led to the hut where I'd been told the hermit lived. The word *ramshackle* was indeed an apt description for Bill's simple hut, I decided as soon as I saw it, and its outward appearance somewhat justified the community's concerns for his well-being. It was nothing more than a one-roomed *'humpy'* built of bush-timber and flattened kerosene tins with a steeply-angled, rusting, corrugated iron roof. A small veranda was attached to the front of the building, its roof another rusting iron awning that was held up by two precariously leaning bush-timber posts, and it had holes in it so big a careless possum could have fallen through any one of them. Two rickety-looking wooden chairs had been strategically placed against the wall of the building so that they afforded the best shade from the afternoon sun that streamed through the gaps, - and an old man sat slumped over on one of them clutching a pewter mug in his gnarled hands.

When I first laid eyes on him the only evidence of Bill's ongoing participation in the daily grind of life was the pair of dark eyes that followed me as I pushed open the rusty gate and walked the half-a-dozen steps to the edge of the veranda; they reminded me so much of those in one of the disconcerting portraits people sometimes hang on their lounge-room wall at home. Unnerving though Bill had seemed to begin with though, I soon found out that the diminutive, unassuming man was the most interesting outpatient that I had visited by far, and certainly much more so than I could ever have imagined. Bill and I soon developed a close bond despite the huge disparity in our ages and circumstances, and although I only knew him for a short time, I am proud to reflect now, that I was perhaps one of the very few trusted confidantes that Bill had ever had in his whole life up until then.

I'd learned that he'd been living on his own, with a couple of old horses for company, at that tiny rural community of Innot Hot Springs about thirty-five miles by road to the south-west of Herberton for about fifteen years. It was on my second visit the following week that we had our first real conversation.

"Got time for a cuppa, Sister Mary," he said after he'd answered my standard questions about his general health. He always called me 'Sister Mary' even though I'd told him 'Mary' would be quite adequate as Sister Mary made me sound like a nun, which I certainly wasn't. That was his way, though, stubborn to a fault in his persistence in acknowledging a person's station in life, and steeped in the respect for authority that was characteristic of the attitude of the people of his generation.

"Yes Bill," I said. "How can I refuse; you make such a good cup of tea?" I'd noticed he'd already had the billy can on its hook over the wood-fired stove bubbling away in readiness for my arrival. I glanced over at him as I spoke and the sad smile and the pleading look in his old eyes almost broke my heart, for I became aware at once that Bill didn't just want to share a cup of tea with me; he wanted someone to talk to; - no, it was more than *want*, - he desperately *needed* someone to talk to. I looked at my watch. "I've got an hour to spare before I have to head back to Herberton," I said gently.

That, as I said, was the first of our conversations. Bill mainly talked, and I mainly listened, and we drank lots of tea. We became absorbed in the tales of the Australian Bush and although Bill's small bare veranda couldn't have been further removed from the calming effect of the yellow glow from a campfire, perhaps on the bank of a

4

billabong or out on the windswept plains of the Channel Country. It didn't matter to either of us, for Bill crouched over his rickety chair as if he was sitting on a log, staring at some imaginary campfire with his teacup clutched in both hands as he spoke of those times long ago that were still fresh in his mind, and I faced him from my perch on the other generally unoccupied visitor's chair like the young awestruck stockman that he must have once been.

I had always been a good listener anyway and I learned so many little facts about events that I'd taken for granted or hadn't even heard of throughout my life; the appalling statistics of the First World War and its aftermath; the Great Depression; the Shearer's strikes, and much more, but it was Bill's own story that affected me the most. The more he spoke the more it became obvious to me that Bill had kept the details of his life's history under wraps for most of his years and perhaps now felt that he'd almost left it too late to relate what *he* wanted people eventually to know and think about him; you will note that I said *eventually,* and that is for very good reason, as it will become evident later in this chronicle.

Bill knew it was almost time for him to ride off into the never-never as old stockmen do. "I have a lot to tell you before I can rest in complete peace, you know, - and maybe there's not enough time left for me to say it in," he said to me more than once, so I knew that the circumstances surrounding his life's story were continually playing on his mind and it was important to him to set the record straight. You see, Bill knew, better than any doctor or nurse that the time had almost come when he would no longer be able to keep the secret he'd guarded so fastidiously from *most* people throughout his life. He was more relieved than regretful that the truth *must* come out, I believe, and content that he wouldn't have to live under false pretences any longer, but he was also afraid that he'd open up his heart to someone who'd listen to him and then perhaps portray him to the world as a fraudster, - or something worse. Past encounters had given him cause to believe that something along those lines could very well happen to him, and he didn't want to earn a dubious place in history as someone who'd duped people into believing he was something he wasn't for personal gain or notoriety.

Bill wanted to talk to someone whom he could *confide* in; someone who would respect his right to be allowed to die with dignity and without any *'hullaballoo'* in the newspapers, as he said more than once. He chose that 'someone' well, or perhaps he just got lucky - for I turned out to be everything he'd hoped for as a confidante.

* * * *

It was around the same time that I squawked my way into the light of day, and the end of the Second World War, (won't we ever learn) that Bill Smith slid unobtrusively into Cairns. He arrived with several packhorses, a pony that he rode and very little else. Bill fitted the category of the post-depression, and now post-war, drifter perfectly. Nobody knew or cared where he came from. He was a slight, but tough-looking little individual with a thin, sun-bronzed, clean-shaven face that peeped out at the world from underneath a much weathered wide-brimmed felt hat. Wisps of fine, salt-and-pepper, grey hair fell about his furrowed brow whenever he removed it, which wasn't often, and his finely sloped shoulders and large calloused hands spoke silently of many years of hard physical toil. His willingness to undertake any type of labouring work became evident when, shortly after his arrival, he took a job at the Cairns Brewery, lifting and stacking empty beer barrels for washing and refilling, for it was a strenuous job in the usually hot and humid conditions that Cairns sweltered through for a good nine months of the year.

Most of the brewery workers looked forward to Friday afternoon, for that was when the men were allowed to finish early and enjoy the company of their workmates as well as the keg of beer that was supplied by the brewery management for the occasion. It was a judicious move by those in charge because it was the cheapest and most obvious means of keeping the morale high amongst their loyal workforce, but Bill was never amongst the happy crowd, either gathered around the keg, or sitting at the wooden trestle tables that had been laden with platters of cheese and biscuits. He seemed to shun such close contact with people and although he got on good-naturedly with his fellow workers and had gained their respect and admiration for his significant contribution to the hard work put in on weekdays, considering his fineness of build, they mostly accepted that he just didn't like beer and was an introvert who couldn't be bothered hanging around to participate in the start of the weekend's revelries. His absence generally went unnoticed after a while and wasn't altogether lamented amongst those who did happen to remark on it from time to time. *'Bill doesn't drink; pity about that; too bad for him; more beer for us,'* was the sentiment most commonly expressed. On the other days, straight after the finishing bell was rung, Bill went home to his small rented cottage where he lived alone, or if a cargo ship was docked at the Cairns wharf he headed down there where he knew he was sure to get casual work as a labourer loading or unloading cargo.

Today, the Horse Racing fraternity in country districts across Australia is invariably made up of tight-knit little communities that are difficult to infiltrate by outsiders, and the Far North Queensland racing community, centred on Cairns, but including racetracks in Mareeba, Mount Garnet, Tolga, Innisfail, and Herberton, was even more so in the years after the close of the Second World War. Families grew up alongside each other in compact high-set houses, many with back yards completely given over to roughly built stables and within a horse-leading stroll to the racetrack, and the children grew up and often married into other neighbouring racing clans, forever combining the business of training and racing horses with the familial duties required of such unions. There were the usual squabbles that most extended families have from time to time and these sometimes degenerated into physical altercations, but police intervention was rarely required as the Racing Stewards were more often than not on hand with AR 228 of the Australian Rules of Racing that pertained to *'Conduct detrimental to the interests of Racing',* to quickly sort things out.

The punters came to the races, had a good day or a bad day and then left the course and went home, either in high spirits or with feet dragging along the ground in disillusionment, at least until the next meeting when the whole process started again, but when the dust had settled after the last race had been run and won, the trainers, jockeys, and track workers came together in the bar to discuss the success or otherwise of the day's proceedings, while the stable hands washed and groomed the racehorses in their care.

It was into the outer perimeter of this exclusive setting that Bill gradually insinuated his small presence and began to earn a bit of money from riding trackwork and shoeing horses. He was light-framed, fighting fit, and the trainers soon found he could ride to instructions. If he was told to first canter four furlongs (half a mile) and then gallop his mount at even pace for eight, then that's what the trainer, anxiously timing the exercise with a stopwatch from the stands, got, - to the very second. The main aspect of his overall reliability that pleased and endeared him to the usually exasperated horse trainers, though, was that he turned up *regularly* each morning before dawn, ready to work more than a dozen horses, which was something the more accomplished jockeys felt no inclination to do, since they knew they'd be sure to get the rides on the weekend race-day anyway. Despite his punctuality and general ability however, nobody thought it necessary to get close enough to Bill to get to know him well. After trackwork, he'd give a brief account of his opinion about the horse's work and general fitness that morning, collect his track-work riding fee and then disappear from the course. I think in hindsight, that it was probably this same 'hard to pin down' aspect of Bill's character that was instrumental in his initial acceptance by the racing fraternity, for he showed no interest in anyone else's business and he expected, and received, the same behaviour in return.

Oh, of course, there was idle chatter and speculation about him amongst those who worked around the stables as there was about anyone with comparable eccentric habits, and questions were asked. *'Was he a criminal running from the law, or a man with a dark sordid past whose enemies would eventually hunt him down and he would disappear as suddenly as he'd arrived?'* Bill steadfastly refused to discuss his past life with anyone, - and the consensus amongst the trainers was that he was entitled to his privacy; it didn't matter what *might* happen to him or where he might go the day after tomorrow or the next day after that; he was here today and he'd been booked to ride tomorrow; he was reliable; he could ride, - and the horses needed to be worked.

Rumours began to circulate that he was a past champion jockey who'd won several big races down south in Victoria and New South Wales in the first couple of decades of the twentieth century, but that something had gone wrong in his private life and he'd been forced to quit the high-flying (or should I say high-riding) world of celebrity jockeys for an uncomplicated life in quieter pastures. Bill didn't start the rumours, but he didn't deny them either, and the racecourse Stewards, keen to promote the ailing industry in the wake of the economic downturn after the war, eventually persuaded him to take out a licence to ride, as well as to train racehorses in his own right.

Something *had* gone wrong in Bill Smith, the famous jockey's life, but it was the wrong Bill Smith. It was established later, that a jockey known as William H. Smith *did* ride with great success in the early 1900s, winning two Sydney Cups, two Epsom Handicap's, a Caulfield Cup, VRC Oaks, Metropolitan Handicap, VRC St Leger and AJC Champion Stakes, but *that* Bill Smith had been killed in a race fall at Rosehill during the running of the Rosehill Cup on March 21, 1914.

The eventual disclosure of that unfortunate incident had little effect on Bill's reputation, for by then he'd already established himself as a good, if not exceptional, jockey, and he was still offered plenty of rides on the country tracks around the north despite being considered a bit of a *'different'* character. The other jockeys and trainers had given him the nickname, *'Girlie'* because of, in part, his unusually high pitched voice and his refusal to change into his racing colours in the jockeys' room at whatever racecourse he was riding at. Bill invariably arrived at the course with the colours already on under his normal street clothes and never showered or changed alongside the other jockeys, always heading back to the hotel he was staying at for the night to bathe in private. The racecourse facilities in the small towns he rode at were generally sparse and some were no more than lean-to tin sheds anyway, so his penchant for a good hot tub at the end of a big book of rides was nothing out of the ordinary, but the Cannon Park track at Cairns was a different matter altogether. The facilities there were comfortable, if not appealing, and his absence from the jockey's room was noticed in a way that led to the most persistent speculation about him, both during and after his riding career had finished. *'He's a woman in disguise,'* some jeered, but the old-timers knew differently. *'He can't be,'* they said. *'Look at his physique, it's a man's, - and, in any case, women haven't got the stamina or the strength to control a thousand-pound horse under race conditions anyway.'*

The jockeys he'd beaten on the track agreed, for many of them had seen him from behind. *'I'd always be able to tell a woman from a man on a racehorse if one was in front of me, - if they ever decided to let them ride against men,'* one is reported to have said. *'Women have bigger bums and broader hips you see...'* He then continued his shrewd, if not slightly offensive observation with a derisive laugh, *'...not that I'm ever likely to see one in front of me in a race because none of them would ever be able to handle a racehorse as well as any man.'*

There were other instances of Bill's perceived peculiarities that occurred over the years too that provoked suspicions about his gender and garnered much debate amongst those who witnessed them. One day Bill was thrown from his mount during a race and another jockey who'd come off his horse in the same incident but hadn't been injured went to his aid. Bill lay on his back on the track badly winded and the other jockey proceeded to open the buttons on his racing silks to make sure his breathing wasn't restricted. Bill jumped to his feet and pushed him away saying "No need for that; I'm fine," and began to walk unsteadily back towards the jockey's room. He refused to be examined, but the racecourse doctor stood him down for the rest of the meeting as a precaution.

My father never owned a racehorse. He liked a punt, but it was usually no more than a couple of shillings in any single bet. He also had a part-time job as a bookmaker's clerk and when I mentioned Bill's name to him he said he remembered him well, but like everyone else, knew little about him. *'He was different all right; nobody knew where he came from or where he went after he'd ended his racing career. He just disappeared one day...,'* he told me. *'...just picked up his gear and left town as far as anyone knew. It used to happen all the time in those days. Jockeys got too heavy or got tired of all the hard work and suffering they had to go through to stay at a riding weight for little reward at the end of the day. It was all right for some of the glamour riders in the capital cities, but it was only a meagre living in the bush. Most of the trainers stayed in the game only because they either grew up with it in their blood or just loved working with horses, - or maybe they didn't have any skills at doing anything else and hated it, but felt trapped in a never-ending cycle of early morning rises.'* There was no doubting that Bill wasn't one of those sad cases. He loved horses, as I've already pointed out, and when he left the industry it wasn't quite like my father and others had imagined, as I found out. Bill had somehow managed to obtain a government pension, but in his usual enigmatic and private manner he'd said nothing about it to anyone who he felt didn't need to know, - and that was just about everyone, - except perhaps the racing authorities. He just slipped away from trackwork one day and didn't come back the next, and for many trainers that following morning his sudden departure would have been an inconvenience as they squabbled to get hold of a substitute rider, but simply put down as another everyday occurrence.

It was sometime in the early 1960s that Bill handed in both his trainer's and his jockey's licences and moved to Innot Hot Springs. The ageing and sick ex-racehorses that he took in were cared for, simply for the sheer love of the poor animals. They were his family, as I learned in time through our conversations, - the only family he'd ever needed. The horses didn't judge him as anything other than a friend and companion, and I'm certain they returned the love and affection he had for them many times over.

Four decades have passed since my conversations with Bill at his hut at Innot Hot Springs and I can say that I've enjoyed a full and very happy existence since then. I married a wonderful man and we had three active children who kept me constantly on the run, allowing little time to fulfil my promise to Bill to set the record straight for him. That is my only excuse as to why I have remained silent until now and I hope you will find it in your heart to understand.

My dear husband has passed on, my children have grown up and moved away and I find that I have time on my hands now to ponder the twists and turns of my life and the influences that various people have had on me during its ebb and flow. Bill was certainly one of those people, possibly the foremost one, for *his* life was not of the conventional kind. I think it's appropriate now to reveal to the world what he told me about himself and also what I have gleaned from other sources that he posthumously directed me to, and in so doing, help the world to appreciate the person that Bill Smith was and understand the factors that lay behind his choice to live such a solitary existence on the outer edge of society.

One more thing I'd like to remind you of before I launch into my story of Bill's life is that McConnell was my maiden name and I have used it here to maintain some confidentiality of my current situation, mainly for my children's sake. I hope you will appreciate my reasons for doing that and come to understand that it's not my desire to become someone who may be questioned, scrutinised and perhaps resented for keeping my familiarity with Bill's life undisclosed for such a long time.

I will tell you the story as Bill told it to me. It was not conveyed in a strictly chronological manner, because I believe Bill wanted to *prepare* me well for what he intended to relate to me at a later point in our discussions and I want to prepare you, the reader just as thoroughly; so let me return to the tale that Bill told me as he laid bare his life to a virtual stranger, but one that he trusted, for to me, - that dependable stranger, - his life *was* special and I believe you will find it worthy of the retelling in these pages in Bill's own words.

Mary Jane McConnell R.N. (retired)

1 Bendigo to Barringun

I was working on a dairy farm on the Loddon River north of Bendigo in Victoria when the *'Great War'*, as a Canadian journalist had aptly labelled it, ended, but the tag *'Great'* stuck in people's minds because nobody expected anything as severe to ever happen again. You see, Sister Mary, it had been four years of bloody mayhem that resulted in the deaths of over fifty million poor souls and people around the world heaved a collective sigh of relief when peace reigned again. The carnage wasn't over though, as the world soon found out, for the soldiers who'd survived the fighting on the battlefields of Europe brought back to their homes an insidious new enemy that crept up on the still euphoric population and struck down and killed like no human enemy ever could.

It was in the spring of 1918 when I first read about it; a brief column in the middle of the *'Bendigo Advertiser.'* The newspaper reported that a moderately mild strain of influenza that caused the usual chills and fever had been first detected in Spain, so naturally it had been given the name *Spanish Flu'*, but it had soon gained a foothold in countries like Italy, Britain and France. Younger people affected by it usually recovered after a few days so there was little to worry about in Australia, or so they said, and although there were a few deaths reported, most of those were elderly people who had an existing ailment of some kind that made them prone to having a general weakness in their bodies. By Jove, we'd been led up the garden path alright, for a second, more virulent strain of the virus began to play havoc with the health of the younger men and women too, and by the middle of 1919, it was estimated that more people worldwide had died of the flu' than the fifty million who'd died fighting in the war.

I'd just turned nineteen then, and although I hadn't grown much in height since I was about fourteen, I'd become quite strong with the work I'd been doing, which is something I'll tell you about later. I'd already decided by then to leave the cold and rain of Victoria's winter and head north to warmer climes, but that wasn't my only reason for leaving; no, it was much more complicated than that.

The owner of the dairy farm, my employer, Edward Naughton, had warned me not to go anywhere near any of the big cities to find work because of the dreaded killer flu. "As I've told you, young Bill," he said, "my family has been involved in the dairy industry in this district for the last sixty years and I want you to know that you're one of the best and most conscientious workers we've ever had here. I'm sorry you're leaving, and you're welcome back here anytime lad."

I was more pleased with that little compliment than I would have been if he'd presented me with a gold-plated cigarette case, because I was proud of the fact that I was the type of person who'd always put in a one hundred per cent effort for any boss who'd pay me a fair wage, and Mister Naughton's remark showed that he was happy enough he'd got his worth out of me. He went on to warn me, though, "…but you may only return if you promise me you won't go near the big cities until this scourge is finally over. It's highly contagious and I don't want it brought back here to infect the rest of *our* family."

I felt an odd mix of elation and discomfort with his use of the words, *'our family'*, elated because those inclusive words and his worried facial expression confirmed that he regarded me as someone akin to the prodigal son I'd read about in the Bible and who would return one day to resume my rightful place in *our* household. That was part of the complication, you see, and what caused me the discomfort I felt for misleading them, for Edward Naughton and his wife Eleanor had been good to me over the more than two years that I'd been working for them, - much too good in fact, - and I'd become so comfortable there in their company that I'd *almost* decided to tell them *everything* about my past life. They didn't employ many workers at any time from outside their extended family and I'd been permitted to take my meals with them in the fine dining room on their homestead at Murphy's Creek, Tarnagulla. I'd even been allowed to participate in the daily home school lessons the Naughton children received from old Mr Hegarty, the retired schoolmaster from Bendigo.

I was mulling over all the good times I'd had with this wonderful family and wondering if I'd been too hasty and should have taken the other course of action that I'd contemplated as Mister Naughton spoke, and in my uncertainty about what lay ahead for me, I didn't dwell too deeply on his next words, for he said, "If, on the other hand, you decide to get into something like droving or working as a stockman on any of the big cattle stations in New South Wales or Queensland, just show the boss man this letter of recommendation and say you've been endorsed by William Naughton's brother. Everyone will know who my brother is, I can assure you." He handed me an envelope with the Naughton family crest stamped on the back.

I thanked him and stowed it in my dry kit with the other letters and documents I'd acquired, but privately I shrugged off the suggestion as a highly fanciful chance of coming to anything, because I figured, in my still immature and confused mind, that the issuing of a letter of reference by a dairy farmer in rural Victoria, wouldn't be of much use to me or hold much of an influence in my future pursuit of work

14

hundreds of miles away in northern New South Wales or Queensland, even if it *was* a family who'd built up the best dairy farms and cheese making businesses in Victoria over the previous half a century.

As well as his achievements in the dairy industry Edward Naughton was well known and respected as a horse racing enthusiast in rural Victoria and one of my responsibilities when I first entered his service had been to look after the family's sporty, two-wheeled horse carriage and the four buggy horses that had been used mainly to convey us all to Sunday church services. The horses were all finely bred mares and had been used in pairs on alternate Sundays, but Mister Naughton had been forced to abandon that arrangement when one of the mares was found to be in foal. He wasn't often grumpy, but he certainly was that day. "I'm sure it's that rotten little stallion in the neighbour's yard that's got through the fence and got to my mare," he told me when the vet confirmed the news. "I don't know how he even got up to her. He's so tiny." His suspicions were proved to be correct though when the mare produced a foal the next year that was the image of his little next-door sire.

Tending to the Naughton's horses had been the most satisfying part of my day. Each of them seemed to have a natural fondness for me and took turns nuzzling up to me as I groomed and fed them and cleaned out the stable, but the foal had taken to me even more than any of the others and followed me about wherever I went, neighing wretchedly when I'd finished my chores and closed the gate to the yard. I thought he was the most beautiful little horse I'd ever seen.

Mister Naughton soon noticed my natural affinity with his horses and he began to take me with him when he attended the horse trials in Bendigo. I loved the atmosphere and excitement at the track as the horses galloped around and he arranged with one of his trainers to let me get on a horse and walk it in the yard enclosure. I must have impressed the trainer with my seat and poise on the horse because he asked me if I wanted to come back and learn a bit more about riding. Of course, I jumped at the chance and with Mister Naughton's permission, I began a phase of my life that became so much a part of me that it stayed with me until I retired from the saddle fifty years later. I started riding trackwork and learned how to time a workout; count the post rails as you pass them; a one, a two, a three and so on. I soon learned how to ride to the trainer's instructions. There are different speeds at which a horse moves in training, you see. A 'jog' is the slowest. As speed increases into the 'gallop', the horse runs at 16 to 18 seconds each furlong. If I was told to go even time it meant my horse had to go half a mile in a minute, - there are eight furlongs to a mile so that's 15 seconds to the furlong. I found it pretty easy to do and the trainers were happy; so was Mister Naughton, because the owners had to pay the trackwork rider's fee every morning and of course I did it as part of my job.

It didn't always go to plan though. One morning I remember getting on a particularly fractious two-year-old colt that we'd brought to the track to get him used to working along with other horses. My colt broke away from the handler as soon as we got through the gate onto the course and began to rear and buck with me holding on for dear life. I'd dropped the reins and got one foot out of the irons by the time we'd gone twenty yards and ten yards later I hit the grass, rolled and finished up flat on my back inside the running rail. The jockey who'd been assigned to ride alongside me was on an old mare used as a companion because of her calming nature and he managed to grab the reins and slow the colt down before it had got too far and the only part of me hurt was my pride. I was still feeling a bit shaken when I got back to the mounting enclosure and became worried when the trainer told me Mister Naughton wanted to see me before I got on the next horse. *'This is it,'* I thought. *'My riding career is over before it's even begun.'*

Mister Naughton's face carried a serious frown when I approached him at the foot of the Members Stand. Another man, who looked to be in his forties stood beside him, but he was smiling. "Are you okay, Bill?" Mister Naughton said. "That looked a bit nasty from here."

I put on a brave face and grinned at him. "I'm fine, Mister Naughton, just winded, that's all."

He half turned towards the other man. "This is a friend of mine, Bill, - Mister Johnny Forrest."

"Hello Bill; I'd say it was more spectacular than nasty," Forrest said, still smiling.

I began to feel a little more comfortable because it didn't look like I was going to be sacked. "Hello Mister Forrest," I said. "I'm glad you liked my performance."

Mister Naughton looked relieved. "Johnny's related to Mrs Naughton and he's coming back to Tarnagulla to spend some time with us, Bill," he said. "He's been breaking in Waler brumbies for export to the Australian Light Horse cavalry units fighting in the war in Europe."

Oh," I said. "Walers, eh?"

Johnny Forrest must have noted my confusion for he explained. "They're bred in the wilds of the New South Wales high country; toughest little horses in the world," he said. "They'll take you a hundred miles in a day's ride and not even break into a sweat."

16

I was awestruck; it was my first encounter with a real live expert horsebreaker and I thanked him and turned to Mister Naughton in a kind of a daze that had nothing to do with my recent tumble. "The trainer said you wanted to see me," I said.

He nodded. "I just wanted to make certain you were in good shape, Bill..."

"...Mind if I give you some advice?" Johnny said.

I didn't need to think about it for more than a second. "Yes, - I mean, - no sir, I don't mind...," I mumbled.

"When your horse bucks lean slightly forward," he said. "Grip with your knees and let your upper body sway loosely. Watch his head straight down between the ears. If you can stay on after the first few bucks most of them will give up. There's always the odd one who won't, of course, but you'll learn to handle them when they come along."

I went back to Tarnagulla more determined than ever to spend my life riding horses in one capacity or another and I hung on to every word of advice Johnny Forrest gave me over the month or so he spent with us at the homestead. We even took on a few of our neighbours' unbroken colts so Johnny could 'keep his hand in,' as he said. I learned a lot from him and it stood me in good stead later in my life as you will see. There were a lot of other lessons to be learned too, of course, but I was keen to find out everything I could and I memorised every detail, lying in bed at night thinking and dreaming of the promising future I hoped was ahead of me after the setbacks I'd had as a child.

I was devastated when Mister Naughton told me he didn't want to have the extra expense of feeding the foal that his mare had produced, which he said was too small to be of any use around the farm and so he was going to send him off to the dog meat and glue factory. I pleaded with him to spare the colt's life. "Please don't send him to the knackery, Mister Naughton," I said, with tears running down my thin face. "You won't have to have the expense of feeding him. I'll look after him myself and pay for his feed out of my wage."

Mister Naughton agreed and seemed happy enough with that arrangement, but I was a little confused because he'd never before shown any signs of being miserly. I thought about it later that night though and after a while, I began to understand that he wasn't the penny-pinching, old Scrooge I'd believed him to be in the light of day, but was a crafty beggar who had no intention of getting rid of the foal at all. He must have considered that I might be a bit of a wanderer with the tendency to move on at a moment's notice and he'd regarded it as a shrewd way of retaining my useful services a bit longer.

17

If that was the case he was right on the nail in his reasoning because I remained at the farm just long enough for the foal to grow old enough to be broken in and ridden. He'd turned into a nice little colt by then; dark bay and almost brown with four white knee-high socks and a white nose. The height of a horse is measured in hands, a hand being equal to four inches, and the average Australian working horse is about fifteen hands to its shoulder or about five feet tall. The colt wasn't any more than fourteen hands, fully grown, but looked bigger than he was by the way he carried himself with his head held high; deep and thick through well-sloped shoulders, wide girthed with a short back and long quarters and large, bright intelligent eyes. I'd named him Tom Thumb after the fairy-tale, midget-sized hero of English folklore and in my opinion, we were simply made for each other.

Horses are very clever creatures, you know, Sister Mary and they've got some kind of a sixth sense, so they can tell right away who is going to be kind to them and who will hurt them. Tom knew I loved him and I think he felt that he owed me a favour because I'd saved him from the knacker's yard, for he was the most faithful little animal you could ever imagine.

When I left the farm I took Edward Naughton's advice and headed directly north, staying west of the Great Divide. I'd had no intention of going to any of the big cities like Sydney anyway, even before he'd warned me against it because I would have had to leave my most treasured possession behind or find good and cheap stabling for him, which would have been almost impossible to achieve in the cities. There were plenty of roadside stops for the travelling public, most with at least a fireplace and a rainwater tank if there wasn't a river nearby and when I camped out, which was almost always the case, I never bothered to tie Tom up. The grassed area between the edges of the track and the property fences was known by drovers and shepherds as the 'long paddock' and Tom would graze along there quite happily, but when the bushman's clock, the Kookaburra, caught sight of the first grey band of dawn on the horizon and gave his raucous, hearty chuckle to welcome the birth of a new day, Tom would wander over to my swag and nuzzle me with his little white nose. That nose was the first thing I saw in the mornings when I woke up, and then while I broke camp Tom would stand there patiently waiting to be loaded up with our swag.

I crossed the Murray River at Echuca and kept on a northerly course until I was well into the interior of New South Wales. I had no firm commitment to travel anywhere in particular, but the further north I went the more pleasant and warm the weather became and I was just happy to be free from the monotony of milking cows twice a day in the cold and rain of Victoria. By the end of winter 1919, I'd gone as far as the Riverina area in the mid-west of the State.

I wasn't at all attentive to my surroundings when I first started my journey, but I soon realised as I ventured further that the expansion of cropping in New South Wales was beginning to gain momentum and it had spread westward into previously uncultivated grazing lands. This rapid expansion, I found out later, was mainly due to the Soldier Resettlement Scheme, an ambitious plan set up to get new farmers settled on land in higher-risk, low-rainfall areas. Confidence in the success of the scheme was high and it was helped along by the availability of new drought-resistant wheat seed and government subsidised cheap superphosphate. Unfortunately, soil erosion soon became a major problem and farmers began sowing into crop stubble using disc drills to prevent wind blasting of the seedlings, but the current season had been good with decent winter rains and the crop was almost ready for harvesting.

I marvelled at the endless plain of wheat fields that were spread out in all directions around me and I wandered along the track wondering where I might find some work to supplement my meagre savings. It seemed that many travellers like me had passed this way before because I came upon frequent hostile signs painted on gateposts. *'No Sundowners or Swaggies need apply'*, or *'No freeloaders.'* *'There's no work here, - keep going'*. *'Keep out'*, or the long-winded, *'I hope you've said goodbye to your mother because you're never going to see her again if you come onto this property without a reasonable excuse.'* That particular sign was accompanied by a pair of old leather boots nailed to the fence beside it for effect, as if some rash swaggie hadn't heeded the warning and didn't need his boots anymore. It was all a bit daunting and I began to feel like I was one of a small group of people who were unwanted by any society and destined to be wanderers and beggars for the rest of our lives, but eventually, I came to a gate that had no sign on it to deter me and I daringly rode along a dusty track between two wheat fields that led me to the station homestead. It looked like an impressive building from a distance, but as I got closer I could see how unkempt and sorry-looking it was. It was nothing more than a galvanised iron hut surrounded by a wide veranda with a rough cut timber front door and a brick fireplace chimney at one end. A hand-painted sign at the front gate had informed me it was called Miller's Run and when a couple of friendly farm dogs greeted me with their tails wagging I thought it was a good sign. I tied Tom's reins to a post-and-rail, log fence and strode up the three steps on to the veranda.

The man who answered my knock on the door was taller than me by about a head, which wasn't surprising because *most* adults were taller than I was. He sported what I guessed was a week's stubble of black hair on his chin and I could see beyond his short-sleeved, open-necked, red flannel shirt, a matching tangle of curly hair poking out from his brawny chest and arms, but I noticed too that he was going bald on top when he removed his wide-brimmed hat to scratch his head in astonishment at my sudden appearance.

"What on earth are you doing way out here in the scrub young feller," he said. "A runaway from school, are you? We're fifty miles from the nearest town of any size."

I stood as tall as I could but still couldn't look the man directly in the eyes. "No sir," I said. "I'm nineteen years old and I'm looking for work. Do you know if the manager of this station might have anything that needs to be done around here?"

The man looked me up and down for what seemed to me to be a full minute or so before he replied, "I might, lad. What can you do?"

I glanced over my shoulder at Tom Thumb, who stood quietly at the front gate of the fenced-off area around the homestead. "I've got some experience working with horses," I said.

The man followed my gaze towards Tom Thumb. "We don't run stock horses here," he said. "We've got no work for them. Most of the men have got their own for getting into town, but they do their own grooming and shoeing. I've got a motor truck round the back of the shed; it's a 1910 Caldwell Vale if you're interested."

I was stunned. "You've got a *motor car?*" I said. "I haven't seen a single one on my way here. I didn't think there'd be any as far out from Sydney as this. It must be three hundred miles."

The man grinned. "It's three hundred and fifty to Sydney from here and the roads are pretty rough. You're right about that though; there aren't many cars, but that's all going to change in the next couple of years. The Caldwell Vale trucks went out of production before the war, about seven years ago, - in 1913, I think it was; they were too slow; mine only does about six miles an hour so I'd get to Sydney quicker walking there, but I got it cheap enough. There are plenty of faster trucks coming into the country now and it's going to revolutionise the wheat industry. Times are changing. I can't ride horses anymore, so I need it to get around anyway." He winced in obvious discomfort and hobbled for a step as he came further out from the door opening, and I noticed for the first time that he had a stiff leg, - a *'gammy'* leg we called it then. He must have noticed my eyes widen a bit because he went on. "I came out of the war with a couple of wounds; not too bad mind you, but enough to keep me out of a regular job in Brisbane or Sydney."

I must say I felt genuine remorse for the man's sacrifice in the war effort because he seemed to have made such a great effort to put his injuries behind him and just get on with his life the best way he could. "I'm sorry to hear that," I said, shaking my head. "I do hope the manager continues to employ you and you recover well and have a good life ahead of you. It's what all of you returned servicemen deserve after what you've gone through."

The man seemed gratified by my acknowledgement of his service to the country. "Well, thanks lad," he said.

I doffed my hat in respect and began to walk back to where Tom still stood patiently waiting, but the man stopped me. "Whoa there," he said. "I didn't say I had no work at *all*. I don't run any stock so I've got no work for stock horses, but I do have Clydesdales to pull the ploughs. There's plenty of work to be done around here. I've got five hundred cleared acres to be tilled and sown and another five hundred still under scrub…"

I was confounded. "…You're the owner?" I said.

The man grinned. "I know I don't look much like the owner of a thousand acres," he said, "…but it's true." His chest heaved with what I realised immediately was a measure of pride at his achievement. "I'm not a big-time landowner, - like Sir Sydney Kidman though. They call us *'Cockies'*, - short for Cockatoo farmers because we scratch a living in the dirt like a Cockatoo to survive, but I'm proud of being called a Cockie because scratching a living out of *this* God forsaken land is about as hard an occupation as anyone can take up."

I held out my small hand tentatively, the man took it, and I winced at the strength in the large fingers that closed around mine. "Jimmy Miller's the name," he said. "It's a good name for a wheat farmer, eh, - Miller, I mean?" He laughed, but it was thin and it seemed to me, still a raw teenager, that he was hiding some other kind of pain apart from the leg injury, whether physical or mental, it was impossible to judge.

I hadn't been exposed to the sort of dry humour that I came to expect from the men of the bush later on in my life and I stared at him in some confusion. "What, - a wheat farmer… Miller?" I stumbled over my words.

Jimmy went a little bit red in the face. "Never mind, - what's your name, lad?" he said quickly.

I regained a bit of my composure when I saw his discomfiture. "It's Bill Smith," I said, trying hard to keep my high-pitched voice as low-toned as I could.

"He nodded. "Got any experience working in the wheat-growing industry, Bill?"

I shook my head. "No," I said, "but I learn quickly enough, and my last boss said I was one of the best workers he's ever had." The letter of reference was in my kit, but I didn't think it was worthwhile producing it just then.

He looked at me pensively and nodded again as if he was considering my physical size and wondering what manner of work I could have done to earn that sort of praise. "Who was that, Bill?" he said finally.

I shrugged my narrow shoulders. "You probably wouldn't have heard of him, Mister Miller," I said. "He's a dairy farmer down south in Victoria."

"So, - are you from the cabbage garden too, Bill?" he said with an impish grin creasing his face.

"Cabbage garden?" I said, confused again.

He broke into a hearty laugh. "We call Victorians cabbage-patchers. The whole state is only the size of a cabbage patch."

I laughed too and it seemed to break the ice a bit more. "Yes, then I must be a cabbage-patcher, Mister Miller," I said. "My old boss's name is Edward Naughton."

His eyes lit up in surprise. "Edward Naughton? Is he the brother of William Naughton, the land baron?"

It was my turn to be surprised. "I - I suppose he is," I spluttered. "He told me he has a brother called William who is a beef cattle farmer, but I thought he said he was hundreds of miles away up north in Queensland. Do you know him?"

He shook his head slightly and gave me another quizzical stare. "No, I don't know him personally, but just about everyone in the land between the Simpson Desert to the west and the Great Dividing Range to the east knows *of* the E and W Naughton Company. I read recently that, since the Honourable James Tyson died, the only other pastoralist now with land holdings equal to the Naughton brothers is Sir Sydney Kidman, - and between them, they own about five per cent of the continent of Australia. The brothers split their company assets about ten years ago. Your old boss Edward took up the properties here in the Riverina and in Victoria and William got the properties on the Darling River and in Queensland."

I nodded. "Ah then, so Mister Naughton wasn't just making an empty gesture when he recommended me for working as a stockman on his brother's cattle stations in Queensland."

Jimmy laughed at my unworldliness. "I'd say it wasn't an empty gesture at all, Bill," he said. "The Naughtons don't work that way. If Edward recommended you to William, *he'll* make sure you get employment wherever and whenever you want it. That reference by Edward is worth its weight in gold and I wouldn't take it too lightly. You're a lucky young man."

I was happy, of course, that he thought my reference from Edward Naughton was worth its weight in gold, but, - *lucky?* In my naivety, I wasn't so sure about *that*. I'd worked hard for that reference and thought I deserved it, but on the other hand, I realised that I was probably being a little offhand about it all because the deck of life's cards weren't always dealt fairly, and I knew that some people worked hard and never got any praise or reward for the great effort they'd put into it right up until the day they died. The epitaph *'He was a hard worker all his life and he died penniless but happy with his lot,'* was hardly a fitting tribute to a man's life of relentless and thankless toil. "If I get to Queensland eventually I'll try to get in touch with him," I said, but I knew in my heart that it must have sounded to Jimmy like I'd said it with little conviction.

If Jimmy held a dim opinion of my cavalier attitude, though, he said nothing and just went on talking about William Naughton. "He's not just confined his dealings to New South Wales and Queensland," he said. "Naughton bought six hundred thousand acres in Western Australia and then resold the land for a huge profit after a couple of years of good rains. He must have a nose for when the rain is going to come, because it's not the first time he's done it, and I'm not at all surprised to hear that his brother Edward is such a quiet achiever too, because apart from William's business affairs he's always to the fore with advice and financial assistance in worthy public enterprises. He's a very generous man and is quietly helping forward many deserving projects throughout Queensland and New South Wales, much as Sir Sydney Kidman is doing in South Australia."

"I agree, - they must be a great men then and I'm sorry I've never really heard anything about their public activities before now," I said, quite humbly, because I could sense the admiration Jimmy had for my old boss and his brother.

He wasn't finished though. "Both of the Naughton brothers are patriotic too," he said, "and the soldiers who've returned from the battlefronts of the Great War love them because of their generously given contributions to the various funds that were set up to aid us."

I admit I was shocked. I'd been living under the same roof as one of the richest and most benevolent men in the country according to Jimmy, and yet his modest standard of living had given me no indication of his great wealth. I was equally shocked to learn of his generosity and patriotism for he hadn't worn that like a badge for everyone to see like some others do. "He *was* a good boss," I said in a hushed tone, still awestruck by the discovery. "He never raised his voice to me in anger and always treated me with the greatest respect, - as if I was a member of his own family."

'I want you to know that you're one of the best and most conscientious workers we've ever had here. I'm sorry you're leaving, and you're welcome back here anytime lad.'

Jimmy laughed again. "Well then that's an excellent reference in itself Bill," he said. "Right, let's find out what we can get you to do around here. Ever heard of a stump-jump plough?"

I thought about lying for a moment because bluffing my way through had helped me to get a job before then, but I instantly realised that I was so far out of my depth here, I'd probably be found wanting at his very next question. "No, I haven't," I said honestly.

"I didn't think you would, but I thought I'd ask anyway," he said casually. "You see, the stump-jump plough was invented by a chap called Richard Smith. I thought for a crazy minute you might be related but of course, the name Smith is the most prolific in western culture; - you're a dime a dozen, as the Yanks would say."

I must have gaped open-mouthed at him. "There are a lot of Smiths in America?" I thought briefly about my family tree and wondered if I'd ever be able to resolve the questions I'd harboured in my mind for so long, but Jimmy's laugh broke into my reverie.

"There are Smiths everywhere," he said. "No, it was only because you said you came from the cabbage garden and Richard Smith invented his plough here about forty years ago."

"I'm certain I can't be related to him," I said. "I don't have any relatives in…" I stopped suddenly as I took in what he'd said. "You say he invented it right *here*?" I muttered in disbelief.

Jimmy shrugged his broad shoulders and ignored my juvenile incredulity. "No, not *right* here, I meant in Australia, - in South Australia as a matter of fact," he said. "The land in South Australia's northern wheat belt is far worse than anything we've got to deal with here in the Riverina of New South Wales. There's even a line drawn on a map from east to west called Goyder's line, named after the South

Australian Surveyor-General who had it drawn up about fifty years ago. To the north of the line, the average annual rainfall is usually too low to support cropping, with the land being mainly saltbush and only suitable for grazing. To the south of it, the cover is mainly Mallee scrub, but it's all still hard, stony ground and before it can be cultivated the timber has to be cleared and the stumps and roots that are left behind burnt. The old, English light Rotherham ploughs were no good for the job and even the heavy wooden breaking ploughs they brought in to replace them couldn't get through the ground without snagging on the roots, so the stump-jump disc cultivating plough, pulled by a couple of big draught horses, was ideal for use on that sort of scrub country. That's what we use here too. It's the main tillage implement we use for breaking up the heavy soils in newly cleared areas, and then we use an International Harvester combine drill, with fifteen boots for sowing and 31 tines, to sow the seed and fertilise the soil at the same time."

I didn't say a word and just stood there trying to take in everything he'd said while trying to find something practical to say that might impress him as to my learning ability, but nothing came to mind and I just hoped my attentive expression did the job sufficiently to encourage him to give me the chance that I needed so badly.

He looked me up and down again. "Do you think you could handle something like the stump-jump plough, Bill? It takes a fair bit of strength to control it." There was a hint of anxiety in his voice.

I nodded, relieved that he was at least considering the possibility that I *might* be able to manage it. "I'm stronger than I look, Mister Miller," I said in my most persuasive voice. "Please give me a chance to prove it to you. I *won't* let you down."

Jimmy's concern seemed to have dissipated with my positive response for he grinned again and patted me on the shoulder patronisingly. *'Maybe he's examining me physically to see if he can discern any muscular strength in my scrawny looking body,'* I thought at the time.

Whatever the case was he must have decided to give me a break, for he said, "I'm sure you won't, lad. There are a couple of other ploughmen working for me down in the side paddock, but after you've learned how it's done from them I want you to go up to the back boundary near the Lachlan River and start work in the far paddock. There's plenty of pumped water from the river and you'll have four Clydesdales in the holding yard, so you can work two and rest two on alternate days. There's a small hut there too if you want to use it, but if you find it too lonely down there you're more than welcome to ride over to the main bunkhouse where the other ploughmen live; it's only half-a-mile along the river track. Most people find that they need some company after a while on their own out there when they start having two-way conversations with the horses."

'*There's nothing wrong with that, - I do that already,*' I thought, but I just grinned at him and nodded.

"You can call in here for provisions any time you need to," he said. "I do a run into Lake Cargelligo each week to deliver and pick up the incoming mail and newspapers if you want to write to, or receive mail from any family you've got hidden away in one of the cities."

I was elated. "I don't have any family, Mister Miller..." I said. "...so I won't need the postal service except for official mail, - and I don't mind my own company so I'll be happy to stay in the hut by myself too."

Jimmy looked at me curiously for a few seconds but must have decided that my preference for being alone was none of his business, and he went on to tell me that the ploughing was generally started in the summer months and then the turned ground was left as weed-free mulch until sowing time in the autumn of the following year, a period of fifteen months. That long fallow time offered the advantage of spreading the workload of tillage over many months, so when I was finished with one section I knew I was essentially to go on to the next without any need for instructions or supervision. That suited me admirably because I could go about my work with minimal contact with other people and just enjoy any spare time I had with Tom and the draught horses that pulled the stump-jump plough.

Tom Thumb adapted to his new surroundings quickly and seemed to enjoy his life of leisure. He was dwarfed beside the great seventeen hands high draught horses and he got a bit jealous if he thought I was spending too much time grooming them and ignoring him, but I always made sure I fussed over him and spent extra time with him to make up for it, and whenever I had to go to the homestead for provisions I always took the longer route along the river and past the main bunkhouse so that Tom could have a good gallop and a look around. On those occasions, he'd walk past the draught horses grazing peacefully in their resting paddock with his head held even higher than normal, almost gloating that he was now the centre of my attention and they were not.

After a brief introduction to the stump-jump plough, which I found to be quite easy to handle much to the surprise of the other brawny ploughmen, I became a ploughman too. I must have cut a tiny figure behind that pair of huge Clydesdales, dressed as I was in grey flannel, short-sleeved shirt and tweed trousers, trudging through the

26

newly turned sods in oversized blucher boots. I was happy though and thought that, even if I didn't *look* like a ploughman, there was nobody around to tell me how I was supposed to look, - and I certainly *felt* like one. I'd also grown more healthy and robust than I'd ever been before, with a deeply sun-tanned face and brown, muscular arms that I was proud of when I looked in the little mirror I'd set up on a nail in the wall of my hut.

Lake Cargelligo was a rip-roaring place, especially at harvest time when the farmhands from all the stations around the Lachlan River arrived to let their hair down after a hard day's work. The spur-line railway from Temora had been opened just two years before and J. J. Donnelly, the main grain merchant in the district, had increased the company's tally of wheat sent to London to two hundred thousand bags after its first year of operations.

Jimmy began to make a habit of coming to visit me at the hut a couple of times a month. He said he was pleased with my work and wanted to make sure I was still happy with the arrangement too, but he admitted that part of the reason for his visits was that he was still a bit concerned that I never asked for time off to ride into town to socialise with the other ploughmen and harvesters. I assured him time after time that I didn't drink alcohol, didn't need the social company of others, I was perfectly happy as things stood, and there was no need for him to worry about it, but he still went away shaking his head and muttering about what he said he regarded as 'my eccentric ways'.

I didn't feel too bad about rebuffing Jimmy's attempts to badger me into socialising with the other men, though, because I'd found out after talking to him a few times that he wasn't such a great socialiser himself. He had a wife who was living in Sydney, but she was a wife in name only, for he rarely saw her and when he did, she let him know his presence wasn't appreciated there amongst her high society friends. He said she'd only married him because she could boast that she and her husband owned a huge wheat farm in Western New South Wales, so I was sure he'd known a few other *eccentric* people in his life before I turned up on his doorstep.

Lake Cargelligo didn't have a local newspaper, but the Temora Times was brought in by train each week and Jimmy had got into the habit of bringing a copy to me to read after his weekly visit to the town. He hadn't entirely given up on enticing me to socialise either and seemed forever bewildered by my continued diffidence as if he'd always fully expected me to break down eventually and admit that I needed a break from my isolation.

"Are you quite certain there's nothing else I can do for you?" he pressed me, for perhaps the twentieth time.

I was tired of dodging the question and thought for a while about how I could make him feel a little more at ease concerning my welfare. "Just keep bringing me the Temora newspaper from Lake Cargelligo whenever you're finished reading it," I said eventually. "I suppose I *should* try to keep up with what's going on in the world, although I've got little interest in it."

Jimmy nodded but he looked disappointed. "Anything else?" he said again.

I noted the look of exasperation on his face. "Well then, Jimmy…," I said as an afterthought, "…I read a great bush poem in the copy of the Temora Times you brought me last week. There are eight verses to it altogether and it's attributed to a chap who goes by the pseudonym 'Glenrowan'. I'd like to find out who he is and read more of his work if he has any. The first verse went something like this;

The sandhills north of Barringun stand shimmering in the heat,
The dust is driven dense and dun by forty thousand feet,
And dimly through the clouds that cling, beyond the Border Gate,
The kelpies swing along the wing to keep the leaders straight.
And I remember Barringun of thirty years ago,
A few tin roofs that took the sun as white as driven snow;
Two bush hotels where loafers sat, a butcher's shop, a store,
A few goats feeding on the flat – and very little more!…"

Jimmy grinned. "Well done Bill," he said. "You've recalled the words perfectly." He responded with another ditty of his own for good measure.

"But sling me a saddle on some good horse,
Bred on Belalie or Lila Springs,
With the Warrego mud in his mane, of course,
And the grass-feed green on his snaffle rings.
Over Bourke bridge at the break of day
Let me north where the red tracks run,
And blindfold yet I could find my way
Through Enngonia to Barringun."

It was my turn to applaud. "So you like bush poems too, Jimmy?" I said.

He confirmed that he *was* indeed an admirer of the 'bush bards'. "Glenrowan is one of the pen-names of a bush poet called, William Henry Ogilvie," he said. "He's a Scotsman, but spent a decade in Australia and went back to Scotland about twenty years ago around the turn of the century. He's still writing poems about the Australian

28

outback even now in Scotland and he's very well thought of by anyone who appreciates the old bush poems, - as you and I do." He paused and grinned again, obviously delighted that he'd found something we could both relate to. "I'm surprised you hadn't heard of him though," he said, "he's gained a reputation over the years as one of Australia's top three bush poets, alongside Patterson and Lawson."

"I'd heard a little about Ogilvie," I said, "but never under his penname Glenrowan..."

The conversation continued about the merits of the various bush poets and we both realised then that we'd found something *very* much in common with each other. It was a bond that was to draw us closer together, not just as employer and employee, but as the best of genuine friends.

Jimmy told me that Ogilvie hadn't been just a poet, but a good horseman, jackaroo, and drover too, and was described in the newspaper reports of the time as a quietly spoken, handsome Scot of medium height, with a fair moustache and reddish complexion. During his time in Australia, he'd worked on sheep stations in north-western and central New South Wales, where he'd gained his reputation as one of Australia's top bush poets. He was known as *'Will'* Ogilvie and by the pen names of *'Glenrowan'* and the lesser-known *'Swingle-Bar'*. It had been said that 'Glenrowan' was named for the town of Glenrowan in Victoria and, of course, a 'Swingle bar' is the wooden crossbar between draught horses and a wagon that keeps the chains separated.

I was intrigued. "So where is this Barringun he wrote about?" I said. "He mentioned the Border Gate so I suppose it's in the north of the state on the border with Queensland."

Jimmy nodded. "Barringun's on the New South Wales side of the border, and it's directly opposite Wooroorooka on the Queensland side."

He went on to say that the twin towns had been important Customs centres when the former colonies of Queensland and New South Wales collected Customs dues from one another. That led to them becoming essential gathering places for drovers and teamsters, either taking their teams from Western Queensland to the rail-heads south of the border at Bourke for export to the Sydney and Melbourne markets or moving them north to the better grazing lands in the northern areas of Queensland after the wet season rains. That would have been the case in the 1890s when Will Ogilvie worked there, and even though he wrote that poem just this year he'd composed it about the Barringun of thirty years ago that he remembered.

I couldn't help but think how romantic it was to have such a well-known poet write about the little town he'd visited so long ago with such fondness. "I suppose it hasn't changed much since Will Ogilvie was here; a bit bigger maybe?" I said.

I was surprised by Jimmy's answer. "No, it's nowhere near as busy as it was then, Bill," he said.

He went on to say that from 1885, when the New South Wales Government constructed a railway as far as Bourke in the north-west of the state, farmers at Cunnamulla and other parts of south-western Queensland began to send their wool and beef cattle to the eastern and southern markets via the Bourke line rather than through Charleville, which was then the terminus of the Western railway line in Queensland. The reason for that was that the New South Wales Government offered more competitive rail freight rates than the Queensland Government.

Queensland Railway Commissioner, James Thallon, responded by negotiating with the Carrier's Union to make the cost of transporting goods to the coast via the Charleville railhead more attractive, but his plan was frustrated because the carriers went on strike in support of the 1891 Australian Shearers' strike. Goods continued to be sent via New South Wales, and the situation was made worse for Queensland by new lower freight rates in New South Wales that were announced in June 1893. The Queensland Government responded again the following month by introducing the Railway Border Tax Act which taxed wool and sheepskins crossing the border into New South Wales in a bid to make it too expensive to freight the wool via Bourke, and in 1895, the Queensland Parliament approved the construction of the extension of the Western railway line from Charleville to Cunnamulla as an extra incentive to Queensland pastoralists.

After Federation in 1901, the Customs charges were discontinued of course, and the New South Wales Railway Authorities began discussions about extending the railhead at Bourke across the border to Cunnamulla, but the Queensland Government was still against it because that would have taken revenue away from its existing rail line between Cunnamulla and Toowoomba. The upshot of it all was that pastoralists were still droving cattle across the old border of colonial times, but without any restrictions placed on their movement.

I was fascinated by Jimmy's knowledge of the bush towns and even more delighted when he supplied me with a copy of Will Ogilvie's book of poems, *'Fair Girls and Gray Horses'*, and the two of us shared some of Lawson's and Patterson's poems too after that first conversation between us. I have to acknowledge, however, that Jimmy's greatest gift to me was his eventual acceptance of what he continued to call, my 'eccentric' ways and I was certain that his mind was eased somewhat to know that I was spending my time reading bush poems rather than brooding alone in some kind of self-imposed exile from the rest of humanity that he'd previously imagined was my daily routine.

In the late spring of 1920, more than a year after I arrived at Miller's Run, tractors were beginning to make their presence felt. The Hart-Parr 30 was advertised as only using one gallon of kerosene to the acre. *'Horses eat all the time; the Hart-Parr only eats when it's working,'* the company boasted. It was all too true though; when horses were the only sources of power for tillage, the distribution of work over the whole year was essential because of the time involved with each task, but with the introduction of tractor power, less time was needed for tillage operations. Jimmy had already got himself a new motor truck and he was thinking about getting a tractor, so I knew then that the work would soon dry up and it was time for me to move on, - but there was another very good reason too, which, in hindsight, I realised was the catalyst for my ultimate decision.

It had become evident to me after a few months into my sojourn at Miller's Run, simply by Jimmy's general conversation that he'd suffered much more than I had at first imagined during the Great War, and had found it difficult to revert to the normal way of life that he'd enjoyed before he entered military service. For one reason or another, - perhaps it was our mutual passion for bush poetry, - or he may have perceived what he believed to be my brooding, lonely personality as a reflection of his own, - whatever the case may be, we'd been growing closer as time went on and he took to spending more and more time visiting me at my hut in the evenings after my work was finished.

I was certain that we both knew in our hearts that our liaison was becoming more than mere friendship and I, at least, tried so hard, but couldn't shake off the feeling of comfort, enjoyment and pure brotherly love that I felt in Jimmy's company as I recited Ogilvie and Patterson and he recited Lawson across my tiny kitchen table.

Our preference for one or the other of the great bush poets seemed curious at first to both of us and caused much discussion about the merits of all three, but we eventually agreed that it had nothing to do with the different styles of their works, but merely reflected the differences in our personalities at that particular time in our lives, that is to say, circumstances had coloured our hopes and dreams of what the bush meant to each of us in different ways. That caused even more discussion since Jimmy's initial opinion of *my* temperament had to change because of it. The romantic utopia of brave horsemen and

31

beautiful scenery depicted in the poetry of Will Ogilvie and Banjo Paterson that *I* loved was nothing like Jimmy's favourite, Lawson, whose grim and uninviting view of the outback seemed to express his spirit of despondency and the futility of people trying to live normal lives in a land full of desolation and despair. Perhaps in hindsight, I should have been able to read the signs of Jimmy's troubled existence, considering what happened later, but I was young and hadn't had the experience to recognise depression. Despite our friendly rivalries, though, the recitations often developed into an entertaining contest to see who could memorise the most verses and we laughed and sang our way through many evenings until late, but inevitably, it became more and more challenging for us to say goodnight at the end of a pleasant evening together.

I certainly couldn't put into words the sentiment that I felt as I watched Jimmy walk away from my doorway to drive his truck to his lonely quarters at the homestead with shoulders drooping, and I retired to my own in a wretched reflection of what our two lives could have been like if things had been different. I'd learned long ago, however, to cope with what life had thrown at me by then and was able to draw on that inner strength to make the decision that I knew was, not only in both of our best interests, but vital to my prospects if I was to have any chance of living the life that I'd dreamed of as a wholly *normal* human being.

Jimmy's voice was husky when I told him I was leaving Miller's Run. "Where will you go from here, young Bill?" he said.

I tried not to look directly into his eyes just in case he saw the moistness in mine. "I'm intending to head north to Bourke and beyond through William Ogilvie's Barringun," I said. "I'm still keen to work with horses despite the progress to trucks and machinery and I know from what I've read in the newspapers that there's a lot of work to be had droving cattle and sheep in the border country around Barringun and further up into Western Queensland."

Jimmy looked down at the ground in front of his feet and kicked at an imaginary stone. "Yes, that'd be right," he said after an awkward silence. "I've heard that too, and your old boss's land-baron brother, William Naughton, owns a line of stations between New South Wales and Diamantina Lakes Station on the Queensland-Northern Territory border. He bought them as relief stops to give his droving teams a clear run south to get to the southern markets without having to abide by the six miles a day rule of the stock routes when passing through land owned by another station." He turned his gaze towards me again, but I still averted my eyes, which were now brimming with tears. "You'll be right then, young Bill; you'll have no trouble getting work up north with any of Naughton's droving teams."

I knew Jimmy was trying hard to hold his emotions in check and I tried to sound casual to ease the nervous tension between us. "I'll miss the big Clydesdales," I said. "They'll probably forget me pretty soon, though, I sup..." I choked on the words.

Jimmy smiled, but the curve of his lips couldn't conceal the sadness in his eyes. "Don't fret over them," he said. "They'll soon be retired to graze peacefully on the wheat stubble while the tractors do their work for them." He paused and looked away over the fields of wheat. "I won't forget you though, Bill. You've made a big difference to my way of thinking about life in general, and I now understand that I've got to do something that I should have done a long time ago." He turned and faced me again and another wry smile creased his lips. "I got more than just a leg injury in the war you know: some of my mates didn't make it home, and I often think they were the lucky ones. It's nothing you can see; it's all up here in my head, but it's always there." He put a fist to his forehead and tapped it lightly. "Nights are the worst, though, sleeping is hard to come by and when it does come the nightmares come with it and then I wake up in a cold sweat. The doctors told me it'll pass, but it's not getting any better. I want to thank you for just being here night after night to talk to me and listen so patiently while I ranted about events happening in the world that you probably hadn't even heard of..." He paused again before adding, perhaps as an afterthought, "...and now it's time for me to make the change to my lifestyle that I should have made long ago." He shook his head sadly. "My wife, living it up in Sydney with her snobbish friends, is going to get a big shock when she finds out what I've done."

I wasn't quite sure what he meant by that, but I didn't want to pursue the subject in case it involved something I'd be regretful for initiating. "I'll never forget you either, Jimmy," I said. "I've loved every minute of my time here at Miller's Run, and..." I hesitated, not knowing how to put what was in my mind into words without giving him false hope that I might change my mind and stay. "I love you, Jimmy... like a brother, but I *must* leave you. Maybe one day we'll meet again and I'll be able to explain why, but I must..."

Jimmy gave me that probing look that, at various times in the past had told me that he was still confused about my mindset and motivation for seeking new pastures when I'd admitted to him my fondness for my present circumstances. "The drover's life is a hard one, but I know you've got a big heart in that small chest of yours and you'll do what you have to do to make a go of it," he simply said, "and although I'd like you to stay, I know you have your reasons and I wish you all the luck in the world if that's what you need to do…"

He left it at that, for he was too respectful of my privacy to make any further comments or enquiries. It was a tradition that I was to find common amongst the drovers and stockmen of the bush, perhaps a reflection of their own buried histories. Many a ripping yarn was told around the campfires at night, but they were almost always told about someone else that the storyteller had met, or heard of along the track. It was hardly ever about the yarn teller himself.

Tom was happy to be on the move again after spending such a long time in the paddock, and he danced and skipped like a yearling after I'd packed my swag behind the saddle and climbed on his back, for he was smart enough to know something was up. I mumbled my final goodbye to Jimmy Miller in a voice hoarse with love and affection and turned Tom's head towards Queensland, but several hundred yards along the track I wheeled him around to have one last look at Miller's Run. Jimmy still stood where I'd left him, but he didn't respond to my salute, for his shoulders were stooped and he had both hands clapped over his eyes.

The bush telegraph was often just as swift as the Royal Mail, and sometimes speedier along the well-trodden stock routes between the western towns, and I found out several weeks later what kind of change Jimmy had decided to make to his life, - and he was right; his wife, living it up with her snobbish friends in Sydney, would certainly have received a big shock, for she'd suddenly become a widow. Jimmy was found by one of his ploughmen lying in the middle of his paddock at Miller's Run with a revolver by his side. The Great War demons had claimed another victim and won the battle for his shell-shocked brain, but Jimmy had found the comfort and peace of mind he'd craved for at long last.

2 The Shearing Sheds

It was three hundred miles from Lake Cargelligo to the Queensland border, Sister Mary, and I travelled north-west along a rough, wheel-rutted track through the Lachlan River valley to the busy little copper mining town of Mount Hope. That was the junction with the well-travelled track from the Murrumbidgee Valley to Bourke that later became known as The Kidman Way after Sir Sydney Kidman, the great Australian Pastoralist and Philanthropist that Jimmy had told me about. I turned north and followed it to the main copper mining centre of Cobar where a population of about ten thousand people scratched a living out of the earth, but the prospect of working in a copper mine was the furthest thing from my mind, so I skirted Cobar and continued to the town of Bourke on the south bank of the Darling River.

Like Cobar, there was no compelling reason for me to remain in Bourke for as long as I did either. Henry Lawson had spent some months living in the town. He'd worked as a roustabout in the woolshed at Toorale Station nearby and undertaken a punishing inland trip between Hungerford and Bourke where he experienced the harsh realities of drought-affected New South Wales in 1892. This became a source for many of his stories in subsequent years and was considered the most important trek in Australian literary history, for it confirmed all his prejudices about the so-called 'charm' of the Australian bush.

I retired to my camp at the showgrounds where I'd rented one of the old horse stables. It was a bit run down but it was away from the main show ring and there was a water trough for Tom and a rough but clean toilet block nearby. It was a mild late afternoon, not yet failing light and I lay on top of my swag reflecting on my wretched, but unavoidable motive for leaving Jimmy as abruptly as I did and wondering what he'd be doing at that particular moment. *'Should I have been more supportive of him in what was clearly his time of need instead of backing away from facing the reality of my own complicated pathway through life?'* To be fair to myself now, though, at that point I hadn't yet heard the heart-breaking news of his sad demise. On an impulse, I reached for the book that he'd given me and that had been the foundation and stimulus of our close friendship. I'd been in the habit of opening it and flicking through its pages randomly until some particular poem of Ogilvie's caught my eye and I did so again, not intending to spend much time within its covers, but it seemed like an omen had been sent to me from Jimmy and I arose out of my nostalgia at once when, on the page that fell open, I read the title of Ogilvie's poem, *'Back to the Border'*. It was the one Jimmy had recited to me on that first night of our literary, - *attachment*.

> *'But sling me a saddle on some good horse*
> *Bred on Belalie or Lila Springs,*
> *With the Warrego mud in his mane, of course,*
> *And the grass-feed green on his snaffle rings.*
> *Over Bourke bridge at the break of day*
> *Let me north where the red tracks run,*
> *And blindfold yet I could find my way*
> *Through Enngonia to Barringun.'*

Jimmy's message to me as I was leaving Miller's Run rang again in my mind. *'You'll be right then, young Bill; you'll have no trouble getting work up north with any of Naughton's droving teams'*.

I crossed the North Bourke Bridge over the Darling River, a unique lift-up bridge built to allow paddle-steamers piled high with loads of wool to pass underneath it on their way down the Darling to the Murray and on to the South Australian ports, and once out on the red sandhills of North Bourke I turned north-eastward and skirted the edge of the deep-cut, wagon tracks of the Barringun road. In the heat of the late spring day, the dust floated in the air and soon Tom and I were lathered in red-tinged sweat. A line of tall eucalypts fenced us in on either side of the 'long paddock' and beyond that, the featureless red land of Lawson's *'back o' Bourke'* seemed to stretch forever until it merged indistinctly into the haze of the flat horizon.

I was mindful of Tom's wellbeing in the trying conditions and I let him take his time as he picked his way through the best part of the track. Each night, I camped out at the old Cobb and Co. change stations that were set at twenty-mile intervals along the road, and Tom's ears always pricked up when he saw the windmill and its connected raised water tank in the distance because he was smart enough to know that there would be a water trough below it and it would be full, providing water now only for the odd emu, a pair of dingoes that came to quench their thirst at dusk, or another lone traveller on the road between Barringun and Bourke. There were usually one or two sundowners camped at the old change stations, some of them at least, men whose pasts had caught up with them and who had taken to the roads and tracks to get away from responsibilities that had become too much of a burden to them. They weren't all of that calibre though, as I soon found out; indeed some robust working men among them were making their way to the Queensland sheep shearing sheds from the sheds along the Darling River where the shearing season had already cut out.

At Mungunyah; a lonely bush hotel and mail change on a bend of the Warrego River, the nature of the country changed suddenly. The red, stony mulga ridges gave way to black soil flats. To the left of the road, not more than a hundred yards away, the Warrego River flowed in a torrent of brown water. Black duck and teal flew out of the lignum bushes and circled high above them. I set up my camp fifty yards away from the hotel in a spot that was fairly secluded from the other campers but close enough to the amenities provided for travellers, and had just got my campfire going when the huge empty flatbed dray that I'd passed several miles down the track, pulled along at an even walking pace by a team of eighteen bullocks, arrived and turned in to the compound.

The bullock driver, a short thick-set man with a black, bushy beard and thick hairy arms, cracked a long plaited rawhide whip over the heads of the lead bullocks and yelled in a voice as deep and coarse as the bellow of one of his tired animals, "Come around Darling. Come around Sweetheart, - left, left, go through." The whole team obediently put their backs into pulling the wagon up the slight incline at his command and turned in to the holding yard behind the hotel. "Whoa up there, now Darling, - whoa Sweetheart." He set the handle of the whip into its holder next to the seat, jumped down from the dray and looked around impassively at the men, including me, who'd sauntered over and stood around watching the proceedings. Several of the men were grinning from ear to ear and one, a gaunt, ragged looking individual with a blackened clay pipe sticking out of the side of his mouth, cheekily enquired whether he was going to sleep with either Darling or Sweetheart in the holding yard.

The bullocky ignored the taunt and turned his back on the man as he began to unyoke the lead animals.

"Need any help with that, mister," I said quietly from close beside him.

The bullocky turned his head sideways and stared at my small frame. "Thanks, young lad," he said smiling crookedly through his beard, "but maybe you'd better stand back a bit; these bullocks can be dangerous if they're not handled the right way…"

The man who'd made the comment burst into laughter. "You mean to say Darling and Sweetheart are *both* dangerous," he said between puffs on his pipe. He turned to the others. "Typical females, I suppose, eh lads?"

The bullocky slipped the leather strap through its buckle and let it drop under the bullock's neck. He turned to face the man, his eyes blazing, and took a step towards him. The man stopped laughing abruptly and stumbled backwards, but not before the pipe had been snatched from between his teeth in one quick motion, broken in half, and tossed on the ground. "It'll be your teeth next time," the bullocky said in a low menacing tone. "Anybody else got any smart comments?"

He looked around the group, but the men, as one, turned and strolled back to their respective camps without another word. Only I stayed where I was and the bullocky looked at me and shook his head. "There's *always* one at every camp," he said.

I smiled, partly because I could almost look the bullocky directly in the eyes without having to raise my neck. "I get teased a lot too," I said. "In my case, it's usually because of my height, but I don't think I'd be able to handle it as easily and as quickly as you just did mister...?"

"Bart," the bullocky said, "...known to other bullockies, shearers and roustabouts in my official capacity as Black Bart the Bullocky from Bourke." He looked me up and down. "You're not that short - and you'll probably fill out a bit when you get a bit older, young feller. I haven't seen you on Barringun Road before. Has your dad got a camp around here somewhere? You're not travelling on your own, are you?"

I shook my head. "I *am* travelling on my own, Black Bart," I said. "I passed you down the track a bit earlier today. My name's Bill Smith and I've probably grown up as much as I'm ever likely to. I'm twenty-one years old."

"Ah, right." Black Bart's thick eyebrows were raised as he looked me over again. "I'm not likely to grow much taller either, but I'm nearly as strong as one of my bullocks here, and I don't take any lip from anyone."

"I can see that, Bart," I said.

Black Bart's eyes lit up and he grinned. "Work hard then young lad, build up those little muscles of yours, and I'm sure you'll get through life with as little trouble as I've been able to." He nodded towards the group of sundowners. "You'll always meet characters along the way who want to prove they're better or smarter or stronger than you, but don't let them get into your head; it'll only upset you and in the end, you're the one who'll suffer for it."

I felt a bit put out by his comment about my 'little' muscles but I didn't want to provoke him and kept my voice at an even tone. "I'm stronger than I probably look," I said mildly. "I've been ploughing mulga paddocks for a wheat farmer at Lake Cargelligo and I can handle a pair of Clydesdales without any hitches. Your bullock yoke isn't much different to what I've been used to."

We soon had the bullocks eating peacefully in the holding yard and Black Bart invited me to join him for supper. He produced a good-sized damper and a camp oven from a drawer underneath the seat of the dray and we soon had the billy on the boil. "I bought these two lead bullocks from a woman bullocky over in Moree last year," he explained as the damper began to bake in the camp oven over the fire. "My other lead pair had been slightly injured in an accident, - not too bad mind you, but enough to stop them from doing their jobs, and I had to retire them to the paddock."

"There are *women* bullockies?" I said, surprised.

"Oh yes, there's a few around," Bart grinned. "You wouldn't know the difference between them and the men unless you heard them call out to their bullocks..." He gave me an odd look as if he was about to say something, probably about my voice, but it only lasted a moment and then he went on. "...Tough as nails, they are usually; they *have* to be in this game, because they're not working with men, they're competing against us. She was retiring too, hanging up her stock whip and heading for the bright lights of Melbourne. A lot of bullockies are getting out of it now; it's because of the railways spreading westwards and all these new-fangled trucks starting to come out this way as the roads improve. We'll be a thing of the past one day, but it won't be soon, because they'll have to build a lot more bridges. The trucks can't ford the creeks during the wet season like my bullocks can." He pointed towards the road to where the Warrego's churning waters could be heard roaring beyond the trees. "Anyway, to get back to what I was saying; the woman bullocky had already worked them under the names Darling and Sweetheart..."

I was intrigued. "...They know their names?"

"Oh yes." Black Bart sat on a log and poked the fire with a stick. "We'll be on the boil in a minute," he said. "Yes, Bill, they all have their own names and they all know them and where their positions are in the team. You can't just put them anywhere in the straps, because they'll have no idea what you want them to do."

"So you've been stuck with Darling and Sweetheart?" I said. "I think that's rather cute."

Black Bart grinned. "It might seem cute to you Bill, but you have to be able to hold your own in a fight if you have to yell out names like that when you're half-bogged in a creek bed and trying to coax them out of it with a seven-ton load of fleece on the wagon. What makes matters worse is I called the wagon the *Gypsy Queen* thinking it sounded quite a strong name, but I'm not so sure about that either now."

"But you could coax them with that wicked-looking whip into doing what you want without calling them by name, I suppose," I said.

Black Bart shook his head. "We all carry whips for sure. Most bullockies will walk miles through the scrub to get a good myrtle whip handle because it's been a fundamental part of our traditional gear, but it's only a bit of a status symbol. If you ask one of us to tell you the best way to treat a bullock team most will admit that a good bullocky doesn't use much whip. The more rattled a driver gets and the more whip he uses, the less he'll get out of his bullocks. They get dour and bad-tempered on you and won't try. They respond better with a strong but gentle voice and they'll try their hardest not to let you down if you speak to them kindly."

"What about the others?" I said, "their names are not too embarrassing for you I hope."

"Oh no, I've had them for years. I've got Villain, Rascal, Vagabond, - good old fashioned bullock names that any other bullocky can relate to, - and doesn't get laughed at around the bush camps or shearing sheds.

"Are you going to the shearing sheds up north to pick up a load, Bart?" I said.

He puffed on his clay pipe and frowned before he answered. "Yes," he said. "I'll be picking up a load and taking it back down the track to the railhead at Bourke. It's about the only loads we get now and we're all hoping that the Queensland and New South Wales Governments don't get together and construct the railway link between Bourke and Cunnamulla."

I thought back to what Jimmy had told me. "Do you think that'll happen?" I said.

He shook his head. "Nah, - it's too expensive and too late for it now; the trucks will take over before they can finish it."

Early next morning I walked down to the creek crossing with Black Bart. The creek wasn't flowing but the still water had backed up from where the Warrego had overflowed its banks and was four feet deep across the road with no way around it.

On the far side, about forty yards away, a teamster stood patiently beside his wagon, fully laden with bales of fleece, evidently waiting till the water receded and the road became passable. The bells of his bullocks could be heard as the animals stood impatiently shaking their huge heads at the unscheduled stop. Beyond his team to the north I could see a line of buildings, tantalisingly close, but yet so far away, their tin roofs just beginning to be touched by the first grey streaks of dawn.

"That's Enngonia Township in the distance," Black Bart told me. "That teamster hasn't got anywhere to turn around so he's going to have to wait there till the water recedes, or unhitch the wagon and walk his team back to the holding yard in town."

I looked at him in surprise. "Surely he won't keep them standing there fully yoked. It could be a week before this goes down and he can cross over."

"No, it'll go down in a few hours," Bart said. "They probably got a bit of unseasonal rain up around Cunnamulla a week ago. It takes that long for it to work its way down through the flat channel country to here. It'll be another week before it gets into the Darling and a month till it flows into the Murray, - if it even gets that far; they'd need a bit more follow up rain for that to happen and it's fairly unlikely this time of year."

We walked back to the campsite and Bart began to hitch up the bullocks, which he'd already fed before dawn, apparently confident that the road would soon be passable, - at least for his team. Sure enough, after two hours the other team came across through knee-deep water and up the gentle rise to where Bart and I stood watching. The men knew each other and Bart asked him what the road was like further north.

"Well, you're probably in for a rugged trip, but you'll get through with the Gypsy Queen now," the teamster said. "The Warrego's still running a banker, although it's gone down a bit since this morning. Tuen Creek was three feet deep over Belalie Station's front gate yesterday and I couldn't see the top of the boundary fences in some places. There was a couple of swims like this one between Enngonia and Belalie horse-paddock too." He looked at me. "You heading for the sheds too young feller?" he said.

"I'm going in that direction, but not to the sheds," I said.

The bullocky stared at me curiously for a moment and then glanced at Bart and smiled; perhaps it was my high-pitched voice he thought amusing, or simply the fact that I wasn't doing what everyone else going north on this road at this time of year was doing, - heading for the shearing sheds. He dismissed my vague response with a shrug of his broad shoulders. "The shearing's been held up because the sheep are too wet to shear anyway," he went on regardless. "I suggest you stay here and don't leave until the mail truck comes through just to be safe. I don't want to hear about any of you roustabouts and your horses being found forty miles downstream, stuck up against Ford's Bridge on the Bourke-Hungerford Road. It'll be completely dry here in a day or two so be patient." Almost as an afterthought, he added, "It doesn't pay to tempt the Warrego Bunyip young lad."

"The *Warrego Bunyip?*" I said, bemused.

The bullocky laughed and turned his attention again to Black Bart. "You haven't told him about the famous Warrego Bunyip yet, Bart?"

Black Bart grinned and winked at him, making it obvious enough so that I was able to pick it up. "I'll save that for later, Ted," he said. See you in Bourke next month."

"Don't tempt the Warrego Bunyip?" I said as we walked back up the rise to the campsites. "What does that mean?"

Black Bart laughed. "It's a common saying we bullockies have used along the Warrego River for a long time. It just means be careful, because this river is treacherous. You know what a Bunyip is, don't you?"

I thought about it for a moment. "I think so; it's some kind of an Aboriginal mythical creature, isn't it, - supposed to live in creeks and waterholes?"

"Yes, it's a creature, but *mythical*? - I honestly don't know about that, Bill." He sounded pensive and I looked at him sideways thinking he was having a go at me, but his face remained serious.

"*You* believe in the Bunyip stories?" I said.

Bart seemed uncomfortable and tugged at his hat as he squinted towards the east where the morning sun was beginning to rise above the straggly gums on the flat horizon beyond the bullock paddock. "I'd better get the team moving. You want to give me a hand?"

I agreed and as we finished yoking the bullocks I brought up the subject again hoping it wouldn't offend Bart. "I didn't think any white person believed in bunyips," I said tentatively.

"Well, - I don't believe in *all* of them, of course," he said, "but there've been some yarns about something strange on the Warrego for many years that keep cropping up from time to time, and I know for a fact people have even found skulls and bones that don't look like anything alive today."

I shook my head. "I wouldn't have thought someone like *you* would even…"

"…I don't believe in *all* the stories that are getting around," Bart said again hastily, "but the Warrego Bunyip is different. Some reliable people have sworn they've sighted someone or something that lives along the river, - and they've been stone-cold sober at the time. I'll just keep an open mind on it until I see something for myself; until then I won't tempt the Warrego Bunyip." He shook hands with me and

42

jumped aboard the Gypsy Queen. "Thanks for your company, Bill," he said, "…and for not laughing at Darling and Sweetheart, but if you ever tell anyone Black Bart the Bullocky from Bourke believes in the Warrego Bunyip I'll deny I ever met you." He grinned and turned his attention to the bullocks waiting patiently for his orders to put their backs into it. "Get up now Darling; come around Sweetheart," he bellowed. The ironclad wheels began to turn, slowly at first, and then as the mighty animals strained against the yokes and straps, the Gypsy Queen rolled down the incline and turned towards the still flooded Enngonia Creek crossing. I watched it until the wagon had made it safely across and had climbed the far bank and then I made my way slowly back to my camp, thoughts of Black Bart's elusive Warrego Bunyip crowding my mind.

The mail truck came through in the afternoon of the next day as the teamster had predicted and the driver reported that the road was clear to Belalie Station and beyond. It was my first lesson in the vagaries of the western Queensland weather, and more so, my first brush with one of the many characters who made up the framework of that society that I was about to become a part of. After more than a month on the road since leaving Miller's Run, I arrived at the small twin settlements of Barringun and Wooroorooka.

When I arrived there in late 1920, Barringun's resident population had dwindled to about one hundred, mostly older people who had nowhere else to go and, as Jimmy Miller had told me, that number was a fraction of the population that had lived and worked in the town in the halcyon days of the 1880s when Barringun had three hotels, a general store, post office, school, and a butcher shop, - and at one point even a registered brewery. After federation and the relaxing of the border customs regulations, the only reason for Barringun's continued existence was to support the surrounding pastoral properties and to accommodate the simple daily needs of the travelling workers, and as luck would have it, Barringun Creek was capable of supplying a constant flow of good drinking water from a shallow bore in its bed even during the long periods of low rainfall that the district went through. At some time in the early years, the progressive and astute town committee had put in a public water syphon and amenities for the visiting workers behind the Barringun Hotel, the one hotel that remained open for business.

Across the border in Woorooorooka, the old Customs House was still standing, a small cottage built in the early 1880's and retained partly as a reminder of the original purpose of the towns' presence in the middle of that immense isolation. It was tenanted by the Border

Fence Ranger and his family, whose main task was to maintain the substantial netting wire border fence and its gates for traffic and stock. The gates were left open after Federation, but they were symbolic in that they clearly defined the *actual* state border between New South Wales and Queensland. Nearby, the police station still had an important role to play in the wide-ranging surrounding district that was controlled by the officer in charge. A motor mail service ran twice a week between Cunnamulla and the border, connecting with another motor service on to Bourke, and it wasn't uncommon for six or seven herds of cattle, or flocks of sheep, to pass through the border gates in a day with their drovers and roustabouts, teamsters and wool wagons creating clouds of dust that blew across the flat sandy spinifex country. At times twenty or thirty campfires could be counted at night within half a mile of the town and this usually meant a spirited night or two was to be had with the travellers slaking their thirsts at the Barringun Hotel.

The Barringun Hotel was well known throughout the west and, when the Queensland shearing season was about to get underway each spring, groups of shearers began to arrive early from the southern districts whose season had already ended. The best stands in the shearing sheds were the ones closest to the holding pens where the sheep could be hauled out, shorn and tossed back down the exit chutes in the shortest possible time, and the old hands who knew the layout of every shed in each district made a bee-line for Barringun to be ready to grab their ticket to the stand that would allow them to get the best tally.

On the road from Barringun-Wooroorooka to Cunnamulla, which was about seventy-five miles to the north, there were some huge sheep runs. Thurrulgoonia was owned by the Squatting Investment Company and managed by Mr J. K. McDonald. It carried about eighty thousand sheep and was considered to be one of the most impressive in the state. The station had a picturesque homestead and several remarkable bores averaging a million gallons a day that watered a vast extent of country.

Another old and famous station was Tinenburra, originally developed from virgin scrub by the famous land squatter I'd already heard about, The Honourable James Tyson. It claimed to have the largest shearing shed in Australia, - perhaps even in the world, - and it probably did. It was a remarkable edifice, built in the traditional woolshed shape of a great 'T', open at the sides, with a sharp-pitched timber roof covered with felt, which came down within four feet of the ground. The central part of the 'T' was the mainboard along which the roustabouts worked, taking the newly cut fleece to the waiting wool assessors and pressers at the bottom end, and at the top of the 'T', there were forty stands, twenty on each side, where the shearers plied their trade. The catching and holding pens were built to accommodate six thousand sheep undercover and the exit chutes next to each shearer led out to counting-out pens that held another six thousand that had already been shorn.

The gun shearers or ringers, who were the best paid, usually rode in on horseback with a good packhorse in tow carrying all their shearing gear and trade outfits, the two pairs of special shearer's dungarees with a double thickness of material over the front and lower back leg, the *'Jackie Howe'* singlets with patches under the arms where the sheep's feet were placed during shearing, and leather boots with lacing across the front and a flap to prevent the shearing comb catching in the laces. The roustabouts or common shed labourers, wool-pressers, ordinary hands, and general utility men, often walked from distant parts of the country with swags on their backs, and lines of empty wagons, with teams of twenty horses or bullocks, trudged down the Warrego track from the railhead at Cunnamulla to take the fleece back there for transport to the mills in Toowoomba or Brisbane or, like Black Bart from Bourke, came from the opposite direction and made for the railhead at Bourke in New South Wales.

It had become something of a ritual for the shearers, after securing their stand tickets and picking their team of roustabouts, to head back down the track to Barringun to wait for the appointed 'cut-in' day. That might be a week or two away depending on the weather conditions, for shearing wet sheep was considered a breach of the Shearer's Union rules. With not enough rooms at the hotel, a collection of tents and shelters were quickly erected on a bend of Barringun Creek and it became the temporary home of the ready and waiting labour force who whiled away the time until cut-in playing cards in small groups, or gathered at the Barringun Hotel where the concertina and mandolin could be heard well into the night, while the rhythmic sounds of a good old bush dance taking place on the hotel's wooden dance floor announced the intention of the participants to enjoy their leisure time before the backbreaking obligations of shearing a couple of hundred thousand sheep commenced.

I decided to linger in and around Barringun for at least a few weeks. Tom Thumb's coat had begun to look a bit dull and I wanted to make sure my little mate was in top condition for whatever station work I might find along the track. I found what I thought was the perfect spot; it was further away from Barringun than the drover's and shearer's camps, about half a mile from the Barringun Hotel, but that didn't matter to me. It was close to the running creek and there was a patch of good grass that Tom seemed interested in examining in detail.

A fireplace had already been established with a circle of stones that had been placed by some human hand now gone and a stack of firewood had been left for the next occupier of the camp. Several logs had been dragged from the creek and laid on the outside of the campfire circle and they made a convenient if not totally comfortable seat.

The town itself, such as it was, appealed to my ever-increasing desire for solitude. It was small enough for me not to feel too overwhelmed by the few people I *had* to deal with daily for such necessities of life as I required, and yet the district was large enough for me to set up my camp, keep to myself and not feel the need to have to explain to any concerned or inquisitive person why I mainly preferred to be on my own. At this particular time though I felt I needed to find something to keep my mind occupied, for I'd only recently learned the fate of my friend Jimmy Miller and I hadn't quite come to terms with the shock of his passing in such a sudden and unexpected manner.

There was a lot of noise coming from the Barringun Hotel and, on impulse, I decided to go down and investigate what was going on as a means to deal with my aching heart. I'd already found out that they were the shearers and roustabouts waiting for the start of the sheep shearing season, of course, but I was unprepared for the sheer cheerfulness and comradeship that each man displayed towards the others around him. Mesmerised, I sat on the edge of the hotel veranda and listened in to the old cronies who sat in a big happy group there, talking of times long past. The conversation turned to the Honourable James Tyson, who'd had the Tuen Hotel built on his own land at Tinenburra for the shearers, and I listened enthralled as some of the old-timers recalled various stories about that enigmatic cattle king of the 1880s who, they all agreed, had been Australia's first self-made millionaire. No one ever knew really how much money he'd made in his lifetime, they said, but the consensus was that he'd certainly died a very rich man.

Big Seth, whom I understood from the general conversation, was one of the 'gun' shearers at Tinenburra, said he'd been travelling to Melbourne overland on one occasion and happened to meet 'Jimmy' Tyson on the way. "He was a man of few words and plain dress," he said, "and his manner was that of someone who was completely self-reliant and who needed no company other than his own."

I pricked up my ears at that remark, and I wondered if Jimmy Tyson and I were kindred souls and perhaps shared more than just similar personality traits, for I too needed no other company but my own at most times and I'd been led to believe it wasn't normal to be like that. Maybe there was nothing wrong with my mind-set and it was simply that Jimmy and I, and perhaps others, were just made that way.

Many of Big Seth's old mates had heard the story of his encounter with Tyson before, but it was considered ill-mannered to stop a man from finishing his yarn once he'd got the floor and was wound up to tell it again. "Tyson was slow of speech, as if he was counting each word as it dropped," he said. "He had a habit of giving a person a piercing look, but he was very shy, especially in the company of the ladies. He was an old bachelor, and unless someone had been previously acquainted with him, or had been warned about his strange ways, few people ever took him to be a millionaire. They rather classed Jimmy as maybe a small tradesman or mechanic, unless the conversation turned to flocks of sheep, herds of cattle, or pastures. Then, if Jimmy forced himself to speak, the listeners who didn't know him usually thought of him as an overseer or boundary rider, - anything but the Honourable James Tyson, the great millionaire squatter."

Big Seth broke off to take a deep breath and quaff a half-pint of ale and Squinty Gordon took up the yarn, as it was considered quite acceptable to step in with your own contribution to the conversation while the original yarn-teller briefly rested his gums. "Tyson would often move about the countryside on his own like a swagman or sundowner…" Squinty said, "…and when he was close by one of the stations that he owned and had a manager overseeing its day to day operations, he would camp within a mile or so of it with any other swaggie he'd met on the track, or he'd wait patiently until at least one came along. Then, over a billy-can of tea, he'd turn the conversation to the nearby station. *'That's hungry Jimmy Tyson's place.'* He'd say to the swaggie, by way of discovering the man's opinion. *"What do you think of the old miser?"* The unsuspecting man would either agree with him, *'Aye, it is his place; isn't he a mean old devil?'* or sometimes he'd get the sort of reply he'd wanted to hear, *'No, no, he's a good man, is Mister Tyson, - always helps out a man who's down on his luck.'* This was one of Jimmy's crafty means of discovering how people felt about his station manager's performance."

Squinty went on to say that, "…he might stay in the camp for the night, and then in the morning tell his travelling companion that he was going to call into the station to see what sort of folk Jimmy's managers were. If the advice was *'don't bother,'* he'd march into the station and give the manager his dues for not following his instructions to respond generously to every 'swaggies' needs."

Big Seth nodded his head in agreement, but he wasn't quite finished with what *he* had to contribute to Jimmy Tyson's story and he took up the yarn again when he identified an appropriate long pause in Squinty's exchange, - after all, it *had* been his yarn.

"Yes," he said, "...Jimmy was always a good friend to the swaggies and sundowners, who were mostly men who'd had a hard time of it, but I'd swear an oath he had no time for slackers or freeloaders when he found out that's what a man was." He paused again, but resisted the temptation to take another swig of ale, for he'd been around the traps long enough to know that he had to make the breather too brief for Squinty, - or anyone else, - to cut in. "When Jimmy wasn't visiting one of his stations or travelling about the interior of the continent, he lived in a cottage near Wagga Wagga in central New South Wales. Wagga, as the residents called it, was a small township then, and Jimmy lived a simple existence, without any extravagance of any kind. He was a particularly hard man to pin down, especially when he got wind that any charitable organisations were keen to talk to him about their fundraising activities, so when a proposal was put forward to build a church in Wagga, and subscription lists arranged to see if sufficient funds could be raised for the building to be commenced, Jimmy would be nowhere to be found. The church ladies were to the fore, as they always are in charitable matters, and one, not knowing of Tyson's attitude towards handouts of that kind, suggested that they ask him to head the donor list, as it would give their fundraising efforts a good start. The tricky part of that little matter was the effort required in cornering him to put their case, as Jimmy had a habit on most days of leaving his home early in the morning and returning late at night. Eventually, however, they were rewarded for their long patience when four of them managed to surround him in a corner. *'Oh, Mr Tyson, we think it is quite the time we had a church in our township.'* One of the ladies said hopefully."

Big Seth had told many a yarn in the past, but it was still a great source of mirth to his listeners when the giant of a man did his vocal impersonation of one of the sweet-voiced ladies pleading their case to Tyson. Several of the men sitting around the circle blew him mock kisses and whistled in approval, but that only served to make Seth, - a natural entertainer, - even more animated in his actions. He stood and curtsied to the gathering and then continued in the same exaggerated tone of voice.

"Jimmy already knew all about their plan to corner him and what they were after, of course, but he wasn't going to let on about his prior knowledge to them. *'How are you going to build it?'* he asked.

'We are about to start making collections and have come to you, thinking that if you would head the subscription list with something

48

nice, it would give us such a good start,' the sweet-voiced lass who'd been nominated for the job explained."

It would have taken little imagination on the part of any of the witnesses to his performance to recognise that Big Seth was play-acting, even if they'd been visitors in Barringun for the first time as I was, and it wasn't just his bushy red beard, his deep-throated laugh and huge bodily proportions that were the main deterrents to any adverse doubts about his manliness. Big Seth gave off an aura of palpable masculinity which allowed him to maintain a safe buffer between his perceived character-acting and his real-life personality, and I wondered idly, while I joined in with the crowd's appreciation of his performance, what kind of a reception a small *'girlish'* person like me with a naturally high-pitched voice would have received if I'd tried to pull off the same yarn and capped it off with the same theatrics.

I knew what the answer to that question would have been almost as soon as the thought crossed my mind. It was, in fact, most likely that a performance of the same kind as Seth's on my part would have been greeted with an embarrassed silence and suspicious side glances, and I decided there and then that I would take care never to engage in any kind of behaviour that might draw attention to my evident girlishness. Having come to that momentous, but obvious conclusion, I turned my attention again to Big Seth, who had continued his yarn.

"Tyson regarded the sweet young lady with one piercing eye," he said. "The other was half-closed, as was his way of sizing up a person's commitment to their cause and, without even a hint of a smile to give the young lady some slight confidence in his big-heartedness, he said, *'What sort of a Kirk were you thinking of building, and what will it cost?'* The young lady was still bright-eyed, and seemingly not put off by Jimmy's brusqueness as she illustrated the plan, *'Well we thought that £1000 would be ample to build and complete the whole thing.'* Any other less wealthy man would have recoiled in shock at the amount of money involved in her request, but Tyson merely said, *'Alright then where's your list?'* and when she produced it from her purse he went into his little office. He returned a short time later and said, *'You think if you could collect £1000 it would be enough to build the Kirk you desire?'* She assured him that it would be quite enough, and then, lo and behold, he handed over a cheque for the whole £1000 and said, *'Go away and build it then.'* He left while the ladies stood in astonishment inspecting the cheque and before they could even thank him."

Big Seth was so dry from talking by then that he had no option but to empty his mug of ale and he looked around for Squinty over the top of it to see if he might take over his yarn again, but Squinty had slid off to the bar to replenish his own mug so he continued, somewhat relieved, knowing that he was almost there and that the tributes would be his alone to enjoy. "The news soon spread that Jimmy had given £1000 to build the church and his rare show of open-handedness was echoed far and wide for hundreds of miles. Some said, *'Tyson must have gone off his nut at last.'* Others of a more charitable disposition said, *'Tyson - a woman-hater, eh? What do you think about him now?'* All sorts of reasons were given for the sudden burst of generosity, but nobody was any the wiser. The church was built in due course, and it was no mean structure, either, but as usual, items of all sorts not included in the contract were added until the money was all expended with still some extra furnishings required. A committee was formed to evaluate ways and means to accrue the extra funds, but without result until the previously successful sweet-voiced young lady suggested at last that they should try Tyson again. They did, and after waiting and waiting, caught him and explained what a nice little church it was and how beautiful a gift it was from him, and so on. Then the crucial test came, when she of the sweet voice said, *'We have some extras to put in and thought you would, no doubt, wish to complete your good work.'* Jimmy was too cagey a bird to be caught out a second time. *'Oh, yes, I see,'* he said, *'Well you assured me that a thousand pounds would do the job. Now you want more money to put lightning conductors on the roof, eh? Well if God Almighty thinks fit to send a storm with thunder and lightning and knock the kirk I paid for right down to the ground, then let Him do it. I can't be held responsible if some of you ladies have incurred His wrath by your sins; - it's none of my business. Go away, ladies.'* They did go, and very crestfallen they were too at his blunt rebuff, but Jimmy had ridden away into the Never-Never long before they completed the extra accessories for the church and he took his money with him to the grave."

Big Seth had finished his narration and he seemed satisfied as he accepted the congratulations from his comrades on another tale well told. It was then time for a few songs and the group settled in to sing the bush songs that everyone seemed to know the words to, - except me of course. I longed to be a part of it all, but I couldn't bring myself to join in with them in their merriment, dreading that my high-pitched voice would be out of place and plainly heard amongst the low and discordant tones of the others. I listened well though and sang them to myself during the evening, and I learned some of the shorter ditties off by heart that very first night, marvelling at how many subjects and how many verses there were that dealt with all kinds of droving incidents, mining romances, and lost loves.

It seemed to me that every traveller in the western districts was a poet or a minstrel who'd lost someone or something of great value and had taken to the bush tracks to share their sorrows in song or verse with others who'd found themselves in similar circumstances, and it was this camaraderie that made me feel even more of a kindred spirit with them. The sense of association was, in fact, so strong that it convinced me to return the next evening to learn more about these rough and tough, but essentially gentle folks and their way of life expressed through song and verse.

I knew that they were all aware of my presence, lurking in the background, of course, and although most of them left me to choose my own level of familiarity, much as they would an apprehensive, inquisitive possum in the veranda rafters, some tried in vain to gain my confidence. "Come on young Bill," one would coax me. "Have a tot of rum with us and we'll teach you another ditty. I'll bet you haven't heard, *'My Lovely Kate of the old Coach Stage'*, or *'Jack the Genteel Stockman'*."

Someone else would chime in with, "What about *'My Old Bush Hut on the Far Bulloo'*, or *'Mulga Jim'*?" and then they'd unanimously decide on *'My Old Brown Hat and Shoes'* and roar out the chorus, with rousing effect.

'Give me my old brown hat,
A pair of my old brown shoes,
Pots and pots of money, and
Tons and tons of booze.'

There was always much emphasis on the chanting of the last line, accompanied by the banging of fists on the table, of course, and by then they'd forgotten that I had even been there, so I was able to slip away unnoticed to sing the ditties I'd learned that evening to Tom Thumb as I rode back to my camp. I didn't care that I sang in a pitch that was much too high for the manly renditions I'd heard at the pub either, because there was nobody else around to hear me except Tom, and I knew he didn't mind. "What about this one, Tom?" I'd say.

"Out on the board, the old shearer stands,
Grasping his shears in his thin bony hands,
His bleary eyes are fixed on a blue-bellied yoe,
Saying, If I get you, gal, I'll make the ringer go."

Tom's ears would twitch and swivel in my direction and I knew that at least *he* was enjoying the sound of his master's *'girlish'* voice.

"Click go the shears, boys, click, click, click.
Wide is his blow and his hands are moving quick,
And the ringer looks around and he's beaten by a blow

51

And he curses that old snagger with the blue-bellied yoe."

One evening when I got back to my camp and set Tom contentedly free on his patch of good grass, I set about preparing my simple dinner and had just finished eating when a form materialised out of the darkness.

"Hello mate," a voice said. "Care for some company?"

"Yes, of course," I said, although I would have preferred to be left alone, but *that* wouldn't have been polite and I accepted that it was the way of the bush to greet someone who didn't want to be alone for at least a little while with tolerance and patience.

"I won't stay long," the voice said. The man came into full view and I stood up to welcome my visitor. He'd been tall and well-built in the past, I thought, judging by the still broad chest and wide shoulders, but now he looked well past his prime, the once-proud muscles of his upper arms wrinkled and sagging and the unruly crop of white hair and full beard straggling down over his singlet. He approached slowly and with some difficulty, seeming to hobble along in a gait that spoke silently of many years of back-breaking work. He carried a pannikin of tea in one hand and what looked like a lump of cheese in the other.

"I'm Pat O'Leary, known as Long Pat to most other shearers in the district. I'm camped just over there," he said, waving the hand with the cheese in the direction he'd come from. "Maybe a hundred yards, I suppose."

"Nice of you to come over; Bill Smith's my name," I said.

"Yes, I saw you down the Barringun earlier…"

"…You were at the Barringun Hotel?" I said.

"Yes, I left shortly after you did. Had my old nag tied up behind the hotel, - that'd be why you didn't hear me coming along behind you, - that and your singing, of course." He sat down heavily on the log on the opposite side of the campfire to where I stood, open-mouthed and embarrassed.

"You heard me singing?" I said, feeling quite uncomfortable.

"Fine voice you've got too young Bill," he said. "A bit higher than my range I reckon, - if I ever tried to put a verse or two together, - but a good one nevertheless. That was a decent rendition of *'The Blue-Bellied Yoe'* I must say.

I tried to hide my mortification that someone had heard me sing after all. "I didn't see you at the hotel, Long Pat," I said weakly. "I don't like to be heard, - *singing*, I mean."

Long Pat chuckled. "Well then, as the old saying goes, *'little girls should be seen and not heard,'* but…" He hesitated and looked at me mischievously, "...that doesn't go for little boys, I suppose, even ones with higher than normal voices, does it?

"I, - I guess not," I stammered.

"I can see why you don't like to be heard though; you would've been a bit out of tune with the rest of the company at the Barringun if you'd joined in, - what with Big Seth and his baritone, - you would've sounded like a budgerigar amongst a murder of crows at sunrise."

"A *murder* of crows...?" I said.

"That's what a bunch of crows sitting around together is called." Long Pat laughed again. "Oh, don't worry about it, young Bill. I didn't come here to criticise your singing voice or talk about murdering crows. Have you got a two-toother in your paddock somewhere up north then, or are you thinking of hanging around for a bit in Barringun and moving on to the shearing sheds in the district? I suppose you've come for the start of the 'cut-in' at Tinenburra and then Thurrulgoonia after that's done."

I'd got over my humiliation at Long Pat's amusement regarding the odds of my high-pitched voice playing a part in Big Seth's pub choir, but I stared at the old man in confusion. "...A *'two-toother'* in my paddock?"

"It's a common enough saying in the sheds, Bill," Long Pat said. "I'm surprised you haven't heard it, but maybe you haven't been around the shearing sheds long enough. A two-toother is a young ewe that's just become fully grown. If a shed hand has a two-toother in his paddock it means he's got a girl waiting for him at home when he finishes the shearing season."

I shook my head in wonder. "No, I haven't got a two-toother anywhere and I didn't come here for the shearing, although I must be the only person in Barringun who hasn't. I was thinking I might stay around here for a few weeks until I've cleared the Darling River red dust out of my throat," I said. "I've just come from working a stump-jump plough on a wheat farm near Lake Cargelligo in the Riverina of New South Wales."

"Ah, I see," the old man said. "The way you sang, *'The Blue-Bellied Yoe'* I thought you must have been a shed worker of some kind," the old man said.

I laughed. "No, Long Pat, I sang the words, but it must be obvious I don't know any of the shearing terms," I said. "I've got a good memory for verse, though..." I broke off and sighed as the memory of my many happy evenings sitting with Jimmy Miller at the small table in my hut at Miller's Run came flooding back.

Long Pat nodded. "A blue-bellied yoe is an old ewe whose wool is so thin on her belly that you can see her bluish skin through it," he said. "A 'snagger' is a clumsy shearer who cuts the sheep he's shearing..." he hesitated before continuing. "...or an old shearer who's past retirement age, but refuses to put down the blades."

I studied my visitor, but sipped my tea and said nothing, fearing that any comment I might make about age or retirement might sour the discussion.

I heaved a sigh of relief as Long Pat changed the direction of the conversation. "Maybe you *should* try to get a job in one of the sheds, Bill," he said.

I shook my head. "I don't know anything about shearing at all, Long Pat, except what you've just told me," I said, "... so I doubt that I'd be able to get any kind of job around here. I might have to keep going on the road until I find something that suits me."

"Oh don't be so sure about that, Bill," Long Pat said. "They're always looking for an extra 'tar-boy' in the sheds, - mainly because nobody else wants to do it." He must have noticed my questioning look for he went on to explain. "A tar-boy carries a jar of Stockholm pine tar and a brush, and daubs the sheep with it if its skin gets accidentally cut by the shears. It seals the wound and keeps the flies away. Good shearers make the tar-boy's job easy because they don't cut the jumbuck's skin and the tar-boy is then free to help the roustabout collect the fleeces and deliver them to the sorting table. It makes it all the more efficient, you see."

I suddenly remembered another verse from 'The Blue-Bellied Yoe' and broke into an impromptu recital, although I was careful not to break into song.

"The tar-boy is there and waiting on demand
With his old tar-pot in his tarry hand.
Sees an old ewe with a cut upon her back,
This is what he's waiting for, come tar here, Jack."

Long Pat laughed. "You'd make a good tar-boy, Bill." He changed tack again. "I know the Lake Cargelligo area," he said as he took a bite out of his lump of cheese. "I used to do a lot of shearing at what we called the *'downriver'* stations along the Darling below Bourke. Each station had its river landing and the fleece was sent to the coast on barges. We'd cut-in Yalladora Station first and if the weather was fine, we'd shear a hundred thousand in six weeks, cut-out of that shed and then be ready to move on to Tambara Station. Tambara was probably the biggest on the river; the biggest that I've worked at anyway; two hundred thousand sheep were shorn there every season."

I was awestruck. "Three hundred thousand at two stations? - that's a lot of sheep," I said. "There'd have to be plenty of shearers on hand to shear a mob of that size."

Long Pat shook his head and grinned. "We usually had thirty or so working on the Darling River stations. It sounds like a big job, but even a rookie shearer could do from a hundred to a hundred and fifty sheep each day, and at the rate of one pound per hundred, you can see what a nice little cheque would be coming to every man when the season ended."

I nodded, meanwhile doing some quick calculations in my head. *'Three hundred thousand sheep at the two stations, - thirty shearers; that's ten thousand sheep each, at one pound per hundred, so each shearer can earn one hundred pounds.'*

"That *would* have been a nice little cheque," I said, "…a hundred pounds each?"

"Well done, you know your sums Bill, but it didn't quite work out as tidily as that in those days. It was before the Shearers' Union started their strike actions around the country and everyone was paid on a system called *'piece work'* whereby each shearer's whole team got paid on how many sheep he put down the exit chute. If you were lucky enough to get into the *'ringer's'* team, - that's the fastest shearer in the shed, - you'd make more money because he usually shore more than two hundred sheep in four runs in a day; that's four, two-hour stints on the board, and it's about twenty more sheep than the next *'gun'* shearer might shear in the same time."

I grinned. "I suppose everybody wanted to be in the ringer's team," I said.

Long Pat nodded. "That's right. I always had plenty of people hanging around me begging to be on my team; it made me feel like I was one of those great actors on the stage when I was on the board and running up a good tally with my team cheering me on, but those days are long gone, Bill. Now they say I'm just an old snagger." He shook his head slowly as if the term was an affront to his sensitivities. "I may be old and a bit slower than I used to be, Bill, but I don't snag too many jumbucks even now."

I looked at him in genuine awe. "You were a ringer?" I said.

"Oh yes; I was *one* of the quickest in the world with the blades, young Bill," he said. "But that's not such a grand thing, to be honest. We, - the colonial shearers that is, - were always better than those from other places anyway because of the way we held the sheep upright between our knees, a style that's made us considerably faster than those who hold the sheep down flat on the board, and when the machine

55

shearing came in about thirty years ago I took it up like a duck takes to water, but I wasn't *the* best, that would've been…"

"…now let me think," I said. "Ah yes, - you're going to tell me about Crooked Mick, the giant shearer. He'd shear five hundred sheep a day; even more, if it were ewes. He worked so fast his shears ran hot; he'd have half-a-dozen pairs of blades in the water-pot at a time, cooling off, right?"

Long Pat laughed. "You've been listening to Crooked Mick yarns at the Barringun Hotel. Crooked Mick wasn't that great as far as the tar-boys were concerned; he was a bit rough on the sheep sometimes. He kept five tar-boys running all the time he shore, dabbing on Stockholm tar each time he cut a sheep. They say that once, in the old Dunlop shed, the boss got annoyed at the way Mick was cutting the sheep and said: *'That'll do, you're sacked.'* Mick was going all out at the time, and he had a dozen more sheep shorn before he could straighten up and hang his shears on the hook."

We both laughed heartily, for Crooked Mick stories were always appreciated the more outlandish they became, - and that was often the case. "No, seriously," Long Pat said. "There *was* one ringer none of us could ever beat with the blades or the machine and I believe his 1892 world shearing record will stand for a very long time to come. His name was Jackie Howe and he shore 237 sheep by machine in one day at Barcaldine Downs station early in October, and then shore 321 weaners with the blades at Alice Downs a week later. During that week he'd shorn 1437 sheep in 44 hours. We all tried to slow him down by tickling him and jumping on his back and a few other measures besides, - all in good sport of course, - but it made no difference to Jackie. He was a great physical specimen of a man; he weighed 18 stone, had a 50-inch chest, huge biceps and hands the size of small tennis racquets. He was no slouch on the track either, so if you were silly enough to give him a bit of lip and he *did* decide to teach you some manners, you'd need to have had a good head start to get clear of him because he could run 100 yards in eleven seconds in his socks. He was also known to have won prizes for Irish dancing so he could have given you the toe of his boot with a high kick without even slowing down, but luckily for us, he was a gentle giant. He was so admired amongst the other shearers that the navy singlets we all still wear in the sheds are called *'Jackie Howe's'*, - have you heard of the great man in your travels?"

I shook my head. "No, I haven't, Long Pat, - maybe I'll have the honour of meeting him one day, - I suppose he's still shearing like you are," I said.

"Oh no, he gave up the shearing twenty years ago and bought the Universal Hotel at Blackall. He held it until last year and then he bought Sumnervale and Shamrock Park, pastoral properties near Blackall, but his health was already broken by then and he died in July this year at only fifty-eight years old."

I frowned. "That's sad. I wonder what went wrong with his health."

Long Pat shook his head slowly. "He had a lot of pressure put on him by his so-called union friends. Jackie was an enthusiastic member of the Queensland Shearers' Union and prominent on its committee and he remained a loyal member of the Australian Labor Party all his life. It took its toll on his health in the end, I believe. He and I weren't close friends, but we respected each other, - although we disagreed on some things, - and the way the Shearers' Union went about making all squatters toe the union line in the early 1890s was one of them."

"You all have to be in the union now, don't you?" I said.

"Yes, we do, Bill," Long Pat nodded, "… and I don't mind following the Union rules now because things are run fair and square and anyway there's no other way to still be involved in the shearing game, but I still remember the mobs who burnt down the squatters shearing sheds if they wouldn't abide by the union rules and pay wages at the rates they demanded. There'd been a long drought leading up to the 1890s and times had been tough for everyone. Wool prices were falling and sheep sales were so bad that the squatters were boiling down their ewes, and selling legs of mutton for a shilling apiece. There was a big meeting held at Wagga Wagga, which was the Shearers' Union headquarters in the Riverina district, to discuss what could be done to keep wages at their current level, but I was concerned that the squatters couldn't go on paying a pound a hundred when the economy was so bad, and I thought they would just shut up shop and destock their runs. That, of course, would have meant none of us would have had jobs. I voiced my opinion to the meeting that, when the price of wool rose, competition amongst the squatters for labour would understandably raise shearing wages as had always happened in the past, but the union bosses were adamant. If the squatters got away with cutting down wages, they said, there's no saying what they'd do next, and the union would see to it that those squatters who defied their demands wouldn't even be allowed in their shed to stand over the workers."

"They were going to be locked out of their *own* sheds," I said, shaking my head in amazement.

Long Pat sighed. "That's what it had come to, Bill. I told the meeting, *'Jim Adams, the squatter at Narraween I worked for last season, won't stand any nonsense. You take my word for it. He's always been a good employer; no man here can deny that. He pays good wages, supplies good rations, and pays cash on the nail when the men want it. He doesn't even give cheques, and that blocks the publican because a chap can pay as he goes, and needn't hand his cheque over the bar counter, but I know what he'll say to the union delegate or any other man who tells him he's not to be boss in his shed. He'll tell them to go away and mind their own business and leave him to look after his, in words a bit stronger than what I'm using here; he'll tell them that he'll see the Shearers' Union and everyone connected with it in Hell before he'll give up the right to manage his property in his way.'* I was shouted down by the unionists, though. *'We'll show him who is going to Hell,'* they yelled at me. *'His property? Who made Narraween what it is today? Who dug the tanks and put up the fences, and shepherded the sheep before the paddocks were fenced, - and built the shearing shed. His property? We say it's our property, - all of us. We made it with the labour of our hands and we ought to have the biggest say in the managing of it. Let them walk off the land they've squatted on and built up with our labour at a miserable dole. We'll take it over and divide it up into nice small-sized farms, that'll give us a thousand fifty-acre lots. See what a crowd of families that'd help to keep happy and contented. Everyone would have their own two hundred sheep to shear for themselves and there'd be no more begging to the squatters for fair wages,'* they said."

Long Pat shook his head. "The union delegates wouldn't listen to reason. *'Miserable dole?'* I said, *'That's a dashed fine name to give free rations to the tune of half-a-dozen sheep a night, and a couple of bags of flour a week, which I know Narraween did at the last shearing. And what if this drought continues,'* I said. *'How about the happy and contented families then? I've seen sheep dying by hundreds on one place - and the whole forty thousand they were running on that station would have died in another month if the rain hadn't come. Small farms in a dry country like this would never survive. They'd be all fighting each other for water after the first year and there'd be bashings and even murders over it; it's nothing short of foolishness.'* I knew I was wasting my time though when they said, *'Time enough to think about that when it comes, Long Pat. Are you with us or are you going to side with those 'scab' strike breakers?'*

I looked at the old man and sighed. "Were you the only one to stand up to them?" I said, breathless with anticipation.

"Oh no," Long Pat said. "There were quite a few like me who were happy with everything as it had been and didn't like the idea of a mob of lazy scoundrels getting paid for causing trouble where it mostly wasn't due. I remember the shearers' quarters on Tarraweena Station in the early ninety's. It was a long, well-built structure, in a pleasant high spot overlooking the Darling River, and it was big enough to hold thirty men comfortably in the two rows of bunks along either side of the room. At that time there were about twenty of us lounging around in it after a hard day's work. We were mostly younger men of between twenty and forty, all different nationalities and languages, English, Irish, Scottish and Australian, a Frenchman, two Germans, a coloured American, but all at ease with each other's company through our common occupation of shearing. We'd had a good feed, and were relaxing in the ordinary dress of the station hand, tweed or moleskin trousers and Crimean shirt. Some had coats because it had been a bit cold, but the majority of us were in our shirt sleeves, - except for the English, of course; they were in the formal after-dinner attire of top hat and tails you'd expect from such gentlemen of the old country."

I spluttered my tea and stared at him in astonishment. "They were dressed in *top hat and tails*?" It was only then that I saw the twinkle in Long Pat's eyes reflected in the light from the campfire. "You're having a go at me," I grinned through my teary-eyed congestion.

"Yes, Bill; I was just making sure you were paying attention. The English shearers always *did* seem a bit over-dressed to some of us, though," the old shearer said. "You're not English yourself are you?"

I looked at him curiously. "No, I'm not..." I started.

"...Oh, I just thought..." Long Pat looked a bit ruffled. "Well, you always seem a bit over-dressed too. Most of the young men like to get around in their 'Jackie Howe' singlets to show off their muscles, but you always seem to keep yourself well covered up. Some of the lads at the Barringun have been wondering..."

I laughed, but the implication made me quite uncomfortable. "Well, I have got some foreign blood in me after all," I said. "I don't know much about my parental background, but I'm more likely to be something other than English I think. I've certainly got fair skin so I don't believe in exposing it to the sun if I can help it."

"That's what I thought, and pretty smart of you it is too." Long Pat said. "I've told some of the other youngsters they should look after their skin, but they won't listen to an old snag..." He stopped mid-sentence and sighed as if he couldn't bring himself to say the word *snagger* in reference to himself and my heart went out to him, for I knew he'd love to have had those years back again when he was the ringer. "Tell me if you don't want to hear any more on the subject of the shearers' union," he said.

"No, no; I'm interested." I was quick to reassure him and to steer him away from any further discussion about my reasons for keeping myself covered up.

Long Pat nodded. "I've been a bit long-winded, I know, but I wanted you to get a picture in your mind of how contented we all were in our surroundings. There was a fireplace with a glowing wood fire at one end of the room, around which several men were sitting or lounging, mostly smoking. Others were seated at the long, solid dining-table reading, for some fairly well-filled bookshelves took up one corner of the room. One man was writing a letter. A few were lying in their bunks engaging in quiet conversation in their native languages. There was no loud talking, swearing, or rude behaviour of any sort, and despite the bare walls and plain surroundings the whole room was steeped in an air of relaxation."

"I've got the picture alright; you were certainly all comfortable," I said, "but I guess it didn't last very long."

"No, it didn't, Bill. All of a sudden the door opened and a man in a tweed suit entered without any ceremony or invitation. It wasn't the station manager or the overseer, but he looked around at us as if he owned the place and was greeted by one of the younger men who'd had dealings with him before. He was inclined to be teasing, this young man, and he exclaimed, *'Hello, my honourable union delegate, what brings you here to our humble quarters? Have you come to call out the shearers on strike, and play the devil generally, eh? You've come to the wrong shop if you've got something like that in mind, - we're all steady-going coves here.'*

"The union delegate was used to that sort of opposition though and answered him sarcastically. *'I don't suppose you're speaking for everyone here, Joe Bracks. Some of the men might be game to stand up for their rights and I reckon you'd be happy to get the benefit of their loyalty to the union by getting your wages raised if the union does that for you?'*.

Young Joe Bracks wasn't going to be swayed by the delegate's scorn and he was up for an argument with the pompous scoundrel. *'If the union does that for us?'* he said; *'You and your union crowd haven't done any great things for us so far, except make bad blood between us and the squatters when everything was peace and goodwill before.'*

"The delegate just shook his head and tried to dismiss Joe with an arrogant wave of his hand. *'We can't get any improvement to our working conditions without fighting for it and I reckon we're going to*

60

have a bit of an all-out war this time; - yes, believe me, - war it will be, and a dashed good thing too. It's a violation of our basic human rights when unionists have to take orders from their fellow men and be worked like slaves into the bargain.'

But Joe hung on to his argument like a young horse breaker on the back of a brumby stallion. '*I see what you're getting at honourable delegate, - convince all the gullible ones amongst us that we've been trodden on, and starved, and treated worse than slaves so that you and your cronies can strut around with your bowler hats and watch-chains, and get four pounds a week for nattering to each other around a table while us fools do all the hard graft. That's your game, isn't it?'*

"The delegate turned to the other men looking for support. '*What do you say, Paddy?'* he said to a man who'd been writing a letter at the table.

The man rose from his seat and stood by the fire. I knew him well. He was a tall individual, not as broad in the shoulders as Jacky Howe, but with a steady expression, lit up by a pair of piercing blue eyes and a ruddy complexion, which effectively declared his nationality as Irish, but one who had been working in the heat of the Australian sun for a very long time. '*I say that this strike business is nothing but a damned rebellion against the stability that the workers have enjoyed for a long time, and it's being organised by a bunch of stooges to achieve their own ends at the expense of the rest of us, - just like Joe said. They're the parasites that feed off the working-men who are mugs enough to believe their rubbish, not the squatters, who've mostly worked hard for what they've made and spent it generously enough to make their workers comfortable. There's not a man here that's got anything to complain about. We're well paid, well-fed, well catered for, and as comfortable in our own way as the boss is in his; more in fact, for I've noticed we've got a shingled roof on our quarters and his homestead's roof is box-bark. The travellers' hut is shingled too, so is the roustabouts' but he's never had time to have his place done up, though he lives like a gentleman, as we all know.'*

"The delegate was a bit stunned, but he gathered his wits together enough to say, '*Well then, weren't you the rebellious scion of a gentleman's family yourself, Paddy? You'd know a bit more about rebellions than most of us here if I'm not mistaken...'*

"Before the last word was fully out, Paddy took a couple of steps forward with his big fists clenched and such a bitter glare in his eyes that the delegate stumbled backwards and almost fell over the foot of a man who'd been standing behind him. '*You infernal crook,'* he cried. '*Don't ever dare to mention my family again, or I'll kick you from here to the woolshed and drown you in the wash-pen afterwards. I've done a common man's work since I was sent to Australia as a lad of sixteen, though I wasn't brought up to it back home in Ireland, as you say. I've nothing damaging to say against the squatters who've always given me an honest day's pay for an honest day's work, and whose meat I've eaten, but scavenging bootlickers like you are ruining the good relations we've had with our employers. You're worse than a dingo, for a dingo doesn't beg, but you come to this station and whine for free food, and then try to bite the hand that feeds you. I'm sure I saw you over at the store to-night, waiting for a handout of grub, like the other travellers?'*

"The delegate had his hand on the door-handle and it must have given him some sense of security that escape was within reach, for he continued in a condescending tone of voice. *'It's no wonder you don't take any interest in the workers' rights, - the men who make the wealth of this country, and every other country in the world. You and your like are the makings of a first-class 'scab' and if the other chaps here were of the same mind as me you'd be put out of every shearer's hut on the river...'*

"Paddy had taken another step forward, but luckily for the delegate, young Joe Bracks stepped between them. *'We're not on for a sermon to-night, honourable delegate,'* he said. *'Paddy's got his monkey up, and it'll be bloodshed in here for sure if you don't clear out.'*

"The delegate opened the door. *'Yes I'll go now,'* he said, *'but this is not over, - not by a long way.'* He went out and slammed the door shut and we all just looked at each other in a kind of daze as if to say, *'Did that really happen tonight when we were all nice and relaxed?'*, but the delegate was right, - it wasn't over, and some of us, young Joe Bracks and myself included, took the brunt of the repercussions more than others who were in the room at the time. I was surprised that Jackie, either couldn't see that it was all heading towards violence, or chose to ignore his personal feelings in his blind allegiance to the Union cause."

"Maybe he did, but by that time it was too late to do anything about it," I said.

Long Pat went on as if he hadn't heard. "I broached the subject with Jackie when he and I were by ourselves one evening. I said to him, *'We've been treated well in the past by most squatters, Jackie, haven't we? - and now you want to turn against those who gave you the work, just as if you were one of those layabouts and spielers who come to the stations because they've run out of drinking money. They're only interested in finding out how much they can get away with by gambling and stealing and if they have to do a little work to cover themselves it's done badly so they'll get paid off and go on their way to the next. A lot of them are going about the country asking for work, and praying to God they don't find it, and abusing the people that feed them on top of it all. I wonder the squatters don't stop feeding travellers altogether. I would if I was boss, except for the old snaggers who've been working for years and I know are genuinely looking for work. I say it's downright ungrateful and foolish besides, - and if you follow whatever the Shearers' Union tells you to do, then mark my words, you'll live to rue the day. You can't get big wages out of small profits, but your union delegates don't seem to have common sense enough to see that. I'm ashamed of you, I really am, Jackie.'*

He seemed to be listening to me, nodding every so often, his big blue eyes fixed on me like a schoolboy to his favourite teacher, and when I told him I was ashamed of him, his face grew red and he looked down at the floor as if he'd been caught red-handed lying about his homework; it was as if *he* was ashamed of himself too. I don't think anyone had ever spoken to the big man like that in his whole life before and he didn't quite know what to make of it. He just said quietly, *'Well, thanks for bringing it to my attention, Long Pat, but I must go now. I daresay the squatters will give in before long, and there'll be no more to it than that.'*

"He was wrong, of course, because the violence got worse as time went on. Those squatters who wouldn't bow to the union demands had their sheds burnt down. At Murwell, the roll of shearers was about to be called, and fifty thousand sheep were ready for the shears when it was set on fire and burned to the ground. At Abingdon Downs, a station hand was shot. The Netallie shed, with eighty thousand sheep ready to be shorn, was doused with kerosene and set on fire, but the plot failed, and when the free labourers began the cut-in the unionists rioted and tried to abduct them. It was the same at Grasmere woolshed where the police were forced to use firearms to stop them from torching the place in broad daylight."

I shook my head. "So this great man that everyone admired still turned a blind eye even after the violence started?"

Long Pat nodded. "Maybe you're right though, Bill; it may have been too late and he regretted it in the end. We'll never know, I suppose. I used to think that Jackie was crazy for giving up the blades when he was at the top of his game, but now I'm not so sure that he *wanted* to give it away. I think maybe he *had* to because of the way things were going with the union's standover tactics. It was affecting his health, but it got to him in the end anyway. Jackie's circumstances were a bit different to mine too; he had a family to look after so he had to be in work. His wife Margie and his six sons and two daughters are still living in Blackall and I'm on my own with nobody else to worry about so I shouldn't criticise his conduct. I'm still alive though, and he's not." He smiled wryly. "Maybe I'll just keep on doing what I enjoy till I drop off the board or they won't let me into the shed. If I'm lucky I might get one of the last boards at Tinenburra, but if not I'll just wait for the next shed to cut-in at Thurulgoonia; maybe I'll be lucky there."

I marvelled at the old man's perseverance and his calm acceptance of whatever fate held in store for him.

"What about you Bill?" Long Pat continued. "I'm sure you must have the intention of finding work *somewhere*. I can't picture you being one of those shirkers who go from place to place cadging food and drink from the squatters."

I shook my head forcefully. "I've never asked for anything for nothing in my life so far and I have no intention of ever doing it, Long Pat," I said.

"I thought that would be the case, Bill," the old man nodded gravely. "Yes, I was right about you; you're a navvy if ever I saw one."

I looked the old man directly in the eyes as a thought formed in my mind. "Would you take me on as your roustabout or tar-boy, Long Pat, - if you do manage to get that last board at Tinenburra, that is?" I said.

Long Pat beamed. "How'd you know I was going to ask you that, young Bill?" he said. "Of course I will. It might be tough work though because my back's not quite what it used to be, but my arms are as good as anyone's half my age and as I told you, I don't open too many cuts on the jumbucks even now."

"Don't worry about me, Long Pat," I said, my voice shaky with excitement. "I'm a lot tougher and stronger than I look. I thought for a moment and then added, "I don't have to wear one of those Jackie Howe singlets, do I?"

Long Pat shrugged. "No of course not, Bill. You can wear whatever you feel comfortable in. Some of the roustabouts have taken to wearing them nowadays, but traditionally it was only the shearers who wore them, - as a kind of a badge of honour I suppose." He didn't notice my sigh of relief. "Things have changed over the years since the great shearers' strikes of the 1890s."

Long Pat and I stared into the campfire for a few minutes, each deep in our own thoughts, until I broke the silence. "*You* were Paddy the Irishman, weren't you Long Pat?" I said.

Long Pat nodded and quaffed his tea. "The delegate was right even though I didn't like to be reminded of it. I was a boy of fourteen from a hard-working farming family in County Kerry in Ireland, and I saw first-hand how severely my father was treated at the hands of the bailiff for the absentee landlord who'd never set foot on our island nation. I was a big lad and it was easy to put my age up to eighteen. I got involved with the so-called 'Fenians' and I learned from our leaders how our people had suffered centuries of enforced poverty, and cruel misery and how our rights and liberties had been crushed by a foreign aristocracy who'd seized our lands, and removed its honest workers to make room for their cattle. Our people had been driven across the ocean to try to find the means of living and the political rights that had been denied to them at home. Our leaders organised an uprising against the injustices, it failed and we were arrested. I was convicted of insurrection and sentenced to seven years transportation, even though it was contrary to an agreement made between the British and Western Australian Governments. I was sent out on the Hougoumont, the last convict ship to Australia, with some of the other political prisoners in 1868 and locked up in the Convict Establishment in Fremantle, Western Australia. Some of us were pardoned after a year or so; others escaped, helped by the American Fenians, and were taken to the United States on a schooner called the *Catalpa*."

"You were pardoned?" I said. "Why didn't you go home to Ireland?"

Long Pat shook his head and stared at the ground in front of his feet. We were pardoned, but the British Government made it clear they didn't want us back. The official line was that it was too expensive to organise our return and the British negotiated with the colonial government to relinquish jurisdiction over us; in effect, although we'd been exonerated of any crime, we weren't allowed to return to our homes, - probably so that we couldn't be held up as heroes or examples of the failure of British justice. At the same time, they relinquished control over the Convict Establishment and it was renamed Fremantle Prison. It was a harsh lesson for me in my tender teenage years; I was only sixteen by then and trapped in a foreign land with nowhere to turn for help."

I felt a tear run down my cheek and was glad Long Pat couldn't see it, for I remembered painfully my situation at age sixteen and could see the parallels between us. "What did you do then, Long Pat," I said quietly.

"The only thing I *could* do, Bill." Long Pat raised his eyes to meet mine. "I was too honest to steal and too proud to beg, but I knew first of all that I was the only one in the colony who cared whether I survived or not, and secondly, if I was ever going to see Ireland and my family again it would only be through my own effort. I worked hard, - harder than I'd ever done at home on the farm, even though the principle instilled in me by my father throughout my childhood, that the reward for hard toil would be the attainment of true happiness, if not in this life, in the next, had been shattered. I'd quickly realised that justice was often denied to the most honest of workers due to the greed and cunning of those slackers who wanted nothing more than an easy means of making money. Yes, Bill, I was Paddy the Irishman in the hut that afternoon and I was only speaking my mind from my own experiences. I hope you can understand that and not judge me too harshly because of what I said to the union delegate."

I held his gaze, not concerned now if Long Pat saw my tear-stained face, because I knew that everything the old man said was true. Happiness was not *always* the reward for hard toil and sometimes the most honest of workers had to fight back for the sake of justice, - if for nothing else. "I would never judge you harshly for seeking a fair day's pay for a fair day's work, Long Pat," I said, "nor for standing your ground against the slackers who want to take away from you what you've earned by honest toil."

"Thanks, Bill." Long Pat grinned. "I never got to see Ireland again," he said. "It's been such a long time and things have changed. The Irish Free State has just been proclaimed and an Anglo-Irish Treaty is to be signed later this year. If I get a board at one of the stations, it'll be my last and I'll go back home and put my feet up by the fireside in a little cottage in County Kerry. I feel that it's time for me to find that true happiness that my father told me about and enjoy my remaining days in the peace of my island home."

* * * *

The weather had been miraculously fine. No late spring storms had come out of the cloudless sky, not even so much as a 'Darling River shower, - four drops on five acres, - had sprinkled the dust of the plain to give the union delegate the excuse to declare the sheep too wet to shear, and so lose a day's shearing. Long Pat bent his back and lifted out a new jumbuck every few minutes from the pen with as much apparent ease as if the big, struggling ninety-pound wether had been a rabbit. He shore each animal as if his life depended on it and I gathered up the fleece and sprinted along the board, heaving it on to the sorting table for the assessors to grade it and pass it to the wool pressers.

On the evening of the tenth day after cut-in the holding pen handlers gathered near the board to watch the final cuts, their jobs finished. The *'cobbler,'* the very last sheep, the worst one to shear, and so left for someone else by every man who picked his next jumbuck out of the middle pen, was lifted aloft by Long Pat amid the cheers of the other shearers, all of them preparing to rest their stiff backs and aching sinews for a full week before they struck the next shed at Thurulgoonia.

"That's right, leave him to me, lads," Long Pat said, eyeing the closely wrinkled fleece, "I'd do him justice even if he was covered with barbed-wire." He set to work and shore so quickly and with such careful precision, that it could, to the recently arrived pen handlers, have been his first tally of the day. He trimmed the cobbler's belly, ran the shears down each shoulder and then with a whoop of delight delivered the final long blow up the back that separated the jumbuck from its woolly load. I grabbed the fleece, sprinted to the sorting table with it, threw it over the rail to the waiting presser and raced back along the board to pick up the tar-pot.

"No need for the tar-pot Bill, he's clean," Long Pat said as he sent the jumbuck tumbling down the chute of the exit pen with a harmless punt from his boot. "Goodbye, and God bless you, old man,"

The other shearers still cheered and shouted their appreciation, for they all knew that they'd witnessed something special that day. An old snagger, who'd only just managed to get on to the last board in the Tinenburra shed because one of the shearers had downed one ale too many the previous night, and the small, innocuous-looking roustabout that I was, who'd never been seen around the traps before, had made the highest tally in the shed for that final day, even beating Big Seth by a margin of one, and if he hadn't hauled up the cobbler at the last, they'd have been equal, shearing jumbuck for jumbuck all day long.

The cut-in at Thurulgoonia was even better. News of Long Pat's tally and exceptionally clean shearing at Tinenburra had preceded him and the shed manager at Thurulgoonia had awarded him a board nearer the centre of the shed; that was a bonus for me too because my run to the sorting table was much shorter and I'd learned by then how to make Long Pat's job easier by holding the struggling jumbuck's hind legs still while the old man twisted it into position and gripped it between his knees.

"First you take the belly-wool and niggle out the crutch,
Go up the neck, for the rules they are such,
Clean around the horns and the first shoulder down,
A long blow up the back and turn her around."

The shearing had cut-out at Thurulgoonia after two weeks; the shearers, sheep-washers, rouseabouts, pen handlers and tar-boys were paid up to the last hour of the last day and a great silence settled on the district. The wagons, drawn by the bullock and horse teams and piled high with their consignment of fleeces, had rolled away, and the shed labourers had departed to wherever each spent their time in the off shearing season because Thurulgoonia was the last of the sheds to cut-out. The shearers had ridden off with their pockets bulging with money, full of good spirits at the success of the season and no doubt looking forward to the rest and recuperation that lay ahead of them until the next. The great shed, empty but for a few of the regular farmhands who'd been retained to undertake the final clean-up, was carefully locked up, as were the shearers and roustabouts huts.

Long Pat held up his mug of tea as if he was proposing a toast to a new business deal. "I can't thank you enough, Bill," he said with a happy grin. "We made a great shearing team together and it's a great pity it has to end, but I'm going home to Ireland a happy old snagger."

I grinned, but the sadness remained in my heart, for it had been such a rewarding time for me and it was all over. I knew I'd never see my old friend again, but Long Pat was right; we'd made a great team and I was happy I'd helped the old man to get that last top tally he'd waited so many years to recapture. "You're not an old snagger, Long Pat," I said, the first tears beginning to run down my cheek. "You're a true-blue ringer," and I meant every word of it.

3 The Warrego Bunyip

It was in about March 1921, Sister Mary, when I took the track that followed the eastern bank of the Warrego River to the railhead town of Cunnamulla, which was about seventy-five miles north of Barringun. The track was gravelled and in fair condition, but there were few bridges over the dry creek beds that crossed it at regular intervals to find their way into the Warrego and I remembered Black Bart's words and wondered how the new trucks that he'd said would replace his bullock drays were going to manage. The river was rarely further than two hundred yards on my left and I thought about the discussion Black Bart and I'd had with Ted the teamster on the Bourke-Barringun road south of the Enngonia Township as we'd waited for the Enngonia Creek backup water to subside.

'It rained up around Cunnamulla a week ago. It takes that long for the water to work its way down through the flat channel country to here.'

It had only taken a couple of days at the most for the water backed up in Enngonia Creek to revert to its usual dry-bed status so there was little incentive for the road makers to build expensive bridges, and travellers had to make do with formed floodways. The Warrego itself was mostly dry when I got an occasional glimpse of the watercourse's sandy bed through the trees and I'd taken to turning off the main track each afternoon when I saw a well-worn sidetrack leading to a grove of tall white river gums that told me of the existence of a billabong, for the presence of even a small pool of stagnant water was a welcome relief to the wanderers who used them as overnight camping spots.

I'd been on the track for a week, taking it in easy stages, for I was in no hurry and had plenty of provisions to last me until I finally got to Cunnamulla, where I'd been told that my Thurulgoonia cheque would be honoured without a moment's hesitation. I knew that the shearing season would have ended on the stations around Cunnamulla too, as it had in Barringun, and there would be no wool loading work to be had. It was simply a matter of finding out what my options were when I finally got there.

I figured I was only about three miles south of Cunnamulla when I noticed a recently used wallaby track leading down to the river, an assurance that there would be at least a damp soak where the animal could scratch a depression in the sand to find enough water for a drink, - if not an actual waterhole at the end of it, - and I congratulated myself on my ever-increasing awareness of the signposts of nature. It was so close to the town itself that it was unlikely that anyone would have stopped there for the night, and that theory was strengthened when I saw no sign of any man-made side-track. That suited me perfectly and I decided to pitch my camp and enjoy the solitude of the river for the last time before I again had to deal with the apprehensions and difficulties of mixing with humanity.

When I arrived at the river bank I dismounted and stood admiring the view, for the wallaby had chosen its path well. I'd come out onto the mid-point of a gentle bend and when I looked upstream and downstream the sandy bed of the river disappeared between the trees a hundred yards in either direction. Past floods had built up a high sandy bank on the side that I was standing on and it sloped gently towards the water's edge where the wallaby tracks stopped at the brink of a clear, placid pool that hugged the opposite bank. The clarity of the water and the few large stones that diverted its lazy course momentarily, creating a tiny ripple, told me that the water was running and about knee-high at its deepest near the opposite bank. It seemed to me that the reason the water was so clear was that the tiny stream emerged from the sand a little upstream of me and then disappeared again a little further downriver, *'What a perfect spot,'* I thought, *'a peaceful little paradise that possibly no one has visited in a long time, - except the wallaby.'*

It was dark in the shadows of the trees on both banks as the sun began its descent to the western horizon and I suddenly felt a strange uneasiness. It was nothing sinister, yet an odd feeling that things weren't quite as they seemed, and it was made the worse when Tom snorted and whinnied softly as if to let me know that he felt it too. I glanced at him and noticed that his ears were erect and pointed in the direction he was staring, downstream along the nearside bank. I gazed intently at the dark line of trees too, but nothing moved and the only sound to break the silence came from the cries of far-off birds somewhere further along the river to the south. I tried to shrug off the feeling, but something *had* spooked Tom, and the little horse, his head raised and nostrils flaring, continued to stare at the tree line. Thirty yards downstream, a wallaby darted out from the undergrowth and bounded along the sand towards us, but when it sighted us it made a sudden right turn back into the safety of the scrub.

"Come on Tom," I said, shaking my head in disdain at my unjustified fears. "You and I are like a pair of little boys frightened by our own dark shadows on a wall." I tugged on the reins and urged him back up the bank to where a patch of lush green grass swayed invitingly in the light breeze that had sprung up in the open reaches of the watercourse. Tom was soon happily chewing on it and I crouched by my swag and began to prepare my simple rations, but the uneasiness hadn't completely left me and the reason for it became apparent shortly after. I stood up suddenly when the shock hit me, - there it was; the smell of smoke from a campfire and the familiar aroma of damper baking in its hot coals, - and not too far away either. We had company.

Tom was still engrossed in tucking into his feed; the smell of damper baking in a campfire was something he was used to and he wouldn't have thought it out of place even in this remote setting, but to me, it was nothing short of astonishing that some other traveller should be so close. I retraced my steps the few yards to the river bank and looked along the edge of the tree line again, searching for a tell-tale wisp of smoke, - and lo and behold, there it was, hardly noticeable unless you concentrated on that particular spot, a thin bluish-white thread wafting imperceptibly amongst the higher branches of the giant paperbark trees, maybe fifty yards away.

I gave the coo-ee call that was the traditional means of giving a fellow sundowner or swaggie fore-warning that a stranger was approaching his camp, but there was no answering call. That, in itself, was odd enough, as most swaggies were happy for a bit of company and a chat even if only briefly before bedding down for the night, but to not respond in any way could mean the person was sick or incapacitated in some way. I walked along the sand and coo-ee'd again, but there was still no answer, although the aroma of damper filled the air. An animal track led off from the riverbank and I saw the footprints of many wallabies in the sand, but there were also the footprints of the invisible damper baker where he too had gone back and forth between his camp and the river. I entered the leafy tunnel with some feeling of nervousness; the silence was so profound that I felt I could hear my own heart beating in my chest. Ten yards in I came to a small clearing. Tall river gum trees ringed it all around, and the whole space was in deep shade. It was a roughly circular piece of ground and I stood rooted to the ground in surprise, for at the foot of a big white-gum was a strange sight in that lonely place. It was nothing more or less than a small tent. The flap of the tent was down, and there was no resident of the camp to be seen, but all about were signs of occupation. From the stout low hanging boughs of two trees dangled a rough hammock, made of sacking, while a water bag hung from another convenient branch. A fallen log had been placed against a tree in such a way that it was used as a chair and a well-blackened billy hung from the tent's ridge-pole. Close by, a heap of dry sticks had been stacked neatly, - and there it was, a little farther away, the ashes of the campfire still smouldering, issuing the fine wisp of smoke that had alerted me to the camp's position. Over it, a blackened bough was suspended, supported by two forked sticks showing that the billy had been boiled there quite a few times. The camp was all very neat and tidy. *'It looks like quite a decent little home,'* I thought. *'It's certainly not an overnighter. Somebody lives here...'*

Suddenly, as I examined the surroundings, the flap of the tent was raised and a figure emerged. My first impression was that he was an elderly man who perhaps would have been more at home in a rocking chair on a cool veranda somewhere other than this lonely outpost, for he'd had to bend almost double to get through the tent's opening and seemed to have great difficulty in straightening up again as he clutched his lower back with one hand. He wore no hat, and his hair, hanging down to his slim shoulders, was long, unkempt and white as snow. Thin brown arms protruded from a kind of sleeved woollen coat that hung over loose, three-quarter length trousers and his pair of spindly legs seemed out of proportion to the large brown miner's boots on his feet. As I stood there transfixed, not knowing what to make of it all, the old man walked slowly across to his little fireplace and carefully raked away some of the ashes with a stick. He drew out a damper from amongst the coals, raked the ashes together again, and placed some sticks on them, after which he brought over the billy, and hung it above the fire to boil. The fire was soon ablaze, and he picked up the damper and walked slowly back to the tent, where he paused to blow the dust from the result of his cookery.

I figured that I had to attract his attention before he disappeared from my view, for it would have become an invasion of his privacy if I'd disturbed him after he'd entered his tent. "Hello there sir," I said. "I coo-ee'd, but got no..."

The old man started violently. He dropped his damper and gazed around, pale blue eyes under bushy white eyebrows darting from side to side. "What on earth's that?" he said. "Who's there?"

"It's me, - out here by the river bank," I said. I stood in plain view, but I suddenly realised that the old man was probably short-sighted at the very least and perhaps near blind.

"*Me*, is it?" the old man said, in great bewilderment. "*Me*," he repeated. "Don't you know that no one ever comes here except wallabies and possums and *me*? Not you-*me*, but me-*me*! How do you account for you-*me* being here?"

"I'm camped for the night just upriver, sir," I said, a little alarmed by his peculiar retort.

72

"May the angels of God defend us, - and I thought I had found the back of beyond, where I would never see anything more civilized than a bunyip. May I ask the name of my 'you-*me*' visitor who frightened me-*me* so much I dropped my dinner on the ground?" He bent down stiffly and picked up the damper, brushing the dirt off as he rose again.

"I'm sorry I frightened you, sir. My name is Bill Smith." I said, still feeling quite uneasy in the presence of this strange old man.

"*Bill? Your name is Bill?*" you say. The old man seemed confused. "You don't sound like a *Bill*. I was sure when you spoke you were more of a Nanny than a Billy." He broke into song in a scratchy voice;

'Patrick McGinty an Irishman of note,
He fell into a fortune and he bought himself a goat.
Goat's milk says Patrick I'm going to have me fill,
But when he got the Nanny home he found it was a Bill.'

He opened the flap of the tent and tossed the damper on to a makeshift table inside. "There now," he said, wiping his long bony hands on an old towel that hung on the ridge pole. "I couldn't smell anything but the damper cooking before now, otherwise I would have known you were coming to visit me. Come closer to me Nanny-Billy, and hold your hand out so that I can smell it just to be sure you really *are* who you say you are."

I laughed, but it was more out of nervousness than mirth; this was nothing like the quiet uneventful evening I'd expected I'd have. I did as I was told and the old man sniffed the air and then peered at me closely through eyes that had looked faded from a distance but twinkled brightly as he moved closer to me.

"Hmm!" he said. "The jury's still out on whether you're a Nanny or a Billy, but you've got a friendly smell. I can almost always tell, you know."

I laughed again but with more confidence this time. "Then you're right again, sir," I said. "I am a friendly person who wouldn't do you or anyone else any harm, although I'm bushed if I know how you can tell I'm friendly by sniffing my hand."

"Ah," he said, "it's quite simple, Nanny-Billy; animals do it all the time. The good Lord saw fit to give me a set of eyes that are only useful for finding stones to trip over and a pair of ears that are only there to stop my hat from falling over my face, but my nose now, - it's as good as any possum's, although not as prettily pink. I've learned to *smell* danger, you see, - and a lot more besides, but when my dinner's

73

cooking I usually let my guard down for a little while; that's why you startled me. Where have you left your horse? I know it's nearby."

"It's just upriver fifty yards away," I said.

"No it's not," the old man shook his head. "It's closer than that. It must have followed you along the riverbank."

Just then I heard a quiet snort and looked around to see that Tom had indeed followed me and he stood at the edge of the riverbank surveying the surroundings. "That's a truly remarkable gift you have, sir," I said, shaking my head in astonishment. "May I ask with whom I am sharing this riverbank camp?"

"That's an entirely different matter, Nanny-Billy," the old man said, stroking his chin and looking decidedly bewildered. "I certainly had a name once, but I quite forget it sometimes. I have an excellent memory for forgetting. What do the fine residents of Cunnamulla say about me?"

"I don't know, sir," I said. "I'm on my way to Cunnamulla now. I've come from further south in Barringun, and over the border in Bourke before that."

"Ah, Barringun and Bourke; you've come up the Warrego from its confluence with the mighty Darling; - the *very* furthest part of my own territory, although I shall never be seen there again..." He paused and shook his head, as if a fleeting, but poignant thought had crossed his mind and then he added as an afterthought, "...probably not while I'm *alive*, anyway."

I was becoming alarmed again at the way the conversation was going. "Are you all right sir?" I said. "You're not sick, are you?"

The old man grinned. "How I wish you'd *not* call me *sir*, all the time, Nanny-Billy Smith? Do forgive me, for I have to call you Nanny-Billy until I've made up my mind about *who* or *what* you are, - but I will forgive you for your mistakes, for if you've not been to Cunnamulla yet then I can understand that you may not have heard of me, although I thought I was as well known in Barringun as elsewhere on the Warrego." He paused. "Maybe not now though, for it's been a long time since I travelled that far south and my travelling days are over, but when you *do* go into Cunnamulla and tell them you met the old *man* Bunyip who calls the Warrego River home and you called him, *Sir*. They'll say, - you must be mistaken; there's *no* old man Warrego Bunyip. Perhaps you've affronted the old *woman* Warrego Bunyip? And what will you say to them then? I suppose you'll then say, ah yes, I've *offended her*. I thought she was an old *man* Bunyip."

I remembered the bullocky's friendly advice as he said farewell to Black Bart and me on the road to Barringun, and Black Bart's evasiveness in discounting the theory about the existence of something or someone living on the river.

'*Don't tempt the Warrego Bunyip.*' The adage had been around for a long time amongst the bullockies who plied their trade along the Warrego and here I was facing the … "*The Warrego Bunyip?*" I said, bemused. My mind was in a whirl as I tried to follow the old man's strange way of speaking until finally, it dawned on me. "The Warrego Bunyip isn't the feared creature of nightmares; you're a - *woman?*" I said. "Oh, I'm so sorry..." I was the one confused now and I stammered, "I mean, I just assumed…"

"…that *all* sundowners, swaggies and fearsome bunyips are *men?*" the old woman cackled. "And why would someone like *you*, in particular, assume *that* to be the case Nanny-Billy? Do you think women can't live in the bush just as well as men can? Annie Bags did, you know."

I shook my head and looked at her in the light of her surprise confession. "I'm sorry, I haven't heard of Annie Bags," I said.

She regarded me with eyes that were clouded, but still showed her disbelief at my admission. "What? You haven't heard of our famous Annie? Why she's better known and much better loved than the Prime Minister, - and what's more she's an admirable example for all women everywhere. She was rumoured to have been a lady once, but she dressed in rags and wandered around from one town to another for many years; she walked everywhere, pushing an old baby pram with all her belongings in it and learned to survive in the bush without having had any prior knowledge of it. She showed that *we* women can do it on our own if we dare to try, Nanny-Billy."

I was intrigued. "There must have been a reason why she lived that way…"

"…Well, of course, a *man* was involved somewhere along the line. A man had done her wrong and she couldn't look any of them in the eyes after that. I believe she's gone to a better place now, though, - lucky woman, but she's still talked about today and will be for a long time." She shook her head and unconsciously pushed a wisp of thin white hair away from her face, before she added, seemingly as an afterthought. "I usually stay clear of men too, - or *they* stay clear of *me*, more's the point - but I think I like *you* Nanny-Billy. Now why would that be, I wonder?"

I smiled, but I'm sure my eyes reflected a touch of sadness that she couldn't see and somehow I felt that this old woman was indeed someone that had seen through my defences and I could confide in her "I think I'm a herm…," I started.

"...A *hermit?* No, you're not a hermit, Nanny-Billy," she said waving her thin bony hand in the air to dismiss the mere thought of it as absurd. "Hermits don't come visiting old women bunyips; they keep to themselves, you see. I'm not a hermit either, or a swaggie, although some people might say I am if you ask them." She shook her head emphatically as if to emphasise the point. "No, I've chosen the Warrego River as my home for a very good reason. I always worked hard for my keep when I was young and now I'm a..." She thought for a moment. "Yes, - I know; I'm a pensioner. Good old Andrew Fisher, our first Queenslander to become Prime Minister of Australia granted me a pension so that I wouldn't *have* to become a swaggie or a sundowner and cadge for food, but he didn't say that to get it I had to live in an old folk's home. All I have to do is walk into the Cunnamulla post office with my old cart, - just like dear old Annie Bags, - every fortnight, to pick up my pension and buy my supplies of tea, flour and sugar. Miss O'Hara the postmistress knows what I need and has it ready for me so I don't have to talk to anyone else, but I'm sure they all know I've been there."

I felt a strange affinity with this odd, old, - *woman bunyip,* and thought I'd humour her. "Ah then, when I get to Cunnamulla I'll be able to say I had a yarn with the Warrego *woman* Bunyip," I said in a light-hearted way.

The old woman's eyes lit up. "My dear Nanny-Billy," she said, "yes, you *can* tell them we had a yarn; - they'll know me; yes they'll know who I am if you tell them you met the old Warrego *woman* Bunyip, - I think."

She looked confused. I told her I'd pass on her regards to the people of Cunnamulla and she seemed pleased, but then a frown creased her brow. "Being any gender of a bunyip, though, has its shortcomings," she said suddenly. "My resources are scanty, but enough that I hope you will stay and have a billy of tea with me, then we *can* exchange yarns around the campfire just like *real* stockmen would do."

I laughed. "I'll be happy to stay here tonight and share some yarns with you as *real* stockmen would do, Miss Warrego Bunyip, but then tomorrow I must depart for Cunnamulla and after that, I've got a mind to go on to Charleville where I'm hoping to get some work as a *real* stockman."

"Oh yes, - Charleville." The old bunyip clapped her hands together. "I remember now; I was born in Charleville, Nanny-Billy." She paused for a moment. "Ah, - and that's it too, - my name..."

"You remember your *name* too now?" I said.

76

"Yes, Nanny-Billy; it's Charlotte. I live in the bush just as Annie Bags did, and from what I've heard about her we have a few traits in common, although I wouldn't dream of putting myself in the same category as the great woman herself. Annie managed to put whatever bad memories she'd had out of her mind, and so have I; that's why I said to you I have an excellent memory for forgetting, but the memories do come back sometimes, - and sometimes too when I don't want them to. It only takes something like mentioning the name of a town, - or one word like 'flood' said offhand by someone to bring it all back, - and that's another excuse for not living in an old folk's home; the constant chatter and reminiscing around me would send me sillier than I am now."

She laughed. "You see, I was one of the first white children born in the district and my parents were so proud of me they called me Charlotte. If I'd been born a boy I would have been Charlie, the Warrego *boy* bunyip." She shrugged her thin shoulders and looked away towards the river as if another unwanted memory had suddenly entered her head. "...but then if I'd been born a boy perhaps I wouldn't have *had* to become a bunyip at all." She shuddered and then took a deep breath. "Right then, let's get this pannikin of water boiling while I try to remember what I was going to tell you."

She fussed about getting the tea ready while I took the gear off Tom Thumb's back and then went back to my camp to retrieve my billy can. When all was ready we settled down side by side on the fallen log and stared in meditative silence into the dying embers of the fire, - just like *real* stockmen did.

It was me who eventually broke the silence. "If your memory permits, and if you want to, can you tell me a little about your life in Charleville, please?" I said as I sipped the hot strong liquid.

Charlotte closed her eyes for a moment and I wondered if perhaps I'd blundered in asking her to bring back memories she didn't want to think about, but she smiled and rocked back and forth as she recalled her youth in Charleville, and then she spoke slowly and deliberately as if the memories were coming back to her just a little at a time. "In the very early 1860's a lonely inn stood on the north bank of the Warrego River, near where Charleville is now," she said at length. "It was the meeting place of squatters, drovers, shearers and teamsters and along with many thousands of square miles of the surrounding district was the leasehold property of the millionaire land baron, James Tyson."

"Ah, - the Honourable James Tyson," I said, "now I hadn't heard of your famous lady, Annie Bags, but I *have* heard of Mr Tyson." I laughed.

"Shame on you, Nanny-Billy," Charlotte scolded me gently. "After Tyson died without making a final will the land was handed back to the Queensland Government, it was broken up into smaller holdings and as usual, where there were vast, rich pastures to be had by squatting, pioneers naturally sought them out. A business and official centre grew around the original inn, with banks, other hotels and inns, stores, a school and a church. Around this centre, residences sprang into existence as people, including my father and mother, continued to move in. There were good times and bad times in the years before federation. The district boasted some of the wealthiest and largest pastoral properties in the Commonwealth in the 1880s. The population of the town grew to be close to four thousand. Money was plentiful. Business, as a consequence, was brisk, with people of all trades and professions coming and going, but although Charleville was going through a prosperous period at that time, there were other occasions when misfortune was reflected in a depression in business in the town. The great federation drought that lasted for ten years from 1893 and affected every State and almost every district in Australia was particularly savage, but Charleville quickly recovered when the rains eventually came, business revived, lost progress was soon made up and the wagons and motor lorries, piled high with bales of wool again trundled down the main street on the way to the railway station. I was born shortly after my parents arrived in Charleville and I was given a good education there."

Charlotte sipped on her tea and nodded to herself contentedly. "Yes, a good education for a girl, Nanny-Billy." She smiled serenely, revelling in the memories of her childhood and I guessed that it must have been a happy one, - so unlike my own bitter recollections of my youth. I thought back to my childhood and a feeling of sadness almost overwhelmed me as I remembered my mother's words.

'I can't put my finger on it, but something's not quite right with that child.'

Charlotte went on. "I grew up thinking Charleville was the centre of the world and my parents were the best people in it, but that was a very long, long time ago, - *antediluvian* it was."

I must have gaped at her. "Aunty who?" I said.

"Antediluvian; - it means *'before the flood'*." She grinned. "It's a private joke between me and the possums, you see. The term refers to the great flood of Noah that's recounted in the Bible, but to me, it means another flood altogether." She looked back at the river and tossed her head. "The Warrego isn't always the quiet little stream it looks like it is now, Nanny-Billy."

"I was going to ask you about that," I said. "I met a bullocky down in Enngonia in New South Wales who told me the Warrego, which was a raging torrent at the time I came through, floods occasionally and takes everything in its path..."

"It does, Nanny-Billy." She nodded sagely. "Cunnamulla and Charleville and the other towns on its banks have been flooded many times, but what you saw would have been a fairly minor one compared to the first one I can remember in 1877, but I was only eight years old and didn't understand what was going on, to be honest. The flood of 1886 though, - now that one I do remember very well because it changed the whole course of my life."

"For the better, I hope," I said.

Charlotte shook her head. "Sadly not, Nanny-Billy. It turned me into the Warrego bunyip you see before you now."

I continued to stare into the campfire, but my voice was tense as I became alarmed about what might come next. "If you don't want to talk..." I said.

"...Yes, I do, Nanny-Billy; I'm quite prepared to tell you about it," she said. "It's not as difficult to talk about it now because the years have healed the wounds and I've learned to love this river so much that I'll possibly never leave it, except..." She sighed before sipping on her tea again. "The trouble started with a fairly heavy downpour on a Thursday in July, that lasted well into Friday, and a couple of the old Bidjara Aboriginal stockmen tried to convince the authorities that we were going to get 'big one bad river flood' and had better prepare to evacuate the town. A meeting was held and it was decided that the amount of rainfall that had fallen around Charleville didn't seem to warrant that kind of drastic action and it was only later that we understood what they'd been trying to tell us, - that *they* knew there'd been substantial and continual rain in the upper Warrego around Channin Creek in the Carnarvon Range in the previous week. It wasn't the rain around Charleville they were concerned about; it was the flow from upstream that was slowly making its way down the river."

"The town wasn't evacuated in time?" I said.

Charlotte shook her head. "No, the town wasn't evacuated at all, Nanny-Billy. The other factor I should mention about Charleville is that it's unfortunate in not having much high ground close by for people to get away to at such times, but in any case, it would have been too late for the authorities to organise the evacuation of the whole town because the river had divided it by the time they started to realise that the old stockmen were right, - this was going to be *big one bad river flood*. The greatest fear initially was that the river might break over into Deverill's paddock as it had in 77, join a gully which runs at the back of the town, and flood out the houses that had been built near it since the 77 flood."

I gasped in surprise. "Houses had been built on the river's flood plain?"

Charlotte looked away, but I saw a flicker of pain cross her face momentarily. "On Saturday things began to look a bit more depressing, as the Warrego had reached an abnormal height and was just below its record, but the rate of rising had slowed and the townspeople were still hopeful, with the general opinion being that it would drop away as quickly as it had risen by the next day at the latest."

"As it did at Enngonia when I came through," I said.

Charlotte nodded. "That's what it had usually done in the past, but on Sunday morning it was still rising slowly. The three churches in the town were almost empty of Sunday worshippers and those whose prayers hadn't been answered instead spent their time watching the river, or in going to the paddock to see how far their fears of it spilling into the gully were justified. That evening the women were paying constant visits to the water's edge to measure the height of the flood against the wooden pegs that had been fixed at various places to test the rate of advance while some of the men were busy constructing a raft."

"A raft?" I said, confused. "Why would they start building a raft at a time like that?"

"The reason for building that raft lay in the wretched fact that the Divisional Board's lifeboat that had been bought a few months before for just such emergencies had been smashed against a gum tree by the force of the water; it had watertight compartments, but it seemed to be held down by the weight of water and it capsized. Its boatload of ten people, who'd been rescued after being stranded by the rising waters on a little islet in the middle of the stream at about 3 pm, had been thrown into the swirling water. Most of them had succeeded in scrambling into the tree branches, but one old woman wasn't strong enough to hold on and she dropped into the eddy circling the tree, caused by the boat's fourteen feet length slowing the current. Her drowned body turned and twisted in all sorts of grotesque and ghastly positions for fully fifteen or twenty minutes, till it got into the outside body of water, and was swiftly borne away. The only other casualty, or so we thought at the time, was that of a boy who jumped or lost his grip on a branch and tried to swim ashore, but he was carried down to another tree, which he managed to get to and hang on to for some time. At last, he was forced to let go and, with a cry of despair, met the same fate as the old woman. His cries while he hung on to the branches of those trees had been appalling, and I'm sure most of the people who heard him would have carried the sound, as I have, in their hearts for the rest of their lives."

I shuddered, imagining the suffering of the poor child, but Charlotte went on in a kind of monotone as if she'd told the story a hundred times, - which she probably had, - though to her furry, passive audience. "The river was about half a mile wide at that point, and the distance between the banks was continuing to increase. As night fell, fires had been lit and the work to build the raft continued in a somewhat frenzied manner in consideration of the precarious positions of the miserable survivors holding on with the tenacity of despair to the tree branches. At about midnight the river level had begun to drop and by daybreak, on Monday the raft was launched, but it had been built with Cypress pine logs and they turned out to be so big and heavy that the first crew to get on it was ankle-deep in water immediately. It was then decided to fix barrels to it so that the thing would float better, but just as they were about to do so the news arrived that all the survivors had been rescued from their perches on the tree."

I was puzzled. "It turned out to be a happy ending for most of you after all then?" I said. "Did you know the two people who died?"

Charlotte shook her head. "I knew them, but not well. It *should* have been a happy ending for all but the families of the two casualties, as you say, but it didn't end happily there for me, Nanny-Billy. I was seventeen and I'd been working as a maid and cleaner at the Warrego Hotel for the previous year while I waited for a position to come up at the hospital where I'd had an interview for a career in nursing. I sometimes stayed in a little room at the back of the hotel's scullery if it was a particularly busy time and on this occasion, I'd been helping wherever I could, bringing tea and sandwiches to the men working on the raft and generally making their lives a little more comfortable. When I finally got to go home to where I'd lived with my parents for eight years, which was near the gully behind Deverill's paddock…"

"Oh, no," I said, knowing that what was to come next wouldn't be pleasant to hear.

She nodded slowly as if to confirm her previous statement about the houses being built near that gully. "I learned that the houses had indeed been flooded and one had been completely washed away. I hadn't given any thought whatsoever to the consequences of that happening in my enthusiasm for providing comfort to the men and I was devastated to find that it was *my* home that had gone."

81

I was shocked. "Oh no!" I said again. "And what of your parents?" But I knew the answer before I'd got the words out.

"My parents were missing," Charlotte said in a matter-of-fact tone. "The police and volunteers conducted a search that lasted several weeks, of course, but no trace of them was found and eventually they called it off. There was a memorial service, as there was for the other two missing people, but it wasn't enough for me. I refused to give up and continued my private search, scouring the river banks between Charleville and Cunnamulla in the hope of finding *some* trace of them. I wanted closure, you see. My dream of becoming a nurse ceased to mean anything to me from that time on and although I realised after a while that it was a fruitless search, I kept going. Occasionally I found something, - a fragment of a plank of wood, or a battered tin bucket, and my hope was renewed, but those things could have come from anywhere and as the months and then years dragged on I travelled even further south. I crossed the border into New South Wales, finding cleaning or housemaid work in hotels I came to along the river. The Warrego had become my home by then, you see; my parents were there, - and somewhere along its nine hundred mile length, I knew they were lying at peace. Someone who'd seen the whole tragedy unfold had told me they'd been washed away holding tightly to each other so I knew that at least they were together."

I shuddered. "Don't you get lonely here by yourself sometimes, Charlotte?" I said, choking back tears

Charlotte looked at me gravely. "Not as much now as I used to, Nanny-Billy," she said. "Before this happened I was quite a social person. I'd had a budding romance with a young stockman from one of the stations nearby. He used to come and see me at the hotel after I'd finished work for the evening." She smiled serenely and then sipped on her tea as more memories returned. "We were in love, Johnny and I, and I was close to inviting him home to meet my parents when the river took them from me." She shrugged her thin shoulders again. "He was away droving in the channel country when the flood came and I don't know what happened to him after that." She sighed and abruptly changed the subject as if it was something she'd often thought about and wanted to put out of her mind. "Sometimes now and then I feel that I'd like to hear a human voice again, and to feel a friend's arm around my shoulders. Oh, there are times when I talk to myself, or yarn to old Slippery, my pet goanna, just to hear the sound of words again even though they're only my own, but when these bad outpourings come upon me I know it's time to go and fish in the river for my dinner to help me concentrate on other things." Her tone became good-humoured and animated momentarily. "The Warrego River is one of only a few rivers where silver perch breed naturally and would you believe I've also caught golden perch and Murray cod here? They must come up against the current during the floods." She settled down again. "When I've had my fill of fishing I go to sleep, and when I wake up I feel refreshed and am quite as cheerful as a bunyip can be once more."

"But you're still alone." I insisted.

She hesitated. "...it *is* isolated from other *humans* here, but that can be a good thing in many ways," she said after some thought; "There's no one to trouble me; no one to treat me badly or to be hateful or malicious towards me; no bitter enemies, and no false friends, who are so much worse than enemies. I'm not *really* on my own either; the wallabies come and hop about me and the birds too, and I know that it's because I've never frightened any of them or raised my voice, even when they try to steal my damper. To gain an animal's trust you have to be consistent; you can't be friendly one day and angry the next. Animals can sense anger just as they can sense danger. I live amongst them as one of them and they can smell that I'm a friend, just like I can smell their trust and friendship towards me. Oh, I can smell danger too, and can hide or defend myself as the case may be; old Slippery slides his ugly head over my knees, and I know he doesn't care a button whether I'm a man or a woman or if I have anything he can take from me, - and that's far, far more than you can say of many human beings."

The conversation continued into the night; Charlotte and I perfectly contented in each other's company, and it was with an odd feeling of fulfilment that I told her *my* own story, - *all* of it, - because Charlotte already *knew* me. She'd known me from the very first minute I'd come into her life, - and liked me for who or what I was, and had no expectations of anything beyond my companionship for the evening. She called me Nanny-Billy, but she *knew*, and she wanted me to be the one to tell her who I was. We cried together and embraced and then laughed and cried again. We talked of many things, me of my past and the uncertainty of my future, Charlotte only of her past because, as she said, *her* future was certain.

"What will you do if the river floods again, Charlotte?" I'd asked her, and even though I believed I'd got to know her so well after the evening's yarns, I was still shocked by her answer.

"It's not *if* the Warrego floods again Nanny-Billy; it's *when*, - but I don't bother much with the little floods; no, they wouldn't take me far enough. I'll wait for another *big one bad river* flood like the '86 to take me home to join my parents downriver," she said. "My future is certain; it's up to the Warrego alone to decide when it will happen and how far downstream it will take me." She smiled sadly. "It might even take me as far as the Darling, but I don't care; I'll be happy then, Nanny-Billy."

My heart was heavy as I bid my friend goodnight, but it was only heavy because the evening was over and there were so many things that had been left unsaid. It had been a chance encounter, a fleeting moment of true love and harmony never to be recaptured but to be remembered for a lifetime, and tomorrow we would go our separate ways, or at least I would go and Charlotte would wait for her destiny; in any case our lives would diverge away from each other once more and it was unlikely we would ever cross paths again. It had been that way with all the others I'd learned to love and trust, Jimmy Miller, Long Pat and the Naughton family; oh and of course the Pavetto's that I haven't told you about yet, and I had no doubt it would be that way again, because that was what seemed to be my destiny.

The campfire had died down to a dim red glow and both Charlotte and I were forced to admit that we were too tired to continue our yarning, but I, nevertheless, lay awake in my swag for many hours thinking about the remarkable woman who slumbered peacefully in the makeshift tent not ten feet away from me. How had the legend of the Warrego Bunyip become so distorted? This innocent woman had been wandering along the Warrego for nigh on thirty years with an ache in her heart that it seemed could never be healed and the misguided yarns had grown up around her, but she didn't know anything about that and probably wouldn't have cared if she did. She had everything she needed except for her lost love; she had enough food to sustain her; she was surrounded by her animal friends who would never judge her or let her down and she had no concerns about whatever other people might think of her chosen pathway through life. Charlotte understood that she couldn't change anything that chance had thrown her way and she accepted and embraced it as *her* destiny. I knew that it was a lesson that I needed to heed in my own life if I was ever to be rewarded with the peace of mind that I yearned for so much and so it was with a sense of something like envy mixed with sadness that I finally drifted off into a troubled sleep.

4 Abingdon Downs

I leant against the middle rail of the cattle-yard, trying to make myself look as tall as possible, probably with not too much success, and hitched my thumbs into the band of my braided belt for further effect, but the swagger and self-confident stance I'd adopted was wasted on the man who'd just lowered his gaunt frame down gingerly from the top rail of the branding chute for he either ignored me or didn't seem to have noticed I was there.

"Hey mister," I yelled, trying to make myself heard above the commotion of the lowing and bellowing cattle milling around in the yard. "Can you tell me where I might find the boss stockman, please?"

Even then the man didn't look up immediately, but stuck the branding iron amongst the hot coals and took off his wide-brimmed felt hat, revealing a sparse crop of greying hair. He dusted it off on his leather apron, wiped his sweating brow and then his hands on a rag that hung on a rail and yelled to the men who'd been driving the steers one at a time into the branding chute. "Have a half-hour tea break lads." He replaced his hat and only then casually turned and walked towards me with a curious look on his sunburnt face. I was about to repeat my question, thinking he may not have heard me the first time when he said, "Don't need to, - you found me yourself. You're looking for work I suppose, young feller."

He looked like he might be in his mid to late-fifties, I decided, but he displayed the broad shoulders and thick forearms of a man who was still used to hands-on heavy agricultural work. I nodded and stepped forward to meet him. "Tom Clancy, the agent at the District Land Office in Charleville told me that I might get a job here; he said you'd be taking a mob to the railhead at Quilpie in a month or two."

The man looked me up and down. "That's right; this Channel Country is great for fattening cattle, but it's a long way from anywhere when we're getting them ready for the Southern and East Coast markets. The Queensland government had a grand plan to build a Great Western Railway between Cunnamulla and Darwin in the Northern Territory about fifteen years ago. What with the war and all that they only got as far as Quilpie and that's where the terminus remains. We've given up hope that it'll be extended from there. We'll be taking a thousand head of beef cattle to Quilpie and we'll need half a dozen extra hands for the drove; stockmen, drovers, and a bullocky. Are you any of those?"

I shook my head. "No, none of them; I've been working as a roustabout and tar-boy in a woolshed down Barringun way," I said.

"Oh right; that'd be grand experience for the drove." He shook his head and looked me up and down again. "Tom Clancy must have gone a bit soft in the noggin sending a boy like you that's never mustered before out here. Can you at least ride a horse, lad?" he asked, with a frown," ...or does he expect us to teach you *that* as well?"

I grinned at him and flicked my thumb over my shoulder to where Tom stood, his head down, chewing on the green grass that stuck out from underneath a wire fence surrounding the station garden. "I learn fast and that's not a bicycle tied up to the gate over there," I said.

I began to relax, for the conversation seemed vaguely familiar and then I suddenly felt a lump come to my throat, for I realised that it was the same kind of reception I remembered receiving from my departed friend, Jimmy Miller, at Miller's Run.

The man nodded. "It doesn't look like a bicycle, for sure, but it doesn't look much like a horse either. That's a pony if ever I saw one."

I bristled a bit at the insult to my pride and joy. "He'll go further and faster than any of those nags I saw in your horse paddock back there," I blurted out before I could stop myself.

The stockman smiled, ignoring my disparagement of the station's horses; many people in the bush were proud of their horses and it wasn't polite to disrespect them if their pride in an animal showed through, - no matter what your personal opinion might be of its visually appealing qualities.

"What's your name lad?" he said. "I haven't seen you hanging around the pub in Jundah. Maybe you're too young for this kind of work just yet, eh? Tom Clancy might have told your dad to send you west to the Channel Country for a bit of work to tide you over for the school holidays, would that opinion be close to the mark?"

I shook my head and sighed. *'Here we go again'*. "My name is Bill Smith," I said. "I know I look young and probably a bit scrawny to you, but I can work as hard as any man twice my size, and probably even harder than most of them. I'm nearly twenty-two, and I don't drink or smoke so you wouldn't find me in a pub in Jundah or Charleville, or anywhere else for that matter."

He smiled at me again. "You're pretty sure of yourself. One of a kind you must be, young Bill."

'One of a kind? You don't know how close to the truth you are mister.' I grinned. "That's been said before now." I held out my hand.

The man took it and then raised his eyebrows. "I'm Johnny Hooper, the manager of this station," he said. "You certainly have a stronger handshake than I expected, young Bill."

I pretended to ignore the compliment if that was what it was, as if it was beneath my manliness to give lip service to it and looked up at the sign over the front gate of the homestead yard again. It said *Jedburra Station.* "The agent said the main homestead was on Abingdon Downs Station, Mister Hooper," I said. "That's further north along the Thomson River, isn't it?'

Hooper nodded. "Call me Johnny if you like Bill. We're all on first-name terms here. Yes, Abingdon Downs is twenty miles further on and it *is* the head station of the Downs blocks. This one, Jedburra, and Berimpa are under the control of the head manager, Paul Waters at Abingdon Downs, but I'm the station manager here and there's another manager at Berimpa to conduct the everyday business affairs."

I looked around. "This is a pretty imposing setup for an outpost station," I said, genuinely impressed.

Hooper laughed and flicked his thumb over his shoulder. "If you think this is impressive you'll think Abingdon Downs is extraordinary. The homestead over there has a large vegetable garden and there's a slaughterhouse on the property where they slaughter their meat and salt it to store or send it to the other stations. There are stables for twenty horses, harness buildings and horse yards,..."

"...Now you're talking my language," I said, recalling his unfavourable remark about Tom. "I can ride anything from a brumby to a racehorse. Have they got a horse-breaker there?"

"Funny you should say that," he said. "They've got a horse stockman there who goes by the name of Horace 'Horsie' O'Donnell. He's supposed to be the best horse breaker in the business. I'm sure he'd like to meet someone of your obvious capabilities." He grinned in a patronising sort of manner as if to say, *'We'll find out soon enough if you can ride, young feller, or if you're all wind and no rain.'*

He went on with his description of Abingdon Downs while I stewed on his words. *'I'll show them.'* "They're pretty well self-sufficient, with paddocks and milking pens for their dairy cattle, and chicken coops for their hens. As well as the manager and his family, there's a couple who look after the house and a boy just to do the garden. They've got a cook, a general handyman and about ten stockmen. The stockmen are mostly aboriginal and they live on Abingdon Downs with their families.

I took a punt, more or less to stop him from going on and on about the place, which he evidently loved talking about. "I don't suppose it's all owned by a man called William Naughton,"

Hooper looked at me curiously and then shook his head. "No, William Naughton hasn't got his hands on the Downs yet, although we've heard he's interested in parts of it. The firm of Collins & Sons holds the lease at present.

I must have looked a bit absorbed as I tried to take in the magnitude of the operation because Hooper continued talking but in a more guarded tone. "I don't suppose you're a troublemaker sent by Naughton to find out how we're going here, are you, Bill? You're not a stockman and don't look much like you'd know one end of a bullock from the other, lad."

I stared at him in some confusion for a moment and then burst into laughter. "You think I'm a spy for Mister Naughton, Johnny?" I said. "You just told me I don't look like a stockman; I think William Naughton would agree with you. He wouldn't have picked someone like *me* to spy for him."

Hooper laughed too, but it was hollow and didn't sound like he was convinced. "No I suppose not, Bill, but it wouldn't be the first time it's happened, although I'm not saying it's Naughton who's been to blame. We've had a few so-called stockmen come looking for work from time to time and as soon as they've sounded us out and found out how we operate they scurry back to their bosses in whatever agency they've been sent by and we then get an offer to buy us out at some ridiculously cheap price."

"I'm certainly not one of them, Johnny," I said. "I've only heard of William Naughton because I worked for his brother, Edward, in Victoria. I was given a reference by him. He said I was one of the best workers he'd ever had and he told me William would give me a job if I mentioned his name. That's the only reason I've mentioned him. From what I've heard though, they're both regarded as fine upstanding men and I don't think they'd be involved in something dishonest like that."

Johnny seemed impressed by my show of loyalty to the Naughton's, no matter what his personal opinion of William might be. "Very well then, Bill," he said after a moment's thought. "We give people a fair go here, but we don't employ people who don't fit in, - especially when we're on a drove; the drovers have to work together as a very close team who look out for each other's welfare, you know, and we'll be so isolated out there where we're going it's hard to give somebody the boot once we've started on the trip. Well then, let's see what we can do with you. You said you're not a drover, stockman or bullocky. Are you a bait-layer by any chance?"

I must have looked a bit confused. "A...what? Do you lay baits for dingoes while you're on the drove?" I said.

Hooper grinned and shook his head. "A bait-layer's a cook, - although he's more like a rat exterminator according to what some of the drovers claim, hence the name bait-layer. Can you cook?"

"I could give it a go," I said uncertainly, "but you'd all probably finish up with the Barcoo spew. I've heard that Chinamen do most of the cooking on the big stations and drovers camps."

"You're right there, the Europeans come in all types, good, bad and indifferent, clean and unclean. The Shearers and Stockmen's Union demand good wages for them, but they get lazy and dirty and often end up drinking too much, - mainly because they're working on their own back in the camp and the boss drover can't keep an eye on them while he's out droving. The Chinese are much more reliable." He chuckled. "Don't worry; I was just testing you to see what you thought of having your tucker served by a Chinese cook. We've already got one; his name's Willie Ah Foo, but the men call him *Wil-ful*, because they reckon he's a wilful murderer." He grinned again. "Wilful hasn't murdered anybody yet, but the drovers swear he tries hard to poison them with his cooking every time they come down with the Barcoo rot."

"It happens often then, I suppose," I said.

"Too right it does," Hooper seemed to take some delight in relating the bad news. "You'll get the Barcoo rot after the first week on the drove no matter who's cooking your tucker. Most of the drovers get a dose of it even if they've been droving for years; they're just too vain to let on to anyone else and try to hide it. It usually only lasts a few days..."

"...I can take that," I said, trying to make my eagerness to fit in with the team obvious. "What happens after the first few days?"

"Oh, you'll get better after that, - or you'll die, - either way you won't have the Barcoo rot anymore."

"You can *die* from it?" I was a little disturbed by the way the conversation was going.

"Sure you can, and if you do then we give you the honour of being buried on the banks of the Barcoo River itself." Hooper laughed. "Anyway, it saves us the cost of carting your rotting carcass to the railhead for burial in Quilpie cemetery. I'm guessing you haven't copped a dose of it before now."

"No, I've only heard about it in Barringun," I had to admit. "It's some kind of vomiting sickness, isn't it?"

Hooper nodded. "You wouldn't get it in the shearing sheds in Barringun because the catering conditions are quite different inside a shed to what they are on a drove; those shearers are a spoiled bunch of whingers compared to the drovers and will have nothing but the best of tucker presented to them right on time from what I've heard; tea and cake at each two-hour break and all the luxuries supplied at dinner time. Drovers' cooks have to be more adaptable; it's not easy to cater for a drove and most of the time out there we're eating cold stew or bully beef and damper out of a tin pannikin and spitting out the dust and at least half of the flies. The drovers always blame the cook when they get the rot because they always think they're too tough to have got it from anything they've done themselves, but the poor old bait-layers have to do their job under pretty trying conditions at times. There's always an army of flies trying to beat them to the camp oven before they can stir the stew and get the lid back on when the drove is done for the day. Breakfast is the best time to eat."

"I didn't hear about the Barcoo spew in the shearing shed," I said. "It was in the Barringun pub."

Hooper looked surprised. "You said you don't drink, but you heard about it in the Barringun pub?"

"Oh, I never drank there, but I'd sit on the veranda and listen to the yarns and bush poems the shearers recited," I said. I thought for a moment. "Yes, it went like this."

'On the far Barcoo where they eat nardoo
Jumbuck giblets and pigweed stew.
Fever, ague and scurvy plague you,
but the worst of all is the Barcoo spew'

Hooper was impressed. "You might be the next 'Banjo Patterson' young feller," he said.

"I didn't write it," I confessed. "I don't even know what nardoo is, to be honest, although I think I've heard the word in the past, but I can't remember where."

Hooper immediately became serious again. "The Barcoo rot or Barcoo spew can come from a range of things, like tainted food or just the dietary change from what you're used to chomping on from the station kitchen, but eating nardoo won't make you come down with the Barcoo spew; - it's got a more insidious way of attacking your guts. It's important that you learn about it, though, because one day your life might depend on knowing what good bush tucker is and what to stay well clear of if you want to survive."

I frowned, "I know I've heard about..." I started.

Hooper cut in. "...Nardoo is a type of native fern that grows on the banks of rivers and creeks where seasonal flooding occurs out here in the Channel Country," he paused and looked at me gravely. "Do you remember learning about the famous explorers' Burke and Wills when you were at school?"

My eyes must have lit up. "Yes, of *course,*" I said. "Wasn't it *nardoo* the Cooper's Creek Aborigines gave them to eat when they'd run out of food on their return journey from the Gulf of Carpentaria?"

"You've got it," Hooper said. "It's an important food source for the aboriginal tribes who inhabit the drier areas of the interior, - even now, over seventy years after Robert O'Hara Burke led an expedition out of Melbourne on a journey of exploration to cross the continent from south to north."

"Ah yes," I said. "If my memory is correct, and my history teacher wasn't telling yarns, the expedition established a depot camp at Cooper Creek, and Burke, Wills and two other men pushed on towards the north coast, - although swampland stopped them from reaching the northern coastline. The return journey was plagued by delays and monsoon rains, and when they reached the depot back at Cooper Creek, they found it had been abandoned just nine hours earlier."

"Your history teacher was spot on, Bill," Hooper said. "They found the provisions that had been left for them under the 'Dig' tree about two hundred miles south-west of here, but once that was gone they were offered nardoo by the local Aborigines and gladly accepted it. It satisfied their appetite and after the Aborigines left them, they began to prepare the nardoo themselves, grinding it up and mixing it with water to make a thin paste, as they'd seen the local people do."

I frowned. "But they starved, didn't they?"

"Yes, they did," Hooper nodded. "Despite eating up to four or five pounds a day between them they grew weaker and thinner and formed the other symptoms of starvation, like shaking legs and a gradually slowing pulse. They couldn't understand why they seemed to be starving, despite eating so much nardoo. What they didn't know was that nardoo contains something that breaks down the gut's ability to turn food into energy and the Aborigines, over thousands of years, had developed a way of getting rid of it during the process of preparing it for consumption. The Aborigines probably assumed that these white men who'd come amongst them would have known that and didn't bother mentioning it. If Burke and Wills had paid more attention to those little details they might have survived to lead long and contented lives. Remember that Bill; take in every detail of what you observe in the bush and you'll most likely survive; miss out on the finer points and it could be the end of you."

"I'm keen to learn everything about this business, Johnny," I said, "...except maybe bait-laying. I'll leave that to Wilful, your Chinese cook, I think."

"I'm guessing you're willing to have a shot at working as a stockman here on the station until we go on the drove then," Hooper said.

My mind harked back again to Jimmy Miller's words as it had done so many times before.

'The drover's life is a hard one Bill, but I know you've got a big heart in that small chest of yours and you'll do whatever you have to do to make a go of it.'

I sighed. "Yes I'm willing to work as a stockman, for now, Johnny, but eventually my dream is to learn to be a drover."

"Right then, I'll give you the chance to show me that the reference from Edward Naughton was a valid one and not just given to you to make it easier to get rid of you from his employment. That happens a lot, you know. You'll need to prove yourself as a stockman before the drove starts because, as I said earlier it's hard to give somebody the boot once we've started."

Hooper invited me to go with him to the stockyard office that was hidden inside the front corner of the outbuilding to complete the necessary paperwork. It was the place where the stockmen gathered to receive their instructions if and when something outside the daily grind of life on the station was underway, he said. It was an area that would easily fit a dozen men without being overcrowded and Hooper went on to tell me something about the lifestyle and working conditions I could expect at Jedburra Station.

"It's not as isolated as it was before the telephone went in last year," he said. "That's been a real Godsend. The telephone allows Paul Waters at Abingdon Downs to maintain regular contact with me and the manager at Berimpa. We inform each other of the weather conditions, staffing issues, condition of the cattle and cattle movements and Paul responds with advice and instructions from Mister Collins, the leaseholder. There's also a branch line from Abingdon Downs with connections at Eight Mile, Twelve Mile, Cavel Creek stockyards and the Sixteen Mile boundary rider's hut so supplies can be ordered from Abingdon Downs and delivered to the outstations along with the mail. It's mostly a self-reliant lifestyle so we don't need to be constantly going backwards and forwards to Windorah or Jundah. Paul will decide where you're to be placed first up, but I'll warn you now that I think you'll be spending quite a bit of time out on your own riding boundary at whatever outstation he assigns you to until the drove starts in a couple of months. I hope you can take a bit of isolation…"

I must have grinned from ear to ear. "…I'll have no trouble with *that*, Johnny," I said, the tremor in my voice betraying my enthusiasm. "I keep to myself a bit anyway so the more isolated it is the better I'll like it."

Hooper shook his head slightly and gave me a perplexed glance. "We'll see about that," he said, but he must have decided that my preference for being alone was none of his business, and I realised with a strange feeling of nostalgia that Jimmy Miller had given me that same probing look at various times in my stay at Miller's Run. It was that same look that had conveyed to me Jimmy's confusion about a man's mindset and motivation for seeking new pastures when he'd admitted his fondness for his present circumstances, - and it was something that I couldn't easily explain to anyone.

'Maybe it would be best if I don't show so much enthusiasm for being on my own,' I thought grimly. *'Someday someone is going to ask me questions about it that I might not be able to answer easily.'*

"Our stockmen are paid £1/10/- per week in wages plus their keep. I think you'll be happy with that; it's over the award rate. Stow your gear in the bunkhouse behind the house for the time being, Bill," Hooper said. He paused before adding, "…there's no one else there at the moment; the other stockmen are in the separate married men's quarters with their wives, but that shouldn't worry you from what you've just told me. The pon… er, horse, can go in the stable, but he'll have company; I hope *he* doesn't mind."

I laughed, but it was with a degree of embarrassment. "Thanks, Johnny; Tom will be fine with that." I stopped before adding apologetically. "I *do* get along fine with people and I'll fit in with the droving team when the time comes…; it's just that I don't drink alcohol as almost everyone expects these days and it leaves me on the outer fringe of socialising sometimes. I have a very good reason for not drinking. I hope you can appreciate that without me going into any more detail about it."

I must have struck a chord because Hooper nodded. "Yes, I know what you mean Bill," he said. "I don't drink either, - *now*." He smiled wryly. "I'm well aware that it can be a problem for some of us and if anyone gives you any trouble about it, let me know and I'll sort it out with them. The drovers are pretty good though, and I'm sure they won't confront you over it. They've learned to leave me to drink my billy tea in peace and they know that I expect every man to keep within his limits, - the white ones, that is; the aboriginal stockmen are not allowed to drink alcohol at all by law."

'He's a recovering alcoholic and he thinks I am too,' I thought. I was immediately of a mind to explain to Johnny that he had taken my remarks out of context, but then I realised that the tactic of allowing someone to think whatever they chose could sometimes be to my advantage, - *'why not let it be and remain silent at that; it's as good an explanation as any other I can think of, - except the truth, of course, - and that's not an option I want to follow.'* It was a tactic that I'd remember and exploit for the rest of my working life.

Hooper went to walk away but stopped in his tracks. "After you've stowed your gear come back to the yard and I'll introduce you to the other men, Bill. We'll be starting with a bangtail muster tomorrow morning."

"A *bangtail muster?"* I said.

Hooper nodded. "We've sold some steers to an agent in Windorah and we need to herd them into the holding yard ready for him to collect. We cut their tails so we don't count them twice..."

"...You *cut off* their tails?" I said

I must have looked at him with dismay for he smiled patiently as he explained, "only the brush on the end of the tail; it grows back in a couple of weeks," He suddenly burst into laughter. "There'd be an awful lot of ox-tail stew for Wilful to cook if we cut the whole tail off and the flies would have a whale of a time, don't you think? Oh, one more thing; you don't have a bush-bell for your horse I suppose?"

I shook my head. "No," I said. "What does Tom need a bell for, Johnny? He doesn't stray and he always comes to me as soon as I call him."

Hooper was still patient. "He won't need it when we're mustering around the paddocks," he said, "but you'll have to get him used to it before the drove; in fact, both of you have to get used to the other drovers' horse bells, and we also put bells on the old station bullocks we use as leaders. Every bell is slightly different in its resonance or pitch, although most city people wouldn't be able to tell the difference."

"Oh," I said, still wondering what the fuss was about. *'Bells on the horses and the bullocks?'* I imagined being surrounded by clanging bells that drowned out all other noises as we drove the cattle across the plains.

"We'll most likely strike a Bedourie shower, - that's a dust storm that comes with thunder and lightning, but not a drop of rain, - at some time on the drove and the only way you'll know where the lead bullocks and other drovers are to keep the herd moving along together is the sound of their bush-bells," Hooper said. "If your horse is as smart as you say he is then he'll probably learn to recognise and separate the bullock and drovers bells quicker than you will. There are a couple of spares in the shed. Try them out and let me know if you're happy with any of them, but let me know straight away if you're not, so that, if I have to, I can send you into Windorah to buy one that suits you. The old-time drovers used to use the English-cast coach bells with their fancy inscriptions, but now there's a good range of Australian purpose-made bells available. The New South Wales drovers swear by their Morgan's and Mennicke's bell, but the best of all, in my opinion, is the Queensland Condamine bell. Its full title is the Condamine Bull Frog Bell and the first one was made from an old pit-saw by a smithy who'd set up his business in the town on the Western Downs, but it became so popular that later it was made from old cross-cut saws or any other old saw he could find. It's got a hard steely sound, something like the clink of a hammer on an anvil and its carrying tone makes it ideal for belling horses and cattle."

"How will I know what suits me?" I said. "I don't think I'd be able to tell a good bell from a bad one."

Hooper looked at me for a moment with a frown on his face. "You have to find one you *think* sounds right for you; then to test it, put your felt hat on the table with the crown down," he said. "Hold the bell over the top and ring it; if the hat quivers at the ringing then you'll know the bell's the right one for you."

I was astonished at this startling new knowledge I'd been introduced to. "Really, and what if the hat doesn't quiver?" I said.

Hooper had already turned his back on me and was on his way back to the branding yard, and he spoke without turning around. "If it doesn't quiver? Buy yourself a new felt hat as well; your old one has probably gone deaf from the sound of the Condamine bell."

* * * *

The Downs stations together, I learned, that is, Abingdon Downs, Jedburra and Berimpa covered an area of one hundred and sixty-three square miles. The parcels were each made up of excellent grazing land as Johnny Hooper had said, and stock was able to be maintained for most of the year at around twelve thousand head of beef cattle, except in times of extreme drought when they'd been forced to sell off most of their stock to other stations nearer the east coast.

The Macedon Range, with the low peak of Mount Twickenham to the east and Mount Misery on the north, bounded the station, and the tableland that made up the bulk of the estates was well-watered by springs, soakages and waterholes in the Saltern, Home and Sunday Creeks. To the west and south of the blocks the tableland sloped off gradually towards the flat, ancient landscape of dunes and river channels of the Thomson River and Diamentina River systems that had come to be known collectively as the Channel Country, arid for much of the year and sometimes for several years if the country was in drought, but after good, heavy monsoonal rain in the tropical north, an inland sea of countless interlaced channels that captured the water and sent it rushing in a torrent down Cooper Creek towards Lake Eyre in South Australia.

Abingdon Downs Station wasn't much different to what I'd been introduced to at Jedburra, I soon realised; it was built in the same style, but was just bigger. Paul Waters, the manager, turned out to be a pleasant, but talkative man and he was proud of the way the station had improved during his term as manager. The station homestead itself was certainly very appealing, as Johnny Hooper had said I would find it. The principal building, that in which Paul lived with his family, had only a main sitting-room or parlour with a bedroom on each side of it, but the family generally preferred to pass their time on the veranda which ran along the front and down either side of the house. It was twelve feet wide, and the rocking-chairs, sofas, and work-tables, - and, of course, Mrs Waters' sewing-machine, - were distributed along its length. It was, in fact, the place where they lived their everyday lives and the parlour was used solely for taking their meals. The veranda was covered in with striped blinds, so that when the sun shone hot, or when the rains fell heavily, or when the mosquitoes were more than usually troublesome, there was the partial protection of an almost enclosed room. Flowering creepers wound up and around all the veranda posts, which covered the front with greenery even when the flowering season was over.

From the front of the house down to Sunday Creek, a distance of a hundred yards or so, there was a pleasant, but a largely unsuccessful vegetable garden, - heart-breaking, indeed, to the Chinese bait-layer regarding anything that grew above ground, for the possums almost always got to the ripened produce before the cook did and he was left to dig up the potatoes and turnips that the little night raiders couldn't quite get to. The garden did fulfil the function of giving the station a pleasant home-like look though, and it seemed it was important to the emotional well-being of Mrs Waters, but Paul, who was probably unfamiliar with

96

the various vegetables that went into making a good broth, I'm certain, hardly noticed the possum's activities, his wife's reaction and the cook's annoyance at the destruction of their little patch of refined cultivation.

Behind the main house, various other buildings stood apart from each other, forming an irregular quadrangle. The kitchen came first, with a small adjacent bedroom where the poor careworn bait-layer spent his sleepless nights listening for the scratching inside the ceiling cavity that told him his little furry enemies were awake and about to conduct their first raid of the night. Behind that was a cottage, consisting also of three rooms, one of which was used as a sitting or reading room and the other two as bedrooms. The head stockman had been allocated one of these since he was a single man, and the other was kept set up for the use of any guest, or a swaggie or sundowner if one happened to pass through, and across the quadrangle facing them, a cluster of cottages had been built to accommodate the married stockmen and their families.

The store, perhaps the most important of all the buildings, formed the back of the quadrangle. The *shop* was part of the store building, but it had been partitioned off and entry was by a separate door. According to the faded sign nailed to the wall, the shop was supposed to be open for half a day twice a week, but the demands of station work didn't allow for that kind of consistency of trading hours, so it was generally opened on request or by prior arrangement. *Anyone* who came to the shop could buy its products, which included tobacco, pickles, jam, nails, boots, hats, flannel shirts, and moleskin trousers, but the main purpose of its existence was to provide the necessities of life for the station hands, who would otherwise have had to travel or send a family member, thirty miles into Jundah for the supply of their everyday needs. Generally, no money was passed over the counter, but the cost of luxuries like tobacco and rum was deducted from the men's wages. Tea, sugar and flour were given out weekly as free rations, and the meat was supplied to them free of charge from the butcher shop that was attached to the station's slaughterhouse.

Behind the quadrangle and set fifty yards away from the store was a well-made coach-house and horse stables. The stables were almost unnecessary except in the most dismal weather conditions, because the horses generally roamed free in the horse paddock, a compound of about fifty acres, and were driven up as they were needed for one of the two carriages. One horse, on a daily rotation basis, was always rostered to be kept close to the stables in a smaller yard so that it could be easily caught and used to round-up the others.

The horse paddock had been cleared with just a few trees left standing here and there for shade, but what caught my eye immediately was a well-formed track about ten yards wide that circled the boundary and looked as if it may have been used at some time as a racetrack and I remembered Johnny Hooper's words when I asked about a job breaking in horses at Jedburra. *'They've got a horse stockman who goes by the name of Horace 'Horsie' O'Donnell. I'm sure he'd like to meet someone of your obvious capabilities, then we'll find out soon enough if you can ride, young feller, or if you're all wind and no rain.'*

I wondered then if this was the domain of Mister O'Donnell and if this was to be the scene of our wrestle for riding supremacy.

Beyond the horse paddock, the run had been divided into much bigger paddocks, so large in fact, that a new arrival to the station could have wandered in one of them for a whole day and not realise that he was fenced in. There were six paddocks on the Abingdon Downs run, each of which covered an area of over ten thousand acres, and the land contained within the four southerly paddocks was flat to slightly undulating. The greater part of these blocks were open woodlands of Eucalypt and Brigalow in which cattle could wander at will, and men could ride their horses over the coarse grass with some certainty of not coming to grief in a concealed hole or burrow. All its streams were seasonal, though there were several permanent springs, and Sunday Creek and its tributaries flowed from its headwaters on Mount Twickenham through the paddocks on its course to join up with Cooper Creek to the south-west.

The two most northerly paddocks were composed of rocky hills and plains, with the north-eastern paddock in the foothills of the Macedon Range being the highest and most rugged and here and there rocky knolls, crevasses and vine thickets blocked access to anything trying to gain passage in any straight line. No fences were necessary on its outer boundaries, for it was fringed on the northern and eastern edges by thick scrub, so dense that it was impenetrable to a man without an axe, or any but the smallest of ground-dwelling animals and snakes. The north-western paddock was fenced, for part of that boundary was shared with Ringley Plains Station, leased by a Scotsman, Gordon McKenzie, but a strip of land to the west of Ringley Plains was so poor that no lessee had ever taken it up. There were assorted bush trails here and there, and the stock route from the widespread pastoral districts of the Central Highlands further east leading to the Channel Country grazing lands passed across the north-western part of the run.

The main aggravation for Paul Waters concerning that section of the western paddock was the presence of cattle 'duffers' who, from time to time, weren't averse to cutting fences and driving the cattle out on to the unoccupied land beyond, where they could legally claim them as 'cleanskins' not owned by anyone, - even if it was obvious that the A^D brand had been partially covered by another of similar shape.

Waters had told me of such an incident that had been particularly frustrating for him several years ago. A man called Michael Hughes had been charged at the Quilpie Circuit Courthouse with stealing twenty cows and seven calves, the property of Abingdon Downs Station. The cattle in question had been grazing, with a hundred others, in the Western paddock; the paddock was visited daily by the boundary rider and the fence examined to ensure that it remained in good order. One day some cattle went missing, the fence was examined and one panel was found to have been removed, and carefully replaced in its former position. The tracks of cattle, and with them the tracks of two horses, were noticed leading away from the fence. The boundary rider followed the tracks, which led him to a cattle yard, in which he saw the twenty-seven cattle impounded. He immediately recognised them as the property of Abingdon Downs and hurried back to the station to report his discovery.

The court heard that Hughes was at the yards where the cattle were confined when the boundary rider and Waters returned, and the manager claimed the cattle. At first, Hughes denied that the cows and calves belonged to Abingdon Downs and said he bought them at another station, but when Waters examined the brand and challenged him again he changed his story and said that he knew the cattle belonged to Abingdon Downs, but they'd escaped through the fence and he'd intended to send Waters word that they were temporarily confined in his yards. Other evidence was given that it wasn't the first time Hughes had been charged with such an offence and the evidence, on the whole, left no doubt in the minds of those present that the thief had been caught, as it were, *red-handed*, with the cattle illegally in his possession. The charge against the prisoner seemed to have been conclusively proven, but, notwithstanding the overwhelming evidence, the jury returned an irrational verdict of *not guilty*. Early in the case one of the jurors showed, by the questions put by him to the witnesses for the Crown, and his subsequent testimonies, such a leaning towards the prisoner, amounting to bias, that the Magistrate was obliged to call him to order and remind him of the obligation he was under from the oath he'd taken. No case could have been better prepared by the police, or brought before the Court by the Crown, to secure a conviction. The proof was clear against Hughes and the Magistrate commented that *'I fail to see the possibility of obtaining a conviction for cattle-stealing, in any indictment put before a Quilpie jury if the evidence placed before them in this legal action was not sufficient to convince them of the prisoner's guilt.'*

The verdict had been a bitter blow to Waters and Collins, but it wasn't entirely unexpected. Tensions had run high between the big station owners and their near neighbours for many years and it was well-known that many ordinary people felt antagonistic towards those few who owned most of the western lands and had become rich at the expense of what they deemed to be hard-working stockmen and drovers. It was a lesson Waters said he'd learned the hard way and he advised me to heed the warning should I eventually have to defend myself through the legal system sometime in the future. *'You can't expect the court system to always get it right whenever you're relying on people to tell the truth under oath, because an oath taken with the hand placed firmly on the bible means everything to an honest person, but nothing at all to a crook.'*

It was a lesson I didn't think I'd ever have to remember, Sister Mary, but of course I was wrong as you'll find out later.

* * * *

Sheep had been the dominant stock on Abingdon Downs in the 1860s and 1870s. Blocks in remote areas like the Thomson River catchment were unfenced at that time and shepherds managed the sheep. The shepherds lived in small timber or stone huts with bark roofs and earth floors which were named according to the distance from the main homestead, and so at the Downs stations there were Eight Mile, Twelve Mile and Sixteen Mile huts, but they weren't linear and were all located in different directions. At night the sheep were all brought to common yards near the hut where they could be guarded against attack by dingos and next morning they were divided into as many mobs as there were shepherds and taken to fresh pastures, returning in the evening to be yarded. The land had proved to be unsuitable, however; the range of grazing land was restricted to areas close to water which left large areas of the country unable to be used effectively and as areas around sheepfolds became more heavily grazed and the best grasses were eaten out, spear grass tended to take over. Spear-grass and sheep didn't go well together as the spear grass seeds became embedded into the skin of the sheep and devalued the hide and stuck to the fleece making it of inferior quality. The sheep were long gone from Abingdon

Downs, but the shepherd huts still stood, a remnant of the past, re-roofed with galvanised iron, and now put to good use by the boundary riders of the station.

It was to the Sixteen Mile hut that I was eventually assigned, as far from the main station homestead as it was possible to be and still be on the Downs, and close to the western boundary beyond which was the no-man's land of scrubby trees and cattle duffers, but before I was due to take up the posting several weeks later, I made it my business to get to know my nemesis, Horace 'Horsie' O'Donnell, the stockman in charge of the Abingdon Downs stables.

* * * *

When I first met Horace 'Horsie' O'Donnell I wasn't sure how to take him on face value. Horsie, as he preferred to be called, was well named for he *was* certainly an excellent horseman as I'd been told by Johnny Hooper. He was proud of his responsibilities as a stable stockman at Abingdon Downs too, for he earned good wages, Paul Waters was a decent manager, and he was living where he belonged, - well almost. Horsie was the product of an Irishman and a woman of the Kunja tribe whose ancestral lands were spread over some 12,000 square miles of territory along the Warrego River from Cunnamulla in the south to Augathella and Burenda in the north. Their eastern boundary lay about sixty miles east of Charleville at Angellala Creek and their most westerly range lay along the Paroo River. Horsie's birthplace was the railway siding town of Cooladdi, which meant the home of the Black Duck in the Kunja language, but he was born long before the western railway was constructed, which was indeed only five years before in 1919. The Margany were the original custodians of the land Abingdon Downs now occupied, but the tribes were close enough for Horsie to relate to it culturally.

It seemed to me at the time that Horsie had come to terms with the fact that the old ways were well and truly over and the survivors of the Kunja and Margany nations had to make the best of their new circumstances, but I was to find out as I got to know him better that he hadn't quite relinquished his old customs and beliefs in favour of the white man's ways.

He'd been sometimes heard to say that few horse stockmen, even in the best stables in Queensland, had a lot of forty horses at hand as he had, out of which so many were able to carry a man sixty miles in eight hours at a moment's notice, but I could see right away that his stable methods wouldn't have met with such high praise in the Queensland cities or even the rural districts around Melbourne where I'd learned to ride. The animals were never groomed, never hand-fed unless they were sick or very young, and many of them never shod. They were bred to live on the open grasslands, and, as Horsie told me, they were working horses first and one or two of the faster ones only became racehorses twice a year when the annual bush races at Quilpie and Charleville came around.

It so happened that the Quilpie Cup meeting was to be held a fortnight after I arrived at the Downs and Paul Waters had nominated two horses, one in a lead-up race and the other in the Cup, the main event of the day. He and Mrs Waters weren't into horse racing in a big way, but I suppose he figured that seeing his own horses go around would be a nice way to gain a bit of an extra thrill for his wife and the children. These meetings were immensely popular, you see, particularly with the ladies, and just about every woman of any age in Quilpie and the surrounding stations got themselves spruced up in their best outfits and hats and attended them, mainly for the enjoyment of the camaraderie and freedom from the isolation of their everyday lives. The men too wore their wide-brimmed white felt hats and stuck their thumbs into their best western leather belts with the big gleaming brass buckles, strutting about the dusty racecourse like roosters in a fowlyard full of fat laying hens.

Horsie, of course, had been assigned the task of preparing the two horses he'd personally selected for Paul Waters as the fastest of his charges and I'd managed to convince him that I could ride well enough to help him work them each morning. What probably clinched my appointment as his stablehand, however, was my offer to wash and groom them afterwards. They were quite fast all right, I thought, and powerful animals too, particularly Abingdon Prince who was to race in the Cup, but they *were* station horses after all and Paul wasn't too hopeful about the likelihood of either of them winning their respective races against the best horses in the district.

Race day came around and Horsie and I had the horses in excellent condition. We'd taken them down to Quilpie the day before and they were stabled at the Quilpie showgrounds along with the fifty or so other horses who were competing in the seven races on the card. I went around the yard mid-morning and had a look at Abingdon Prince's opposition in the Cup. "There's not a lot of class there by the look of them," I said to Horsie. "I think Paul's in with a bit of a chance with his pair."

Horsie gave me a look that said, *'Yeah right young feller, what would you know?'* although he went back to inspecting the horse's hooves and said, "His feet are right enough; just depends if he wants to use them to run; got a mind of his own, this one."

I said nothing at the time because I hadn't got to know him that well, but the feeling of getting brushed off stayed with me and I thought that one day I'd find a way to make him realise that I knew a lot more about horses than he'd given me credit for. As luck would have it, though, I didn't have to wait long to get my opportunity. Paul had engaged the same local jockey to ride both horses, but the poor fellow had sustained an injury to his arm in the lead-up race and was unable to ride Abingdon Prince in the Cup. There were no other jockeys available either, for the Cup had attracted the biggest field of the day and Abingdon Prince looked like being scratched from perhaps the most important race of his life.

Paul's children were too young to understand what had happened and were inconsolable, and strangely enough, I noticed that Horsie was visibly distraught too. My first thought was, *'Why are you so upset, Horsie?'* and then it hit me. *'You old fox,'* I thought. *'You knew the horse had a good chance of winning the race all along.'*

I was still musing over the unfortunate circumstances that had befallen us all, - for I considered myself one of the Abingdon team by then, - when Horsie looked at me shrewdly. "You reckoned you could ride anything, Young Bill," he said. "Right, you've got the opportunity to show it now if you're game enough."

"You want me to ride Abingdon Prince?" I said, "…but I don't have a jockey's licence."

"Yes, you do." Horsie grinned. "It's being renewed right now, - in Melbourne. There happens to have been a jockey called Bill Smith riding there a few years ago. I don't know where he went, but he's not riding there now, - and what good luck for us; he's turned up at Quilpie and offered to ride Abingdon Prince in the Cup."

I thought about it for a moment and was beginning to warm to the idea, for I dearly wanted to show him my horse riding skills, and of course, I didn't want to disappoint the Waters' children either. "The stewards are sure to find out, Horsie," I said, but my protest was weak and fell on deaf ears.

Do you ride long or short," he said.

"Short," I told him.

He began to readjust the buckles of the stirrup iron straps to suit my riding style. "It's a bush meeting, Bill; nobody checks anything. The steward's the publican from the Railway Hotel in Cooladdi," he said. "He's a friend of mine so he'll believe my story that your licence is on its way. I'll go and tell him right now we've got a replacement jockey who just happens to be visiting Quilpie."

I shrugged my shoulders. "Okay then," I said, "but don't hold me responsible if they get suspicious about the sudden appearance of a Melbourne jockey in their midst."

Horsie laughed and turned to hurry off to the steward's room. "You'll have to learn how to tell a few tall tales to get you through some tough spots, Bill," he called over his shoulder. "It's not too hard once you get used to it."

I stood there and regarded his disappearing back as he pushed through the crowd. *'Yes, I know that Horsie,'* I thought. *'I could tell you a thing or two about it, by Jove.'*

By the time Horsie returned a few minutes later I'd rechecked all the horse's mouth gear and tightened the girth strap under its belly. It wasn't that I didn't trust him to do it correctly; it was a routine I'd been taught from my time in Bendigo. *Always check your own gear because then you've only got yourself to blame if something goes wrong.*

"The favourite's Macedon Chief and he's small but fast, so the jockey would have been told to try and steal it in front to keep him out of trouble," Horsie said. His voice was slightly higher than normal, another indication of his pent up excitement.

'He really does think we can win this,' I thought for the second time.

"He'll be the one with the green and white silks. Do your best to keep our horse near the fence, but let him run freely if he sees clear space in front of him. He loves to be in front and he'll fight hard to keep his lead if anything tries to pass him."

'Well then,' I thought, rather boldly, as he legged me up and I took the reins. *'Thanks for the advice Horsie, but pardon me, for I'm going to ride him the way I see things pan out in the race.'*

Abingdon Prince was a powerful horse as I said before, and the buffeting he got in the first couple of furlongs of the race would have put many a lesser horse off completely, but he'd been bred tough and he came through it and settled down in second place to Macedon Chief as the field entered the first turn. His breathing was nice and regular, and he was just bowling along with his ears pricked so I was happy to let him run at his own pace. When we came into the home straight the field had been stretched out a dozen lengths behind me and Macedon Chief had pinched a break of two lengths on us, but I knew I had a mighty big motor underneath me and with two hundred yards to go, I shook him up and asked him for an effort. Well, - he pinned his ears back, put his head down and sprinted to the post. We won by a neck.

Paul Waters' voice was hoarse when he met Horsie and me in the winner's enclosure. I think he'd had a few bets and had won a lot of money, but the faces of Mrs Waters and their children were quite enough to gladden my heart. "Mister Jockey," they cried. "Mister Jockey, you beat them all."

Horsie and I became a lot closer after that.

* * * *

Horsie and I rode out together to the Sixteen Mile hut so that I could be familiarised with the detailed duties of my new posting. The boundary rider was just as important to any station as a stockman was, - in his own way, of course, Horsie told me. He was responsible for checking that the cattle in his particular paddock had access to water that wasn't contaminated by anything such as dead animals or rotting vegetation at all times and that there was enough water in the billabongs for them to draw to. He was also responsible for ensuring that the boundary fences and gates were maintained in good order. It was a solitary kind of life and he was well-paid for it because the boundary rider's job wouldn't have appealed to everyone.

"No way, Bill," he said when I asked him if he'd ever done a stretch at the hut. "Boundary riding isn't the sort of life that I'm cut out for and I've got the greatest respect for *anyone* who can work under the isolated conditions in *any* of the huts, but the Sixteen Mile is the worst, by far."

"I think I might enjoy it, Horsie," I said. "Isolation suits me sometimes."

He gave me that same look again that had so stirred me up at the racecourse, *'Yeah right young feller, we'll see about that,'* but I knew that in this case, I'd have to bide my time to show him what I was made of, for it was going to take a bit longer than a couple of minutes of a horse race to convince him. Why it was so important for me to prove my resolve to him, in particular, is something I can't explain; - maybe it was because he had the reputation of being a great horseman, - someone I felt I wanted to emulate as I got older, or more likely it was just my sheer pigheadedness. No matter what it was it only served to give me the strength to want to succeed in whatever lay ahead at the hut. Horsie seemed intent on putting me off the posting before I'd even got there, though, and I listened as he went on talking it down until I came to the conclusion finally that it wasn't for my benefit at all; he was simply voicing his own nervous apprehension about the place.

105

"No boundary rider has ever stopped at the Sixteen Mile hut for long," he said. "The solitude is just too intense for them and after a trial of a few weeks, sometimes a few days, men who'd been determined enough to take on the role for the sake of steady and well-paying employment, regularly rolled up their blankets, rode into the homestead yard, told the manager that there was a limit to the deprivation of other human contacts any man was capable of tolerating, and left, claiming the respectable paycheque was not enough to compensate them for the despondency they'd endured at the hut.

"Despondency?" I said, intrigued. "Why would *every single one* of them feel morose just from being out there alone? Surely it's no different to anywhere else on the Downs."

"Oh, it *is* different. There's something about that particular place, Bill," Horsie said.

He went on to tell me that the longest period of continual residence in the Sixteen Mile hut in his time at the Downs was six months, but that particular boundary rider had had his reasons for staying where he was, - well out of sight, for it turned out he was wanted by the police. When his name and a photograph was finally published in the Warrego Times, Charleville's local newspaper, and Paul Waters realised that the man wasn't who he'd said he was when he'd employed him and he'd been inadvertently harbouring a criminal; the man was arrested in the hut and taken to the Rockhampton Prison. The Sixteen Mile Hut remained deserted for a few months after his departure, and when the news came through that he'd been tried and hanged for a particularly cold-blooded murder it had fallen to Horsie to collect and burn the dead man's blankets and scraps of clothing that he'd left behind in the hut. It was a task that, given his Kunja culture, had left him in dread of the possibility that the murderer's spirit might return to haunt the land, and the Sixteen Mile hut's atmosphere as a place of inexplicable menace was heightened to such an extent that the western paddock boundary rider post became even harder to fill than it ever had before.

I reached up and pulled the brim of my hat down just above my eyes, squinting into the distance at the object that glittered in the strong sunlight above the distant belt of dull green scrub. The thing that had absorbed my interest, and which could be seen across several miles of plain scrub, was the galvanised-iron roof of the Sixteen Mile hut, the lodging place of every boundary rider of the western paddock since it was fenced thirty years ago.

"That's it, Bill," Horsie said as we dismounted. "Your new home; I hope you enjoy your stay."

* * * *

One of Horsie's jobs, besides tending to the station horses, was to load the four-wheel dray and distribute the weekly provisions to the boundary riders at the various huts. The Eight Mile, Twelve Mile and Cavell Creek huts were straightforward and easy to get to with well-formed tracks over which his beloved horses travelled with ease, but Sixteen Mile Creek was different; the track that led to it was rough, with washouts on Sunday Creek and its tributaries that had to be crossed, - and to make matters worse the telephone line to the hut had been dead for two days, probably down somewhere along its route due to a fallen tree. I didn't know this at the time though, for I was firmly established at the hut and blissfully unaware that my only connection to the outside world was cut off.

Horsie would check the line when time permitted, but I'm sure he didn't regard it as high priority as he'd told me the boundary riders in each of the huts seemed reluctant to use the new-fangled gadget anyway. He'd made a habit of stopping and having a cup of tea with us, not only because he'd been instructed to by Paul Waters, but because he enjoyed seeing the eager looks on our faces and hearing the exclamations of *'My my, you don't say'* as he told us of any important news that had come through from Quilpie and beyond. He was careful, though, not to divulge too much to those of us who could read, he said because the weekly Warrego Times was included in each man's box and he could have the entertainment of reading it for himself later, - even though the news was at least two weeks old by then. Horsie felt, nevertheless, that he was almost the perfect purveyor of specialised topics related to the news that he dealt out to the white *and* aboriginal boundary riders because he had a foot in both camps, so to speak, and indeed his news summary was quite often very different for each man. The white boundary riders were generally more interested in world affairs than their aboriginal counterparts who usually wanted to know only what was occurring in their communities.

Horsie was still surprised, nevertheless, each time he arrived at the Sixteen Mile hut with my supplies that I had settled down so contentedly after his sombre warning of the intensity and extreme solitude that I was likely to experience, and his message from Paul Waters was always the same. *'If it gets too much for you there's always the option of doing some other work around the station.'* Paul had taken a liking to me, he said and wanted me to be happy in my work, but I continued to assure him that I found the solitude was more than acceptable; the scrubby plains fascinated me and the repetitious march of the sun across a brilliant, blazing sky did nothing to diminish the contentment of life in the saddle and in the confines of the hut that I'd felt from the beginning of my tenure there.

I wasn't there on one particular day when Horsie pulled the dray up at the front of the hut and looked around for any sign of me. It was unusual for a boundary rider not to come out immediately they heard the creaking sound of the dray's wheels trundling along the track and indeed some were so eager for the weekly visit they would often ride out to accompany him the last half-mile or so to the hut, talking and asking questions the whole way. He told me later of his concerns at my absence.

Was he too early? He squinted up at the sun. No, it was past midday, the appointed time of his attendance, and the same time almost to the minute that he arrived every week. He stepped down from the dray, looked around again and cupped his hands around his mouth like a megaphone. His coo-ee rang across the scrub, but only silence and the soft whinnying of his horses answered him.

He tried the door of my hut; it was unlocked and he opened it and stepped inside hesitantly. Nothing moved but no foul smell assailed his nostrils; - that was a good sign. Horsie didn't like intruding on *anyone's* privacy, but in this case, it was a necessary aspect of his job, because he *had* to find out what the reason was for my non-appearance. He could easily have unloaded the rations and then left a note with Waters' instructions for the following week's work recorded in it, although that was hardly necessary, but it was a strict rule of the station that he had to *see* the man and make sure that everything was in order. On the other hand, it was also my responsibility to be at the hut at the appointed time. If he did go back and report to Paul Waters that Bill Smith was missing, a search party would be organised at once to return to the hut and he would be part of it. Besides all that he had some news that he wanted to divulge to me that he was excited about.

Horsie hadn't been further than the front door of the Sixteen Mile hut since he'd shown me around the place a couple of months before, for he was used to having his cup of tea sitting with me on one of the two broad tree stumps that served as chairs under the canvas awning outside the door. This was common practice amongst the occupants of all of the huts, and it wasn't due to any lack of manners or respect for their visitor. The huts were too small even to seat two people and still leave a decent enough space between them, and the outdoorsmen who occupied them naturally were of the disposition that at least five paces apart was the minimum distance in which a conversation could be held with any degree of relaxation.

Almost his first sight on entering the darkened hut was the reflection of his swarthy face in my little mirror, which was neatly nailed to the wall close to the door. Horsie had never been vain, for very good reason, he admitted, but he told me he did pause to gaze at his untidy jumble of black hair and straggly beard for a moment, then he turned his back on the glass, merely noting that it was a strange thing to find in a boundary-rider's hut and that it had not been there a few months ago when the last man had been taken away. He was struck with the scrupulous tidiness of everything. Ration bags all hung up; nothing left lying about; fireplace cleaned out, - daily, by the look of it; pannikins bright as silver; bunk made up. "Bill Smith is surely one of the oddest little men to ever set foot in a boundary rider's hut," he said aloud. "But where are you now Bill? – not here where you're supposed to be, that's for sure."

Suddenly an upsurge of guilt at his intrusion into my private world made him feel so uncomfortable that he opened the door and stepped back out into the sunlight. He scanned the horizon again and saw a small cloud of dust with a dark speck in its centre that seemed to be heading in from the west. "Ah, that'll be Bill coming now." He began unloading the boxes of rations and had just finished when I drew rein and leapt to the ground.

"Sorry I'm late, Horsie," I said breathlessly. "I had some trouble on the western boundary fence I had to take care of."

Horace looked at me and grinned amiably, but then he saw the torn shirt and beginnings of a dark bruise on my face just below my left eye and his grin faded. "It looks like you came off second best in that stoush, young Bill," he said. "Is the fence still standing?"

"The fence wasn't the problem, Horsie," I said. "I caught that Scotsman, McKenzie from Ringley Plains ringbarking trees again."

"That's not a crime, Bill," he said giving me a troubled look. Is that all he was doing?"

I nodded. "But he was on our side of the fence this time," I said. "Paul Waters told him a few months ago he wants the bigger trees left standing in the Western Paddock because there's so little shade for the cattle, but McKenzie said the trees will stop the rain from blowing on to his block when the season changes."

"Oh, right." Horsie's face lit up, "then it *is* a violation of the Common Fences Act," Horsie said. "He's got no right to be on our side of the fence without permission."

"Yes, that's exactly what I told him," I said abruptly, showing my exasperation at his know-it-all attitude.

Horsie didn't seem to notice. "He obviously didn't agree with your point of view in the matter, Bill," he said. "Do you want me to come back with you and have a word with him about it?"

"That won't be necessary, Horsie," I said, still a bit miffed; "I've seen him off and I don't think he'll be back,"

Horsie pointed to my bruise. "He gave you something to remember him by before he left, I see."

I grinned. "He rated me and Paul Waters in language that would have seared the landscape and I got a little annoyed with him. I punched him in the jaw."

Horsie didn't share my delight. "He got you back, though."

"Yes he did," I said, still thinking about the incident with a certain amount of satisfaction, "and that's when I got *really* annoyed. He grabbed my shirt and I took hold of his arm and twisted it until he fell to the ground. I had a hold of his fingers and I warned him I'd break one if he moved."

Horsie raised his eyebrows. "Did he move?"

"Yes, he did," I said.

"You broke it?"

"Yes, I broke it."

O'Donnell was impressed. He'd inherited some of his father's Irish temperament, he said, but not his fighting ability, and he figured, quite rightly, that having one of those qualities was not of much use without the other; besides that, his memory of the one time he'd met McKenzie was that the top of my head would have been about level with his shoulders, although the Scot was a thin, bony looking individual. He told me later that any private thoughts he'd begun to harbour about my manliness when he'd seen the inside of the hut were banished in an instant. "What did you do then?" he said, his tone hushed and bordering on deferential.

"I didn't have to do anything," I said. "I let him go and he jumped the fence and ran away into the scrub cursing me and everyone who had anything to do with Paul Waters." I shrugged. "I feel bad about it, - breaking his finger, I mean, but it was partly his fault; the way he tried to pull his hand clear only contributed to his grief. Anyway, it's over now; how about a billy of tea, Horsie?"

Horace squinted up at the sun. "No, I'll have to pass on that one young Bill," he said. "I'd better start back, - anyway, you're going to have quite a few visitors in three days. Make sure you and Tom Thumb have plenty of feed and rest tomorrow and the next day because we'll be doing a muster of the cattle in the western paddock. I'll be back that morning with the dray to pick up your swag and any provisions you have left over, so have it ready first thing in the morning."

"We're heading out on the drove, Horsie?" My face would have shown my excitement, which was the kind of reaction he'd expected and yearned to see when he gave me the surprise news, but he wasn't quite finished.

"Next week we head for the railhead at Quilpie," he said. "...and you're in luck, young Bill."

"I am?" I said, thinking, *'What could top that bit of good news?'*

Horsie nodded. "You're going to be working with *me*, as my assistant horse drover, - well, at least some of the time anyway, - unless you're needed to fill in for one of the cattle drovers who's come down with the Barcoo rot." He made the statement in a measured, solemn tone as if I'd just been promoted to the second most important job on the drove, - after his own chief horse drover position of course. The effect worked a charm, - almost too well, - for I seemed so happy that Horsie said he thought for an anxious moment that I was going to kiss him, but instead, I grasped his hand and shook it with so much vigour that he almost winced. It was another reminder to him that although I was small and looked a bit girlish, I had the strength of someone twice my size.

* * * *

The droving party consisted of Horsie the horse drover, me his assistant, Willie Ah Foo, or *Wilful*, the Chinese cook, the bullocky Sam Watson, with his team of ten bullocks to pull the supply dray, and twelve cattle drovers, including the lead drover, Johnny Hooper from Jedburra. It was a good choice of leader Horsie told me, for out of all the outstation managers, Johnny had the most experience at managing cattle on a drove. He'd been droving from his teenage years up, and he knew, almost instinctively, how to control a spooked herd, but more importantly, he could control the other stock-riders too, all of whom were of the ordinary run of Australian bushies; long unruly hair tied up with rawhide thongs, tobacco-stained hands and teeth, and subject to the relentless use of coarse language as well as the whip to get any wayward beast to turn in the direction it was supposed to go to re-join the herd.

The men had been hand-picked by Paul Waters, however, and were the best riders that he'd been able to gather together in the district, and although they needed to be kept well in hand, Horsie was confident they'd do their work well. They wouldn't receive their cheques until the completion of the drove and the final amount paid to each was dependant on the successful delivery of the cattle with minimal casualties. It wasn't a long drove by anyone's standards, Horsie told me, least of all by the yardsticks of the men who'd done the Western Plains to Channel Country droves, which could take several months, but those long droves were few and far between now that the Western Railway had been extended to Quilpie and the long droves were mainly confined to Queensland bullocks heading down south to the railhead at Bourke for transport to the southern capitals.

The preparations for the drove were well underway. Flour, tea, sugar and tinned bully beef were laid in, each man's spare boots and pack-saddles, provisions, tents, swags, and general property; medical kits and the all-important casks of rum and water were loaded on the dray. Supplies of tobacco had been bought and secured in watertight containers with names attached by the men who smoked, - which was most of them, - for those sorts of luxuries were not part of the provisions supplied by the station. Whips were checked and the handles carefully rewound, for a stockman without a good *cracker* of a whip was like a schoolmaster with a feather duster instead of a cane in a class full of teenage delinquents.

The horses had been rounded up from the big paddock two days earlier and were confined in the holding yard, because every horse's overall health, but especially its legs, hooves and shoes had to undergo a thorough examination before it was passed fit to undertake the drove. Each drover had three horses assigned to him and they were to be worked one day and then allowed two days' rest, and it was one of our responsibilities, that is, Horsie and me, to ensure that the resting horses were freshened up and kept in good condition for their turn at work. No matter how well the riders reported their assigned animals to be feeling on their trial runs, Horsie insisted on rechecking each animal personally, for he wasn't about to take any chances with our precious charges and he felt that the disposition of some of the younger men was that, *near enough was good enough.*

Dinner was taken before dark and most of the men retired early to the bunkhouse, for they knew that this was the last night they'd be sleeping in a comfortable bed for at least a week. There was no early night or sleep-in till dawn for Wilful, the Chinese cook or Horsie and me, because, for the three of us and Sam the bullocky, the drove had already started. All of the horses, both working and resting, were fed, washed down and turned out into the holding yard, and then, an hour before dawn the four of us were up again, feeding, watering, saddling and belling the working horses for the first day's travelling. Wilful roused the drovers, banging on a tin pannikin with his serving ladle and yelling, *'Gitup now, - you comee bleakfast quick now, - lazee lot,'* at first light and the men filed out of the bunkhouse rubbing the sleep from their eyes and muttering curses about deaf Chinese bait-layers.

During breakfast, Johnny Hooper gave his instructions for the day, although it was hardly necessary for most of the men because they were all well aware of what lay ahead. The first day's drove would be a distance of twelve miles, Hooper said. Camp would be made at the Travelling Stock Reserve at Sheep Station Creek. It would be easy travelling with plenty of good grazing along the Stock Route, which was all fenced. Sam the bullocky with his supply dray and the horse drovers with the resting horses were to catch up once they'd broken camp and go on ahead of the drove to set up the next night's camp.

* * * *

I looked along the road to where the cloud of dust kicked up by the moving herd had already started to settle and the yells and whoops of the drovers mingled with the plaintive cries of calves who'd momentarily been separated from their mothers died away into the distance. "It's all been so orderly, Horsie," I said. "I thought droving would have been a lot more disorganised than this, but the cattle are moving along nicely without any fuss at all."

Horsie O'Donnell hoisted a wooden case containing one of Wilful's camp ovens on to the back of the dray and then turned to look in the same direction. "Yes, there's not too much that can go wrong on a short drove like this one nowadays, Bill. The early drovers had it pretty rough, though," he said. "Depending on where they were they would've had to contend with crocodile-infested rivers in the Northern Territory, droughts, dust storms, floods, poisonous plants and..." He hesitated before continuing. "...sometimes what they used to call *hostile* natives, - that's my mob of course. The explorers and overlanders followed routes along river systems and used the trade routes and trails that my mother's people had been using for thousands of years, even up to as late as forty years ago."

I felt an outpouring of sympathy for him because I could see that his allegiance was torn between the simple and natural way of life that his past had offered and the current circumstances of contentment he now found himself in looking after his beloved horses, but he continued his chinwag with no more than a sigh of acceptance.

"It was first come first served along the routes in those days and if you arrived at a waterhole and another mob had already gone through, you might find that there was no feed to be had close by for the night stopover and you'd have to spread them out for a couple of miles either side of the track."

"That'd be hard work," I said," "I mean, keeping the herd together."

"It meant putting the men on night watch for two hours at a time and lighting fires in a circle to mark the edge boundaries of the herd's run, but sometimes that wasn't enough to keep the herd calm. It could be the smallest thing, - like the little grey ground-nesting bird that looks a bit like a quail. It makes a flapping and whistling sound as it rises when it's disturbed and at night when all is quiet that sudden noise would easily cause a stampede. They'd run for miles before they could be rounded up, but the worst thing I saw was when a herd charged through the night camp where the men were sleeping in their swags."

I shivered involuntarily and saw a slight grin light up Horsie's face. He was either relishing reciting the tale to his dismayed apprentice or just taking delight in the memory of it. In any case, he hoisted another pack onto the dray and went on with hardly a pause for breath.

"Tommy Rafferty was the drover in charge. It was on the Georgina near Lake Nash Station and the men heard the racket and realised that it was headed straight for them. Luckily there was a big old Gidgee tree between them and the herd and most of them scrambled into its branches, but the bait layer was a bit slow and only just managed to crawl behind it. He escaped with a broken leg and the herd kept going for four miles until they stopped at the edge of Lake Nash itself."

I sighed and shook my head. "The poor old cook was the only one injured?"

Horsie laughed. "The drovers reckoned it was divine providence for the tucker he'd been serving up to them, but in truth, they looked after him like he'd been their foster mother until a couple of them got him to the doctor at Boulia, an eighty-mile detour to the east of the stock route. He didn't drink, but they'd poured so much rum and brandy into him to ease the pain that afterwards, he couldn't remember how he'd got there."

I laughed too, but it was tempered with the realisation that in those days the stock routes were lonely and dangerous places and even the slightest of accidents could result in a slow and painful death. As Horsie said, rum, brandy, painkillers and Holloway's pills were used to stave off the inevitable and provide a little relief to the victim, but everyone knew when their days were numbered.

Horsie went on. "The stock routes eventually became so well-used that the colonial authorities had to do something to make travelling over them more reliable as far as obtaining feed was concerned, but at the same time, they had to ensure that the pioneers who'd begun to settle in the districts the stock routes went through were able to feed their own livestock. A new law was passed that required the travelling stock to cover at least six miles a day to make sure the mobs didn't overgraze and clear all the roadside grass along that part of the stock route by a single mob passing through too slowly. The tracks began to be dedicated as roads between the 1860s and 1890s and then after Federation, from the early 1900s, the State Governments began to develop stock route watering points, each located the distance of a droving day apart."

"Ah, I see," I said, "so that's why Johnny mentioned we'll be overnighting at a Travelling Stock Reserve."

Horsie nodded. "A Travelling Stock Reserve is a fenced paddock set aside at regular distances to allow overnight watering and camping of stock. Queensland has thousands of them all over the state." He looked around. "Where's that bait-layer got to now? The mob will be at Stockyard Creek before we get there and the drovers will be clamouring for their dinner if he doesn't get moving soon."

The drove proceeded at an unhurried pace over the level road, the herd following the lead bullocks without any encouraging or persuading, feeding on the road verges as they went. The drovers sat low in their saddles, their whips at rest over their knees. It was a fine day, not too hot or too cold with a light breeze blowing from the east and the whole world seemed at peace as Horsie and I, with the contingent of spare horses, caught up to and passed the herd at noon. At about three o'clock in the afternoon we reached the campground at Stockyard Creek, along with Sam the Bullocky and his team and Wilful the bait-layer sitting happily amongst his pots, pans and camp ovens in the back of the dray. I looked about the site with great interest. A fenced paddock of about a hundred acres stretched in front of me and a snake-like row of straggly looking eucalypts running through it told me where the low banks of the creek were, but from fifty yards I could see no sign of water in its shallow rocky bed; there must have been some moisture around though because the surrounding area was covered with a verdant green pasture. A bore, equipped with a large windmill that turned lazily in the light breeze, clanging and knocking on worn bearings, provided a continuous stream of water from a standpipe to a row of troughs and on a slight rise stood a small square building with a corrugated iron roof.

"That's the long-drop dunny," Horsie told me. "It has to be the regulation thirty yards from the bore for obvious reasons. It's cleaned with kerosene every week so don't go in there for a quiet smoke and throw the lighted match into it. You might finish up blowing the door open and I don't fancy picking you up from the paddock with your belt around your ankles."

I laughed. "You know I don't smoke, Horsie."

"Yes, I knew that," Horsie beamed as he always did when his jokes were appreciated, but then his face became serious again. "It's worth remembering to always close the lid though, Bill, - and check for snakes and red-backed spiders before you sit down."

My face must have shown my alarm. "What will happen if I get bitten?" I said.

"You'll need to find someone to suck the venom from your butt," Horsie said without a smile. "You won't find anyone around here willing to do it, - me included - so you'll probably die."

I quickly changed the subject. "That windmill is fairly gushing water out of the standpipe, isn't it? There must be an underground creek around here, Horsie," I said.

I cringed as he gave me that look of scorn that I'd been the recipient of in the past and that clearly said *'Do you really have to state the obvious?'* and then he must have realised that I was serious. "It's not an underground creek; that water's coming from an aquifer, Bill," he said. We're standing on top of the Great Artesian Basin."

"Oh," I said. "Yes, of course we are; I'd forgotten all about that,"

He grinned knowingly. "You came up through Western New South Wales, didn't you?"

"Yes, I did," I nodded, wondering where the conversation was going.

"Through Bourke, you said?"

"Yes."

He grinned again. "You weren't aware that the Great Artesian Basin's been under your feet the whole way?"

I had to give in and admit my ignorance, and then Horsie relented in his contempt for my lack of bush know-how and went on to explain that the Basin covered about one-fifth of the Australian mainland and stretched east to the Blue Mountains, west to central Australia and north to the tip of Cape York. "Somebody did a count a couple of years ago," he said, "and found that about five thousand bores have been drilled into the aquifers at depths of up to 6500 feet, but the

116

average is closer to 1500 feet. This one is about 2000 feet as you'll see if you look at the brass plate on the windmill base."

The horses and cattle grazed peacefully in the fenced paddock in gathering darkness, and the men sat around the campfire, their work finished for the day. The sounds of laughter and light banter filled the air as the drovers, their bellies full from Wilful's generous helpings of boiled corned beef and fresh damper, washed down with a quart-pot of tea, amused themselves by recounting the latest collection of yarns and poems that were doing the rounds of the mustering camps. A few smoked, rolling the tobacco between the palms of their hands and then lighting the end with a stick drawn from the edge of the blaze. Some produced bottles of rum from their swags on the wagon and poured generous tots into mugs held out to them by their companions, and the sharing was done willingly because everyone understood that it would be someone else's *'shout'* either later *that* evening, the next, or the one after that. It was quite common, in fact, for a bit of competition to develop between the drinkers in cracking the first bottle of the first evening of the drove because nobody would deliberately miss out on his 'shout' for fear of being branded a freeloader and be subsequently treated with some resentment. From that perspective, it was always a good idea for a man to get his round in early just in case the unthinkable happened and the drove ended before his bottle was emptied of its contents; that would be an embarrassment to the holder of the unshared brew and a blemish on his selfless nature that could easily follow him from one drove to the next.

When everyone was settled and the rum commenced to work its magic on the tongues of the younger and the memories of the older drovers I pricked my ears up as tales of long passed expert horsemen began to flow back and forth across the campfire. It was a subject I'd always loved, of course, since my time in Bendigo and I became even more absorbed when one of them, Bob Cox, who was in his fifties but was as wiry and supple as any man half his age, stated quite casually, "Believe it or not the best rider and horsebreaker I ever met was a *woman*."

A few of the younger drovers guffawed and scoffed at the absurd suggestion, but Horsie good-humouredly told them to listen up and they might learn something. "Go on Bob," he said. "You're talking about your old friend, Red Jack, I suppose."

One of the young men sounded confused. "Red Jack was a *woman*?"

"Sure was," Horsie said. "I think she was given the name as a kind of backhanded compliment, I suppose it was something like, *'you*

117

have to have a man's name if you want to compete against us so that it doesn't make us feel so inferior when we get beaten.' That's what I worked out anyway."

Bob nodded and stared into the fire as if it helped his brain to warm up and retrieve the information stored in its inner recesses, or maybe, - I thought later, - he was just composing himself to relate something that held some painful memories for him. "You're probably right, Horsie. Red Jack was born Hannah Glennon at Toowoomba in 1872," he said to nobody in particular. "I know that because her brother, Bill Glennon, had become a good mate of mine while we'd been on a couple of droves together in Western Queensland and he used to talk a lot about her. Bill was a tall, wiry man with a pointed reddish beard, intense grey eyes and an open, honest expression and *he* was well-known for his feats of horsemanship. He was so good that the drovers crowned him the unofficial king of the cutting-out camps. Bill told me he was one of eight children of Irish emigrants John and Catherine Glennon, who were land pioneers in the Toowoomba district and Hannah was their youngest child. It seems that their father had been a fairly successful bullock driver, but he went blind and couldn't work. He died when Hannah was only two years old and within a month their mother Catherine, who was a pathetic drunkard, had remarried a man named Daniel Ryan. She must have sobered up after she moved her children to his farm at Westbrook because they lived well and happy for a decade until their step-father died too. Hannah was twelve then and her older sisters had married and moved away. Bill said he'd left the home too and got into droving in the west, but he'd go back to the farm a couple of times a year and bring some unbroken horses which he and Hannah worked together and then sold at the Toowoomba horse sales. After Daniel Ryan died, their mother, who was fifty-two years old, spent little time grieving after him and married again. Her third husband was a labourer half her age named James Bell, but he was a violent man and Catherine herself was dead within a year."

I shuddered at the thought of the poor mother's fate because I knew something about the utter despair a woman must go through in a violent marriage with nowhere to turn for help. I thought about my poor mother and I could see in my mind her sad eyes pleading with me. *'Now don't ye' go telling anybody at school about this, Billy,'* she'd say. *'It will only make it worse for me if ye' do. Promise me ye' won't say anything to the teachers that will get yer dad arrested; promise me, Billy my love.'*

Bob had taken a short break to sip on his tea. The young drovers had gone silent, perhaps sensing, as I did, that the telling of this

118

particular tale meant something more than just an entertaining, thought-provoking campfire yarn to the teller. Bob's voice had a slight tremor to it as he went on. "The brother and sister combination continued to work the farm for a couple of years, but it became too much for them, - what with Bill being away out west so much, - so they sold it. Bill told me Hannah had become an expert rider and horsebreaker by the time she was fourteen, but like most young horsemen…" He paused and glanced up at the group seated around the campfire. "… I thought it was just another bush yarn, or maybe he was seeing her through the rose coloured glasses that only a devoted brother could see his little sister through. It couldn't be true; no woman or girl could ever ride better than a man. They were still riding side-saddle then in the novelty race events that were specially set up for them at country shows and race meetings."

"They rode side-saddle?" somebody said.

Bob's eyes turned on the speaker and it was clear to me that he thought the young man was a bit thick, but he kept his feelings to himself and maintained his calm expression. "Oh yes, that's how most of the ladies rode horses before the turn of the century, even on long-distance rides - something to do with preserving their modesty, but it was a pretty dangerous way to travel. There were some terrible accidents when women were caught by their skirts and dragged along by their horses when they fell." Bob turned his attention back to the campfire. "I realised Hannah was different as soon as I met her. I'd travelled to Toowoomba with Bill on one of his home jaunts and we found when we arrived that Hannah had gone to the nearby town of Pittsworth to ride in the buckjumping competition at the showgrounds. She didn't know we were there watching from the stands and despite the handicap of riding side-saddle, she won the junior trophy against the boys. I was convinced; Bill hadn't been exaggerating. She was only fifteen then, a trim little girl with a mass of beautiful auburn hair that tumbled from beneath a battered wide-brimmed drover's hat. Bill and I went back out west again and she continued to break in horses while she waited for him to return home, but he never did. She got word that a horse on a Western Queensland cattle run had finally got the better of her brother and Bill Glennon had taken his last ride."

I shivered, although it was a warm night. There always seemed to be death and despair attached to the stories told around the campfires, but perhaps that wasn't so unusual because it was a big part of the western way of life. You'd meet people and become friends and then you'd hear that they hadn't made it back from a drove. The Australian bush can be unforgiving.

"Hannah was grief-stricken," Bob said. "She became a wanderer; just rode off with three packhorses to carry her belongings and six spare saddle horses. All the modesty in the world meant nothing to Hannah after that and she rode astride her horses as confidently as any man did long before it became socially acceptable for women to ride that way. That's when the legend of Red Jack was born. The stories of her exploits were told around the campfires for years after. I heard that she broke in a mob of horses at Wallumbilla; horse-tailed for a drover who was shifting a mob from Charleville to the coast and worked in a ring-barkers camp on the far western Maranoa. It was a couple of years later I met her again at Adavale. She was dressed for work, and a fine figure she cut too in her breeches, boots and spurs. She was still only five foot six inches tall..." He tossed his head my way. "...a little taller than Bill over there maybe, but about the same build."

A few of the young drovers laughed and heckled me. "Hey Bill, how about a date, Girlie?" and, "Give us a kiss, Billy boy," but Johnny Hooper intervened.

"C'mon lads," he said. "Don't get personal. We need to respect each other at the night camp on a drove or we won't work well together when we need to tomorrow."

The laughter died away and Bob looked at me contritely. "Sorry Bill," he said. "I meant no offence."

I waved the apology away and grinned. "No offence was taken, Bob," I said, but the jubilant references to my lack of masculinity by the young men remained in my mind and troubled me. It seemed that no matter how hard I tried to be one of them I was always destined to be the one seen to be different, but then so was Red Jack, - different, I mean, - and she was admired for it.

"I saw Hannah get on a big, black, strong-willed stallion called Mephistopheles that some said had been sent to the ring from the Lockyer Valley just to try her out," Bob said. "It had already thrown Big Peter Rouse, the best of the Logan boys and some of the best riders from the Lockyer Valley. She blindfolded and saddled him in the ring yard, took a lug hold and landed on his back like a fly, slipping the blindfold off at the same time. The gate of the crush was thrown open and the horse gave seven or eight violent bucks and galloped across the ring. It wheeled at the fence and bucked again, but Hannah sat there as unconcerned as one of those swell chaps driving on a quiet Melbourne street in his two-horse carriage."

I remembered the advice Johnny Forrest had given me at Bendigo. *'When your horse bucks lean slightly forward; grip with your knees and let your upper body sway loosely. Watch his head straight down between the ears. If you can stay on after the first few bucks most of them will give up. There's always the odd one who won't, of course.'* The way Bob told it this Mephistopheles was one that didn't give up too easily, but I could picture Hannah swaying loosely with its every move until it tired itself out and in my mind's eye it was me up there, impressing the other riders with my calm and easy seat.

Bob's voice drew me out of my reverie. "I was a pretty good horsebreaker myself by then and we began to get to know each other again, but I remember the hurt I still saw in her eyes at the mention of her brother, Bill. I was a bit disappointed though when I found she'd married a station cook called Thomas Doyle. She was only seventeen."

'A bit disappointed?' I could feel Bob's embarrassment as he recounted his feelings towards Hannah. It was typical of the bushman to downplay his emotions and I wondered how many other old drovers had a similar story to tell, for it reminded me again of the ditties sung and poems recited at the Barringun Hotel and other places, but they were almost always told about other people; for Bob, this was too personal. I cringed as one of the young drovers said indifferently, "Oh well, old man, you never know with some women, do you? Maybe you were the lucky one after all's said and done."

Bob didn't seem to show any annoyance or irritation with the remark and continued his story. "The Glennon hoodoo must have followed Hannah though, because a short time after her marriage, she became pregnant and gave birth to a daughter she named Daisy, but the child died after four days. Within months she was pregnant again and this time her husband suspected the child wasn't his; he became abusive and repeatedly threatened to *'do himself in'*. Hannah got tired of him, took off, and was staying in Adavale when Thomas found her and tried to persuade her to return to him. She refused and he made good on his suicidal threats and shot himself in the stomach."

There were some oh's and ah's amongst the young drovers, who'd got caught up in the story, and I knew that this was one that would do the rounds for many a year to come, maybe being changed a little with each retelling, but this wasn't a retelling, - this was an original, - from one of the witnesses to the events that took place.

"It took him a long time to die from his wounds," Bob said, "but as Hannah knelt by his bedside he used the time he had left to lay the blame completely on her, telling her it was all her fault. The second child, Mary, was born six months after her father's suicide, but Mary died too. I never saw Hannah again after that, although I heard plenty of stories about her. She'd taken to wandering out in the far west again; Red Jack was seen a few times out in the Gulf Country, at Cloncurry, up at Croydon and riding the big black stallion called Mephistopheles into Hughenden, but she generally avoided any close contact with people unless she needed to for one reason or another."

"Is she still alive?" someone said in a hushed voice.

Bob shook his head. "She was mustering cattle near Chillagoe, west of Mareeba on the Atherton Tablelands twenty years ago, probably to earn some money to continue her roving life, when her horse put its leg in a hole and fell on her. She was only a month off her thirtieth birthday when she was buried in the Mareeba cemetery."

I excused myself from the assembly and bid goodnight to Johnny Hooper and Horsie who sat together on a wooden bench a little way off from the proceedings. I felt sad for Hannah, or Red Jack, the woman who rode as good as, or better than the men, but when I rolled out my gutta-percha ground-sheet and bedding on the far side of the parked wagon and lay in my swag looking up at the star-studded sky I thought, *'she had a hard life, but she was loved by Bob at least, and she died doing what she loved; I suppose that's a blessing and isn't that how it's meant to be? I hope I'm more fortunate than Red Jack though and get to live my life the way I want to and then die in peace and contentment even if I never get to be loved by anyone.'* My mixed emotions gradually changed to a kind of euphoria then for I realised that I'd been lucky enough to be doing what *I* loved too despite my small and effeminate frame being a source of mirth amongst some of the drovers. I could take that, - and more, - and it didn't matter how short or how long my life was or how unloved and scorned I was by other people so long as I could have a good horse under me and the winds of the plains on my face. Like Red Jack, if matters got too hard to face head-on I'd just saddle up Tom Thumb, get myself a couple of good packhorses and go, - somewhere, - because I knew that I'd gained enough experience now to survive any undesirable situation that came my way. I didn't know at the time how accurate that would turn out to be, but it was all in the future and I wanted to live for the moment. As it was, I felt I'd never enjoyed anything so much in my life as I had that day and I was determined to continue to enjoy my good luck until some shift in my fortune chanced along to change my perfect contentment and happiness. Finally, the hours spent in the saddle led to a pleasant weariness of mind and body and I drifted off, sinking into a well-earned unbroken slumber which only ended when Wilful woke me an hour before dawn with his usual "bleakfast alleady, Bill."

* * * *

122

The days passed quickly and all too soon the drove had ended and the cattle were yarded at the railhead at Quilpie ready to be loaded on to the train for transport to the east coast. The drove had gone particularly smoothly, there had been no loss of stock along the way and the drovers filled the bar of the Railway Hotel to celebrate their success as tradition demanded. Horsie, Johnny Hooper and I sat to one side of the carousing men.

"The men will be paid off tomorrow after the cattle are loaded on the train, Horsie," Johnny said. "There's a passenger carriage behind the locomotive tender as usual and I'm going to take the opportunity to do some business down in Cunnamulla for a few days. I'll be back on next week's train."

"Sure thing Johnny," Horsie said. "You want the horses paddocked at the Showgrounds yard I suppose."

Hooper nodded. "I've already arranged for you and Wilful to bunk down at the Jockeys' change rooms." He turned to me. "What about you, young Bill?" he said. "I've been very impressed with your work and I'll be sorry to see the last of you, but we've got no more work for you for a while, more's the pity."

I shrugged. "I appreciate everything you and Horsie have taught me and the opportunity you've given me, Johnny," I said. "I'm ready to call myself an experienced drover now so I'll see if I can find the elusive Mr William Naughton and ask him for a job as his brother in Victoria suggested."

Hooper nodded. "Yes, I've heard Naughton's moving stock from the Gulf Country down to the railhead at Marree for the lucrative South Australian market at Kapunda so you're bound to fall in with him…"

"…But before I do that," I said. "I'd very much like to visit a lady friend who lives not too far out from Cunnamulla. If Horsie can put Tom Thumb in the paddock with the other horses I might keep you company on the train."

"A *lady* friend?" Horsie said with a huge smirk on his face. "Well now, do tell, young Bill, - and who would have thought a bonzer little bloke like you would have a woman tucked away in a town the likes of Cunnamulla?"

I realised that my face must have gone a shade of pink for Hooper came to my rescue, scolding his horse drover lightly. "Leave the lad be, Horsie," he said with a sly smile. "You're embarrassing him." He turned to me again and frowned. "Of course I'd like your company on the train, Bill, - but you said your friend lived *not too far* from Cunnamulla. There isn't anyone living near Cunnamulla as far as

I know, - apart from the womenfolk on the big stations, - and they're all married, or far too young for you," he said.

Horsie sniggered. "Maybe the squatter's away and young Bill's been ploughing his paddock for him, - if you know what I mean."

I was sorry I'd mentioned that I had a *lady* friend; perhaps I'd done it as an unconscious means of strengthening my impression of manliness to these hard and seasoned stockmen that I wanted so much to be the measure of, and it had certainly worked with Horsie who was relishing the opportunity to give vent to his mischievousness at my expense, as men of the bush do, but I knew I'd been caught out by Hooper who was shrewd enough to realise there was something more to my remark than a hint of a mere romantic liaison.

I decided to come clean. "It's not the way it sounds," I said, looking from one to the other. "She's an old lady who lives on the banks of the Warrego. Maybe you've heard of her, - she said she's well-known along the river."

Johnny frowned again. "You're not talking about the Warrego Bunyip, are you, Bill?" he said.

"Ah, so you have heard of her." I was relieved that I didn't have to go into detail about the sequence of events surrounding my meeting with Charlotte with the possibility that at the end of it I'd be accused of telling a bush yarn.

"She's a real person? You've met her?" Hooper said, his face alight with curiosity.

I was surprised by his unexpected interest. "Yes, she's real; her name's Charlotte," I said.

Hooper's face had gone a shade of grey and he slumped forward in his chair with his elbows on the table in front of him. Both Horsie and I stared at him in shocked silence until he suddenly raised his head and spoke, his voice hoarse. "Will you take me to meet her, Bill?" he said, his eyes brimful of tears.

"Yes, Johnny. I only hope she's still there." I couldn't hide my sense of incredulity at the turn of the conversation and I stared at the ashen face of the man opposite me with alarm rising in my chest.

Hooper smiled, but the pain in his eyes was obvious. "I'll explain along the way," he said.

5 End of the Bunyip

The wallaby track that led down to the waterhole on the Warrego River was just as I remembered it from my first visit and I jumped down from the two-horse chaise that Johnny Hooper had borrowed in Cunnamulla. Johnny tied the reins to a tree branch and followed me as I headed along it at a brisk pace. "She'll know we're coming by the time we get to the river bank," I said, but a sudden alarming thought crossed my mind. "There hasn't been a flood in the river in the last four or five months has there?"

"Not as far as I know," Johnny said. "It's only October now and the wet doesn't usually kick in before November. Why do you ask? I'm sure Charlotte would have the sense to go to higher ground if the river has flooded, - after all, she's been through floods before..." His voice trailed off and he sighed and shook his head.

I didn't answer right away, my mind on that final conversation I'd had with Charlotte.

'It's not if the Warrego floods again Nanny-Billy; it's when, - and I will wait for it to take me home to join my parents downriver. My future is certain; it is up to the Warrego alone to decide when it will happen and how far downstream it will take me.'

A feeling of dread almost engulfed me. *'What if she's not here? What if she's wandered away to some other part of the river, - or got sick and went into Cunnamulla? Worse still, had there been an out of season flood that Johnny hadn't heard of?'* I hurried along, with Hooper trying to keep up, and when we came out on to the river bank I turned my gaze downstream, searching the near-side bank.

"What are you looking for?" Hooper said, coming up beside me.

"Smoke from her campfire," I said. I continued to peer amongst the trees and my heart skipped a beat when I saw it, a thin blue wisp curling up through the dark green canopy. "Look there, Johnny; she's here," I said, my voice hoarse with relief and excitement.

Hooper followed me along the sand until we reached the opening to the small clearing and I stopped at the edge, unsure of how to make my presence felt without frightening her, for I remembered Charlotte's shock at my sudden appearance the last time I'd visited her and I didn't want her to drop her damper on the ground again.

A thin voice from the depths of the grove startled both of us. "Hello Nanny-Billy; ah, you've come back to visit me." There was a pause and then the voice continued in a hesitant tone. "It is you, Nanny-Billy, - isn't it?"

"Yes it's me, Charlotte," I said as I plunged into the foliage.

Her tone was uncertain. "You haven't come alone."

Johnny Hooper had followed close behind me and he gasped audibly. *"Charlotte?"*

Charlotte had been seated on the fallen log and she got up with some difficulty. "Who's that Nanny-Billy?" she said. "I recognise that voice, - from a very long time ago."

I grinned at Hooper in satisfaction, although I knew Charlotte wouldn't have been able to see it, even in a good light. "A long time ago?" I said. "Do you mean it's an *antediluvian* voice, Charlotte?"

"It *was* before the Flood, Bill." Charlotte laughed. "Yes, it is; it's someone I knew before the flood."

Hooper looked at me and then at Charlotte and I realised that tough man as he was, there were tears welling in his eyes again just like in Quilpie, but this time I knew why. It was a poignant moment and one I've never forgotten. "It's Johnny Hooper, Charlotte," he said. "I've missed you my love; oh, how I've missed you. I didn't know where you went after the big flood of '86. I came back from a drove and you were *gone*. They said you'd left town after your parents were swept away, but nobody knew where you went." He stumbled towards her, took her hand gently in his and she held it up to her cheek. "Johnny, you were, and still are, my one true love. I had so much heartache at that time, though, that I couldn't have promised you my abiding love and affection," she sighed. "And I hoped that you would find someone who would give you the joy and happiness you deserved. I've missed you too, Johnny."

"I fell into the depth of despair when you disappeared out of my life, Charlotte," Hooper said. "I was so devastated I took to the drink and almost ended my life quite a few times, but each time I picked myself up because I knew in my heart I'd find you again. It's been nearly three decades, but there's been no other woman in my life since you left and there never will be in the time I have left in this world. I'd like you to come back with me to the cattle station I manage out in the Channel Country."

'The Warrego Bunyip is no more', I thought as I discreetly turned away from the older couple who were so engrossed in each other's company that I may as well not have been there anyway. I looked out over the sandy bed towards the gentle stream nestled against the far bank. It was so placid and peaceful at that moment that anyone who didn't know its history would never have believed it could transform itself into such a ferocious and destructive torrent that it could sweep away everything that stood in its path. I smiled to myself. *'You won't get the Warrego Bunyip now old man river.'* I thought, and my feeling

of elation was complete when I heard the words I'd been hoping to hear.

"Yes, Johnny," Charlotte said. "I think my dear parents would approve, and my time on this river as the Warrego Bunyip has come to an end."

* * * *

"We really would like you to stay, Bill," Johnny Hooper said. "I can find some work for you around the yard, and Charlotte could do with the company of someone like..." He stopped short and looked back affectionately towards the veranda where Charlotte sat in a big rocking chair, rocking gently as she sang. "I never stopped loving her in all those years, Bill, - and thanks to you we've got a second chance to be happy. I'll leave the droving to the younger lads now and just stick to managing the station and looking after her. I won't let her out of my sight again."

I tightened Tom Thumb's girth strap and adjusted the stirrups before answering. "It's good of you to offer me a job, Johnny," I said, "but I know you must feel obliged to find something for me to do around here considering our mutual love of Charlotte, - and I don't want you to feel that way; I'm just so happy to see that she's here out of harm's way. I do appreciate your offer though, but it's not necessary and I need to feel that I'm useful and earn my keep with a hard day's work. I'm sure you and Charlotte will be very happy together from now on and I'd only become a burden to you in the end."

"She told me why she calls you Nanny-Billy..." Hooper looked away for a moment, seemingly embarrassed that Charlotte had discussed my private life and perhaps betrayed a confidence, but when he turned to face me again I couldn't help but smile at him.

"You know all about my past then, but you still want me around, Johnny?" I said, my eyes beginning to glisten with tears.

"Of course I do; - we *both* do," Hooper said without flinching. "You're a remarkable person, Bill, and from what Charlotte has told me about your past life, you're one of the best examples of a person who has risen above the odds to ever ride with me..."

I pretended to adjust the swag on Tom Thumb's back, but it was only to hide the tears that were now streaming down my face. "...I *have* to go, Johnny," I said. "Say goodbye to Horsie for me when he returns from his rounds of the boundary rider huts. I'll miss our conversations over a cuppa at the Sixteen Mile Hut."

"Yes, I'll pass on your regards, Bill," Hooper said. He smiled reflectively as if a thought had just entered his head. "And *now* I understand why the Sixteen Mile made you feel so relaxed." He looked back at Charlotte still happily singing on her rocking chair. "Come on, Bill; you can't leave us without saying goodbye to the famous Warrego Bunyip, though; - she'd never forgive me."

I turned Tom Thumb's head north-west on the rough track that would take me to the Thomson River stock crossing at Stonehenge. From there the track joined up with the stock route that led to Naughton's Devon Downs Station a hundred miles further west on the east bank of the Diamentina, but a hundred yards along the track I wheeled him around to have one final look at Jedburra Station. Johnny Hooper stood on the veranda with one arm around Charlotte and the other raised in a wave. I sighed, waved back, and then turned Tom's head once more. "Come on Tom," I said, my voice breaking. "It's just you and I again, - just the two of us. *You* understand why I *have* to leave, don't you? I want to be independent and I don't want to be a burden on anyone." Tom's ears twitched and he whinnied softly as if he understood every word and I patted his neck. "Yes, of course you do, probably better than Nanny-Billy does, but don't worry; it'll be alright when we get to Devon Downs. Nobody knows us there and if Edward Naughton was true to his word we should have no trouble getting on a drove and earning our keep. Come on now; I'll sing you a song or two to pass the time."

> *'Patrick McGinty an Irishman of note,*
> *He fell into a fortune and he bought himself a goat.*
> *Goat's milk says Patrick I'm going to have me fill,*
> *But when he got the Nanny home he found it was a Bill.'*

6 The Drove

When I arrived at Devon Downs Station I described my past involvement with William Naughton's brother, Edward, to the head stockman and he took me to a small nondescript hut at the rear of the main homestead that was some kind of a saddlery storeroom, for it smelt of old leather, and various spare saddles, bridles and stirrup irons hung on pegs on the front veranda wall. I wondered if the man had misunderstood me. *'Maybe he thinks I'm a sundowner, dropping Naughton's brother's name to cadge a free feed,'* I thought, but I was ushered into the dark interior and there at an old rickety desk that was covered in paperwork sat the great man himself, for it turned out that William Naughton was as unpretentious and unaffected by his wealth and importance as his brother had been and not given to any airs and graces. He was dressed in the usual stockman's outfit of Crimean shirt and Moleskin trousers and an old felt hat lay where he'd tossed it on the edge of the desk. When he rose and came from behind the desk to greet me, I saw he was wearing neither boots nor socks, but a pair of Cossack boots I'd noticed by the door as I entered the hut were no doubt his too.

"So Eddie gave you a letter of reference lad?" he said, grasping my hand in his own big, rough mitt.

I passed the letter across the table, but he merely glanced at the Naughton stamp on the envelope. "You must be an exceptional worker then because Eddie doesn't give out recommendations to anybody that asks for one. Tell me about what you've been doing since you left Eddie's employment."

* * * *

Devon Downs Station was established on two thousand square miles of dunes, claypans, sandstone cliffs, gibber plains and the numerous river channels of the Diamantina River which passed through it on its way south-west towards Sturt's Stony Desert. The open rolling downs had a frontage of forty-two miles on the Diamantina River itself and had near-permanent, naturally deep waterholes fed by seasonal rains and the Great Artesian Basin so that the extensive grasslands were able to support as many as twenty thousand head of cattle in normal drought-free years. The great centenary drought of 1897 through to 1903 had decimated the stations stock and in another lesser drought between 1914 and 1916, about ten thousand cattle had perished. Suffering financially, the owner, Sydney Kidman, sold the property in 1918 to William Naughton.

Naughton, as usual, seemed blessed by the rain Gods and had restocked Devon Downs with bullocks brought overland from two of his other stations, Savana Downs on the Flinders River in North Western Queensland, and Hollovale Station over the border in the Northern Territory and those additions had increased the livestock numbers on Devon Downs to near capacity. Those herds were fattening nicely on Devon Downs lush Mitchell grasses and were destined for the east coast through the railhead at Quilpie where we'd taken the Abingdon Downs herd. Hollovale was overstocked with fat bullocks too and Naughton knew that the summer rains had renewed the usually arid country of the Southern Trail into a sea of Mitchell and Flinders grasses that swept to the horizon in all directions. It was May, coming into winter and the best time to travel, and he couldn't afford to wait any longer for fear of losing out on the lucrative southern market to his rivals. He'd decided to move a thousand head directly from Hollovale to the South Australian markets through the railhead at Marree in the north of that State. I didn't know any of that until much later, of course, but by the time I'd finished my interview, I knew I'd impressed Mister Naughton, for he offered me a job on the spot.

It was to be a mammoth drove, just like the old times in the 1870s and 80's that I'd heard so much about around the night camps when famous overlanders like Nathaniel Buchanan took vast herds of cattle down the Murranji Track, which became notorious amongst those who came after him as the Ghost Road of the Drovers because of the number of losses due to lack of water, - not just of cattle but of men too. The Murranji Waterhole had been the most vital source of water on the track and if it was dry the cattle and horses faced a thirsty run of over a hundred miles before reaching the next watering point. In one terrible drove I'd been told about, one man died, all but two stockmen deserted the drover and hundreds of cattle and horses died. Things had improved, of course, with wells sunk and windmills and water troughs installed at regular single day travel intervals and the Murranji track was no longer considered a death march, which was comforting to know because we'd be taking that route for part of *our* drove.

* * * *

We started on the southern trail from Hollovale in late May. The conditions were near perfect; clear blue skies, a light breeze fanning our faces and the purified air of the Barkly Tablelands filling our lungs. I was enthralled by the peace and tranquillity of those vast plains. The herd had spread out, grazing calmly in a mile-wide front as it moved slowly towards the Buchanan River, and here and there plain turkeys and emu strutted across in front of the mob, apparently annoyed at the unexpected disturbance to their idyllic existence. The cattle and horses were given a day's rest at the Buchanan and then, after we'd filled up the back of the wagon with logs and branches we headed across the Rankine Plain. I soon found out why we'd stocked up on kindling, for the plain was forty miles of treeless and woodless country with nothing higher than straggly blue bush clinging to life in the dry swamp beds. After we struck the Rankine River we followed that downstream to the permanent waterhole called the Long Hole where we came across hundreds of brumbies grazing. Our station horses became quite wayward and flighty at the sight and smell of them and we had to hobble them and put a guard on them at night otherwise we would have lost a few. The Rankine disappears underground in the limestone formation south of the Long Hole and so we cut across country for a few miles to meet up with it again near its junction with the Georgina River. We followed the Georgina then, crossing the border into Queensland and moving the mob through Headingly and Carrandotta down through Bedourie to Glengyle. The Georgina finally loses itself in the sandy wastes of the Simpson Desert and so we passed on to the Diamentina, following the Murranji track down through Carcoary to Birdsville in south-west Queensland.

After the Murranji we were to travel either the Birdsville Track from Birdsville to the railhead at Marree in South Australia or the alternative Strzelecki Track further east to Lyndhurst just north of the Flinders Ranges. The Birdsville Track skirts the Simpson Desert and the Sturt Stony Desert and in the old days before the artesian bores were sunk could only be used in good seasons when rain filled the few waterholes along its length. During the centenary drought, there were some big stock losses on this route. In one case a drover, from Warenda Station in Queensland started with five hundred fat bullocks, but only had seventy left by the time he reached Marree. If the word was received from the south that conditions were not ideal on the Birdsville a decision would be made to take the Strzelecki instead. That used to be one of the driest and loneliest tracks to transport mobs of cattle to the Adelaide market but it wasn't used much by the 1920s which made it a good alternative if the Birdsville was grazed out by too many herds passing through. It was the track pioneered by Captain Starlight, whose real name was Harry Redford, to drove a thousand head of stolen cattle from Queensland, down the Barcoo and Cooper past Mount Hopeless, to the outskirts of Adelaide where he sold them. He was caught and sent to trial but was found not guilty by a jury fascinated with his great feat of blazing a new cattle stock route through the most difficult country in Australia.

If we maintained the six miles a day rule for travelling stock we would reach the railhead at Marree in about five months I learned, - not long in comparison with the famous drove of the Durack brothers, Patrick and Michael, who trekked across the north of Australia from Cooper Creek in Queensland to the Kimberley region of Western Australia with seven thousand head of breeding cattle and two hundred horses. That drove covered three thousand miles and took nearly three years and there were no artesian bores then. I grimaced as I thought back to my conversation with Horsie O'Donnell, recalling my lack of awareness of that vitally important underground water that lay beneath the surface of the most arid parts of Australia and had made these stock routes *almost* bearable to drove, - according to some of the old hands.

I wasn't too concerned with the horror stories that had been circulating amongst the old drovers for all those years past. The fresh-faced, young stockman I'd been a year ago was gone. I was stronger, much more confident and ready to take on *almost* any possible dangers and difficulties that these stock routes might present. The only obstacle to my thorough enjoyment of the droving experience, I realised, was the constant need to keep my personal situation secret and that meant perpetual diligence. To be otherwise would have put me in an awkward and embarrassing situation, but with closed in long-drop dunnies, water troughs and even washing facilities at many of the rest stops, the likelihood of any accidental exposure was insignificant.

It was a good time to be alive I can tell you, Sister Mary. The drove was completed with hardly any losses, but like all good things, it had to come to an end. Some of the drovers headed back to Devon Downs or went east to catch up with long-suffering wives and children, and others with no familial bonds went on to spend their wages in Adelaide's bars and taverns. Another drought had hit the country by November of that year, not as bad, the old hands said, as the Federation Drought had been, but enough for Mister Naughton to sell up some of his stations and destock others. Tom and I helped move some of the herds to railheads at Moree, Quilpie and even to Rockhampton in central Queensland, but once that was done I knew it was time for me to move on again. In any case, I'd received a letter that threatened to turn my world upside down.

7 A Reunion

14 May 1925
29 D------ Street, South Melbourne.
Dear Bill,

It was so good to receive your letter last month and be able to read it to my dear Luigi whom I fear will not be with me much longer. My poor husband's eyesight is failing and he finds it difficult to even get out of bed nowadays. We have both always had a great affection for you, as I'm sure you are well aware and we talk about you and wonder what you are doing and where your travels have taken you. It was great to hear that you have been finding work in New South Wales and Queensland in these difficult times for I can tell you that things are not going so well in Victoria.

Armand came back from the war very much changed in his temperament. He is not the same person he was before he went away and I worry about him constantly. He spent a lot of time brooding alone in his room at the beginning and we'd often hear him calling out in the middle of the night. He missed you terribly too and couldn't understand why you'd gone away, but I tried to explain the situation as best I could without actually telling him the reason for your departure from our home as I felt that you would not have wanted that information to come to him from anyone but yourself. When he got a little better he tried hard to find work, but it was impossible to get a job in Melbourne; there were so many able-bodied men out of work and the Spanish Influenza closed down many businesses. He read in a newspaper that there was plenty of work for strong, young Italian men cutting cane in the canefields of Queensland (It seems that Italians are better prepared to work in the hot sun than those of British stock), and he is now living and working in North Queensland at a place called Pin Gin Hill near the town of Innisfail. I am not sure where that is or how close you are to it because my knowledge of our vast northern state is limited. (I still find it hard to negotiate the streets of South Melbourne although we've been here for forty years or so.) I only know he is hired by cane farmers to cut cane for them in the harvesting season and he works on ploughing a forty-acre plot of land with his cousin who has come out to Australia from Italy. They are hoping to develop it into their own sugar cane farm. Italy is in a worse position than Australia for work and much of the younger population has been emigrating, mainly to the United States of America, but I've heard that the USA has closed its borders and won't allow any more people into the country for the foreseeable future. Australia seems to be going the same way, as I shall explain shortly.

Armand is almost thirty now and still hasn't found a wife so I worry that I will never have a grandchild to love and call me 'Nona', and my doubts have only worsened since I read the recent headline of a Melbourne daily newspaper to the announcement of an inquiry into Italian immigration ordered by the Queensland government. 'Invasion of the Olive Skins,' it read, and at a congress of Australian women, housewives were told not to buy fruit from Italian shops even if their prices were cheaper. They said that after having done so much to defend 'white' Australia from the menace of Asiatics we now have 'olive' migrants establishing themselves in great numbers in the country. We are such a degraded and low-class race apparently, that Australian women are encouraged not to marry our boys even if they too fought on the front lines to keep Australia free. Why is the world so cruel, Bill? Olive, white or black, I know you will agree that we are all the same under our skins.

I must tell you about my friend, Mavis...

The remainder of the letter was full of gossip about the comings and goings of people whose names I only vaguely remembered, but they were people who were important to Mama Rosa, and I yearned to sit at the small dining table in the neat little home in South Melbourne once more just to hear her happy prattling on about them in her thick Italian accent, for my time with the Pavetto's had been the most cherished episode of my young life. It was signed,

With much love,

Mama Rosa Pavetto.

I folded the letter and put it with the other important papers into the satchel that would be rolled in my swag for safekeeping, for it was almost two hundred miles to Innisfail.

'Armand came back from the war changed in his temperament. He is not the same person he was before he went away and I worry about him constantly.'

Armand had been like a big brother to me until – oh well, - it was best not to dwell on those memories too much. All I could think of was that my experience with Jimmy Miller had taught me that some returned soldiers were doing it tough, - suffering alone, - even in the midst of family and friends, holding their cards close to their chests and trying to struggle through as best they could. It had been much worse for Jimmy out there on his own, of course, but I'd decided I needed to see Armand and tell him how much I loved and missed him before it

134

was too late, particularly if my absence from our South Melbourne home had any bearing on the change in his disposition.

Pin Gin Hill wasn't hard to find. It was five miles west of Innisfail off Palmerston's track to the Atherton Tablelands and on the very edge of the cultivated farmland. I'd enquired at the Post Office and been told by the postmaster, *'Pavetto? Yes, I know him; go to the end of O'Brien's Road, where it starts to go up the hill; go past the last cane farm on the river flats. There are a couple of crazy Italians up there blowing up the rocky hillside with dynamite. Pavetto's one of them; they reckon they're going to put cane in next year. They'll probably blow themselves up, more likely; good riddance to them too. That'd be two less olive skins in the district to take over our land.'*

I thanked the man for the information and left the post office, feeling ill at ease with the sentiment he'd expressed during our brief conversation. *'So Mama Rosa was right after all,'* I thought as I rode Tom Thumb along Palmerston's track and turned into O'Brien's Road. *'Some people at least around here consider the Italians to be an inferior race to their own. I hope he was one of only a few.'*

The farm, if it could be classified as such, was bounded on the south and east by cane farms and the north by the North Johnstone River which flowed swiftly out of the dense tropical rainforest of the Southern Tablelands. To the west, the ground rose gradually towards the low summit of Pin Gin Hill and I noticed that part of the hill's vegetation was in the process of being cleared. Large trees had been cut down and left in orderly stacks on the bare ground ready for salvage while the smaller saplings had been tossed into loose piles for burning. An acre of land fronting on to O'Brien's Road had been left in its natural state, however, and a timber building had been constructed in the shade of several large trees with beautifully coloured new foliage of red and dark pink. I found out later they were Johnstone River rainforest trees called Lilly Pilli, but of course I didn't know that at the time. The building wasn't grand by anyone's standards but it looked neat enough from the street. It was set on eight-foot high timber stumps and had a wide staircase that led up to a covered veranda that was part of the main house under the shiny new corrugated, galvanised iron roof. Bright yellow painted weatherboard walls with white, timber-framed, sash windows and metal window hoods completed the picture of simple elegance.

I dismounted, tied Tom up under the shade of one of the trees and walked along a well-worn dirt path to the bottom of the staircase. It was late afternoon and the sky was darkening as thousands, possibly hundreds of thousands of what I took to be birds soared overhead. I found out later that they were in fact flying foxes on their way to roost in the mangroves at the mouth of the Johnstone River, as they did every afternoon.

"Hello, is anyone home?" I called out, but there was no answer. The area underneath the house was open to the light breeze that wafted up from the riverbank some three hundred yards away and I wandered around to the back of the building where a staircase led up to another wide veranda, similar to the one at the front of the house. I stood at the bottom and called out, but again there was no reply and I looked around, uncertain about what to do next, for it seemed that the place was deserted, - or if it *was* occupied the owner didn't want to open up to visitors calling unannounced. *'Perhaps, in hindsight, I should have written first,'* I thought, my apprehension mounting. *'Maybe I was rash to believe that Armand might want to see someone from his past, - particularly someone like me who, I'm quite sure, confused and puzzled him when we lived and worked together. Mama Rosa said he came back from the war changed in his temperament and isn't the same person he was before he went away. Perhaps I should leave now and let sleeping dogs lie. I can write to Mama Rosa and tell her I couldn't find him, which is not really a lie.'* My indecision was soon dismissed, however, and I swivelled around, surprised when a voice called out from beyond the undergrowth.

"Wait, who's there?" The voice was unmistakable.

"Armand?" I said. "Armand, it's Bill Smith."

Two burly men appeared from between the trees, both carrying axes over their broad shoulders. On seeing me one of them dropped his axe and rushed forward, whooping with delight. "Bill Smith, my little brother, - well, I never thought for a minute I'd ever see *you* again," Armand Pavetto said. He threw his arms around my shoulders and lifted me off the ground in a bear hug, swinging me easily around in a circle. "You're a lot heavier than I remember, Bill," he laughed as he dumped me down on my feet again.

I wobbled unsteadily for a moment and laughed with him, but my enjoyment of our reunion was more of relief than excitement. "It's been ten years, Armand," I said. "I was only fifteen then. I haven't grown much taller, but I was bound to grow out a bit. You've grown too, - quite a lot, I think."

Armand still gripped my shoulders; he held me at arm's length and gazed down at my small oval face, his big dark eyes serious and a deep frown creasing his forehead. "I always knew you would grow stronger just by reflecting on the work you and I used to do at the markets, Bill," he said. "I just didn't think you'd look as muscle toned as you do now. I was beginning to think before I left you were…" He stopped suddenly and laughed, releasing me from his grip as he turned to the other man who'd joined them. "Hey, Vittorio, this is my little brother, Bill."

Vittorio shook my hand and grinned. "*Benvenuto nella nostra casa.* Welcome, - our house into," he said in halting English.

"Very good, Vittorio," Armand clapped him on the back. He turned to me. "Vittorio's learning to speak English very quickly, Bill. You wouldn't have got a word of English out of him three months ago." He changed the subject again. "Hey come on into our *'casa'*. It's not much of a house yet, - not even as good as your old room at the back of mama and papa's place in South Melbourne, but we're working on it and you're welcome to stay as long as you want."

We stepped up on to the back veranda and entered the building through a door that swung easily on well-oiled hinges.

"We shifted it from down the road a bit, piece by piece," Armand said. "It had been flattened in a cyclone and it was given to us on the condition we took it all away. Luckily most of the walls were intact and the floor was still standing. This area gets hit by cyclones more than any other part of Queensland, you know."

"You've done well, Armand," I said. I was genuinely surprised at the work that had gone into refurbishing the outside of the house and I was even more surprised at the interior. A wide corridor ran through the centre of the house from the front to back, passing two bedrooms that led off it, their doors facing each other on either side. Behind that, the corridor opened up into a large dining-sitting room on one side with the door to the main bedroom opposite it and a small separate kitchen tucked away in an alcove at the back of the house.

Armand opened the door to the main bedroom. "I'm sorry about the way this has been decorated, Bill," he said, his face slightly reddening. "It was like that when we moved the body of the house and we thought we'd leave it in case Mama decided to visit us."

I wondered why Armand was being so apologetic, and I was unsure of what to expect, but I understood right away when I looked in, for it was a mainly feminine room, decorated in delicate pastels, with a flowery bedspread and pretty curtains on the window that could be drawn to provide privacy to the occupant from anyone passing along the back veranda. "It's quite nice, Armand," I said. "Mama Rosa should be happy…"

"…Mama won't be coming here now, Bill," he said. Papa's too sick and she won't leave his side. I'm sorry, but Vittorio and I have the

137

front two bedrooms. This one is yours if you're going to stay; I hope you don't mind."

"It'll be fine, Armand," I said in as casual a tone as I could muster, but secretly I was thinking, *'What a beautiful room; I couldn't imagine anything better after years camping in the harsh outback'*. The bathroom was no more than a built-in corner of the back veranda with the original chipped porcelain washstand and a bath that hadn't been used for many a day, but Armand explained that they usually had a shower with a hose attached to a tap on the galvanised iron rainwater tank behind the house. "It's been set up quite private, Bill," he said as he must have noticed my look of concern. "Nobody can see it from the street and you can't take a bath in the South Johnstone River, of course."

"Why not," I said. "I saw it as I was coming here from Innisfail and it looks very inviting."

"Yes it does," Armand said with a laconic smile. "It's a beautiful river, but only for looking at from the bank. It's so full of saltwater crocodiles there's hardly a dog left in the town."

We talked at length on many aspects of what had happened to each of us in the ten years we'd been separated and I began to feel a renewal of the affection that I'd had for him in the past and maybe even to doubt what Mama Rosa had said in her letter about him. I decided to meet those uncertainties head-on and I looked at him across the table. "Mama Rosa's worried about you, Armand," I said. "She thinks you're a different person to the boy who left her to go and fight in the Great War."

Armand shrugged. "Maybe mama's right, Bill; I certainly felt different for a long time when I got back to Melbourne. That cursed so-called Spanish influenza pandemic had closed everything down and the returning soldiers were being blamed for spreading it." He grimaced. "We probably did, but we didn't know we were carrying the extra baggage when we boarded the ships to come home. I'd never been to Spain, of course, and I believe, from what I've read that it originated elsewhere; it was only called 'Spanish Flu' because that's where it was first recognised as a pandemic." He paused and shook his head as the memories of his return to Australia came flooding back. "It was meant to be a triumphant return, with ticker-tape receptions and crowds cheering from the footpaths as we marched to receive the keys of the cities we came from, but it didn't quite work out that way. We were all tarred with the same brush, Bill, whether we'd been sick or not, and what's more, we olive-skinned people suffered more humiliation and abuse than anyone else. Many people couldn't, or didn't want to differentiate between Spanish and Italians; we were all the same to them, - disease carriers who had to be avoided."

My eyes grew moist. "And that was on top of what you'd been through in the war, Armand," I said, my voice full of emotion.

Armand nodded. "Sure it was, and I felt miserable when I found that *you'd* left our family to wander across the country on your own." He spread his hands wide. "Why, Bill? You seemed so happy with me and I had made big plans for both of us. I was looking forward so much to catching up with you again."

"I, - I had to go, Armand; I just had to…" I looked down at my shaking hands. "There are things you didn't know about me then Armand and I thought you might find out and be unhappy with me, - even hate me. I'll tell you about it… someday, but not now."

Armand smiled but the despondency remained in his brown eyes as he regarded me in silence for a moment. At last, he sighed and clasped his hands together as if he'd accepted that things would never be the same between us as they had been before the war. "I would never have been unhappy with you, Bill, - no matter what secret life you had before we met, and I could never hate you, but *you* mustn't worry for *me*," he said. "I'm alright now. I feel like I've got some purpose in life up here in the north where nobody gives a hoot where you come from or what you've done in your past life. We don't get too many people coming out here anyway and there's plenty of work to do that keeps us occupied and out of trouble. We're going to blow out more rocks and stumps so we can plough the cleared paddock to get it ready for next season's cane crop.

I recalled the conversation I'd had with the postmaster; '…*probably blow themselves up; good riddance to them too. That'd be two less in the district to take over our land.*'

"Maybe I will stick around for a while, Armand," I said. "Do you *have* to blow the stumps out? It sounds a bit dangerous to me."

"Vittorio's an expert in explosives, Bill," Armand said. "He learned all about it during the war in Italy; anyway we don't have much choice; all the best land is already taken and we have to put up with what's left, so we have to blow it."

"I can give you a hand, you know," I said. "I've used a stump-jump plough in Western New South Wales…"

"A *what*, - plough?" Armand stared at me in confusion.

"A stump-jump plough," I said, calmly enough, but inwardly feeling immensely satisfied with my superior knowledge, for it was indeed the first time *I'd* been able to teach Armand anything useful; it had always been the other way round in the past when we were teenagers. "It was invented in Australia for ploughing the ground in Western New South Wales and South Australia. Places where there were too many mulga roots and stones for the old, English light Rotherham ploughs that were used before them."

"Hey, you haven't been wasting your time either while I've been away, Bill." His face lit up and he grinned and turned to his cousin. "Did you hear that, Vittorio? Bill's going to give us a hand to get the paddock ready for planting."

Vittorio grinned too and nodded excitedly. "You help us plough the land; we look after you too, little brother..."

"...You'd still have to blow the large tree stumps out," I said, my enthusiasm for the project growing, "but the stump-jump disc cultivating plough, pulled by a couple of big draught horses, will be ideal for use on this sort of country."

"We'll be able to afford the plough after this next cane-cutting season is over, Bill," Armand said in a businesslike tone, "but instead of horses, we'll buy a tractor to pull it. We've been contracted to cut cane for some of the local cane farmers each season for the last couple of years; it's hard work, but it pays well and it gives us enough capital to buy what we need to continue our work on this place in the off-season."

"Can you get me a job too?" I said.

"Sure I can," Armand said. "They're always looking for extra labour, but as I said, it's *really* hard work, and you're... well..." His voice trailed off and a worried frown creased his forehead.

I'm sure my stare was penetrating as I faced him for what I felt would be his final admission of what he thought of our brotherly bond. "I'm what, Armand?" I said; "...too *girlish* for that sort of work?"

Armand's sunburnt face went a deeper shade of red. "No Bill," he said. "I was going to say, - you're too white and not olive-skinned. Most of the cutters *are* Italian, you see; it's not only hard work, it's hot and dirty too and even a lot of the big tough Irish labourers give it away and move back down south to a more temperate climate after a couple of weeks working in the tropical sun."

I was relieved, as I had been on many other occasions in the past. "Oh, is that all you're concerned about?" I said. "You needn't worry about my stamina in the heat, Armand. When I left Melbourne I got a job near Bendigo, but that was too cold for me so I travelled north to the Riverina of Western New South Wales and eventually to the shearing sheds in South West Queensland. After that I went droving in Western Queensland, and into Northern Territory. The heat out there is worse than anything I'd have to suffer in a cane paddock, I'll wager."

Armand shook his head in admiration. "How could I ever have doubted you, little brother? You've got more pluck than anyone twice your size."

* * * *

There were six men in each gang of cane cutters and it was expected that, with no rain delays, a gang could cut, top and load about fifteen tons of cane daily. A steam locomotive delivered a line of empty cane bins, a kind of railway wagon with steel mesh sides, to the nearest rail siding off the main line and the farmer then moved the bins into the paddock with a tractor using a portable line laid by the gang. Three men would work along the face of the furrows cutting the cane stalks at the base, lopping the tops off, and laying them down; a fourth man would stack them in neat bundles and the other two would then shoulder-load them on to the cane bins using a ladder as the pile of cane on the bin grew higher. When a bin was full a chain was thrown over the cane to show the farmer that the truck was fully loaded; the farmer or his overseer then tightened the chain, hooked up the bins and pulled them back to the main line from where the steam locomotive transported the cane to the mill for crushing.

When the gang had finished the harvesting at that farm and it was time to move on to the next, the portable line was picked up, loaded on an open wagon and taken to the main line for the locomotive to deliver to the next farm, where the portable line was again transported by tractor to the paddock, re-laid and the next farm's harvest got underway.

At the sugar mill the cane was crushed, the raw sugar was bagged in hessian sugar bags, each bag filled to the correct weight and dropped onto a conveyor belt, and finally, the bag was stitched closed. The bags were then manually loaded on to wagons and transported by rail to Mourilyan Harbour to be loaded onto ships for export.

It was hard and hot work as Armand had said it would be, but I was happy working alongside my old friend and Vittorio too, who turned out to be as willing a worker as Armand and me; so much so that each day's harvesting became a source of friendly rivalry between the three of us, and by the time the harvesting had finished for that season we were as comfortable in each other's company as it was possible to be.

* * * *

Armand unhitched the tractor and trudged up the back stairs to the house. He seemed a little despondent as he sat down at the kitchen table, took off his wide-brimmed hat and wiped his forehead with a sweat rag. I looked at him with a worried frown. "Had a bad day, Armand?" I said as I slid on to the chair opposite him.

"No Bill," he said, "…at least, not any worse than yesterday or the day before."

That comment made me feel even more worried "You look a little downcast." I persisted.

Armand shook his head and made an effort to smile, but it was short-lived. "I got a letter from Mama," he said, his voice strained.

My heart skipped a beat, remembering Mama Rosa's letter to him. *'I fear my Luigi will not be with me much longer…'* "Is Papa Luigi okay?" I said.

Armand nodded. "Papa's as well as can be expected and so is Mama, but she's been writing to her relatives in Italy about me and they've made some arrangements I didn't know about until now. She wants me to come back to Melbourne in two weeks to meet my second cousin who is arriving from Italy."

I grinned. "Why are you looking so glum then? You should bring him back here. He might be a good help."

"It's not a *he*, - it's a *she*," Armand said, "…her name is Regina and I know very well what Mama has in mind. She's sent me a picture of her." He reached into his shirt pocket, produced a photo and tossed it on to the table.

My mind was racing as I reached over and picked it up. "She looks very pretty, Armand," I said quietly. "What *has* Mama Rosa got in mind for you?" I *knew* what the answer would be before I'd asked the question, but I wanted to hear it from Armand's lips in case I'd misinterpreted his line of reasoning. "Is she coming to Australia for a holiday and then maybe going to live in Melbourne with Mama Rosa?"

Armand shook his head again and stared at me sadly. "I'm afraid not, Bill," he said. "Regina is *not* coming on holiday and she won't be staying in Melbourne…"

"…You mean she's coming to live *here* with you, - without the two of you even having met?" I was dumbfounded at the implication.

"It's been that way in Italy since feudal times," Armand said. He spread his hands wide, palms upwards in a gesture of resignation. "It was often done generations ago to unite families who might have been feuding over land and would otherwise have been enemies. The parents saw it as a way to keep the peace and the engagement was often arranged soon after the children were born."

142

"The engagement?" I said, my mind in a whirl.

Armand's tone became tinged with a note of cynicism. "Nowadays I believe it's just a way for the parents to ensure that on the man's side the family name will continue through another generation and on the woman's side that she doesn't spend her entire life single and maybe shut away in a convent somewhere. There's a shortage of young men in Italy right now, you see. They're all off to America or they've come here to Australia looking for work."

The irony in Armand's voice as he vented his frustration was lost on me, for my attention was still fixed on his previous revelation. *"The engagement?"* I repeated.

"Yes, Bill," Armand's voice had a distinctive tremor to it as he spoke the words that changed my mood of satisfaction and contentment in an instant. "Regina and I are engaged to be married and the wedding day has already been set because Papa is so frail and he wanted it to take place before he dies."

"Oh, I can readily understand that," I said, my mind in a whirl. "Papa Luigi would certainly want to be there for such a big event."

"He won't *be* there for the wedding, Bill, - and neither will I. It's being held in Italy," Armand said, his broad shoulders slumped forward.

I must have gaped at him, my mouth open. "You won't be at your *own* wedding…?"

Armand shook his head. "It's going to be a *'marriage by proxy'* ceremony. It's often done now, mostly because the groom can't afford to go back to Italy or doesn't want to leave his job. In my case, it's because of the urgency due to Papa's illness. The religious ceremony will take place in Regina's village church and she'll be accompanied to the altar by her father. Her brother is going to stand in for me."

I was dumbfounded. "Is that a legally binding marriage?" I managed to stammer.

"Unfortunately it is, Bill," Armand said. "Marriage-by-proxy was authorised by the Catholic Church in the sixteenth century, after the Council of Trento. The law was never repealed and today, it's written in the Italian Civil Code."

I shook my head in bewilderment, searching for something to say that might end this bad dream, for that's what I thought it was, and I hoped fervently that I would wake up and find that everything was as it had been before. "But isn't it still a bit rushed?" I mumbled. "Surely Papa Luigi would understand that you don't even know whether you'll *love* each other," I said, my hopes fading fast.

Armand looked at me oddly. "Love hasn't got anything to do with it, Bill. It's obligation and duty that comes first and foremost in the Italian culture and I want to be an honourable son to my papa and mama and make them happy. That means being a worthy suitor to Regina and the two of us accepting our time-honoured roles and producing little bambino's to carry on the tradition." He continued to stare at me as if he'd just opened a window into my heart and had at last begun to comprehend the ache that lay inside me.

"It's settled then," I said as I quickly looked down at my shaking hands and away from his gaze.

Armand and I sat in strained reserve for what seemed an eternity to me until he finally broke the silence. "Bill?" he said in a soft, low tone. I glanced up at him and his big brown eyes were sad. "I've got serious doubts about marrying someone I've never laid eyes on too," he said, "but I'm surprised *you* don't seem particularly happy about it either. Is there something you need to tell me?"

I shook my head, my eyes downcast again as tears began to form. "No, Armand," I said, my dreams for the future shattered, but still unwilling to tell him the truth. "There's nothing to say really except that, - I won't be here when you get back from Melbourne."

"I thought that might be the case," Armand said. "Mama said you wouldn't take the news too well, although she didn't elaborate…"

"…I've got a job lined up," I said quickly, and *that* at least wasn't a lie. "It's with the Great Northern Railway Company."

"You don't have to go away just because Regina will be here, Bill," Armand said. "We might take over your room but you could have mine instead. There's plenty of room for all of us and I'm sure you and Regina will get on…"

"…The company has been advertising in the Innisfail Advocate for navvies to work on the section of line between Innisfail and Cairns. It's the final section of the tramway to be brought up to main line standard in the whole length of railway from Brisbane to Cairns you know." I rambled on as if to shut out any further protests from Armand. "The sections already built to main line standard have a speed limit of forty miles an hour, and the regional tramways have gradually been brought up to this standard as the company has bought them from the local authorities and cane growers over the years…"

"…I know how you like your privacy, Bill," Armand said. "If that's what's bothering you we can build another room downstairs under the house, - with your own facilities, - just like you had at Papa's place in Melbourne."

I continued as if I hadn't heard Armand's offer, for I knew it wouldn't work, but there was no way I could let him know *why*. "…It'll be hard work on the railway, but I know I'll enjoy it, - chopping out earth and rocks to widen cuttings, breaking metal, laying sleepers and all that sort of thing. It's mostly piece work so I'll make good money and be able to save if I work hard, - maybe up to £35 a month…"

"Bill… Please stay here with us. We'll all be happy together and, - I *need* you…" Armand's face showed his distress. "I thought I'd never hear from you again and…"

His words struck deep into my heart. *'He needs me.'* I thought miserably. *'Oh, you don't know how that hurts, Armand.'* I turned away, unable to face him any longer. "…I can't, Armand," I managed to whisper. "I just can't stay here with you and, - Regina. Maybe one day you'll understand. Maybe one day…"

8 Herberton Hospital

Bill Smith was admitted to the Herberton Hospital in early June 1975. I'd had a few days off to visit family in Cairns and by the time I finally got to see him he'd been there almost a week. He'd had no visitors since his arrival, and had been so sick that the doctor told me he'd had grave doubts about his capacity to live more than a few days. He was so concerned that he urged the hospital administrators to try to find any relatives Bill may have had to let them know that he was close to his last breath, but their efforts were in vain, for he seemed to have none. The doctor was a little out in his diagnosis though, or Bill's constitution was stronger than he'd anticipated, for his time hadn't come, after all, - well, not right then anyway, and he recovered to a sufficient state of clarity of mind and lucidity to be politely questioned by the hospital administrators as to where his relatives might be found, - but he declined to provide any information on the subject.

"There's enough money in my account to bury me," was all he'd tell the senior staff when he was pressed.

Bill never recovered from the illness that led to his hospitalisation. He died on 24th June 1975 and his passing was very much in keeping with the way he lived his life, - quietly and serenely with no fuss or fanfare, like an old drover riding off into the sunset. Bill was not only a small person; he left an even smaller imprint on the planet. He was one of life's forgotten people and with no known relatives to take care of the end of life ceremonies; he was buried the next day in an unmarked grave at Herberton Cemetery with only the hospital chaplain and a few of us from the nursing staff at the graveside to mourn his passing. Several more attempts had been made by hospital administrators to find his relatives through birth records and other methods, of course, but the search was soon abandoned and Bill's case forgotten in the hustle and bustle of the hospital's busy schedule.

That wasn't the end of it for me, Mary Jane McConnell, though, probably Bill's final friend in this world. He'd told me much of his life story, as I have shared with you already in these pages, but he hadn't been granted that little bit of extra time on this earth to tell me *all* of it and put my mind at rest. I'd been thinking during my later visits to his cottage, that he was perhaps having second thoughts about delving any further into what must have been a harrowing account to share with me about his early life. Bill and I had come so far in such a short time; I'd gained his confidence; we'd laughed and cried together, much as I expect he'd done with Charlotte, his Warrego Bunyip in the creek bed near Cunnamulla, and now it was over and I felt empty inside. I couldn't stop thinking about him and cried myself to sleep every night at the thought of the little man's sad demise, so much so that my nursing friends became worried about my state of mind. I was mistaken, though, for Bill *had* intended to go through with the account of his early life to put the record straight and he must have realised in his final days that he had run out of time to tell his story to *Sister Mary*, and the world. He wanted to finish the task he'd begun when he and I started our weekly afternoon yarn sessions, even if it *was* after his death.

Bill's worldly possessions accounted for very little in the way of monetary value and the few goods and chattels he left behind were mainly fashioned from materials he'd gathered from bits and pieces discarded by others. His hut at Innot Hot Springs was found to be on land owned by the council and was reclaimed by them as part of the Nettle Creek Land Trust area. It too was demolished eventually, having little if any worth to anyone, but there was one item of apparently significant sentimental value that remained; a small wooden box full of memorabilia that Bill had carefully marked with the name and address of the person he'd bequeathed it to. That name was mine. The council workers retrieved it from its hidden place in the hut and respectfully got it to me unopened, probably assisted by Bill's contingent of loyal well-wishers in Innot Hot Springs.

I was so upset by Bill's passing that it took me some time to work up the courage to open the box and go through its contents, feeling that it would possibly take me to new depths of despondency, but when I ultimately did, I realised that it had fulfilled Bill's final wishes, and I was able to unravel the story of the secret that he hadn't been afforded the time on this earth to divulge to me. The box contained several time-yellowed newspaper pages from the end of the nineteen-twenties and early thirties, a time when the whole world was on the brink of a major financial disaster, which was followed by the Great Depression that lasted for decades. The pages were neatly folded in chronological order and tied with ribbon, along with some transcripts from court proceedings with notes jotted in pencil in the margins. There was also a recent hastily penned letter to me that explained the *in-between* circumstances of the newspaper articles and conversations he'd had, particularly with his solicitor Mister Sholto Percival Kemp. It was an eye-opener for me, but I carefully replaced it in its box and I have kept it to this day as a memento of the little man who played such a significant part in my life in such a short time.

9 Sholto Kemp's Client

Sholto Percival Kemp had been a Solicitor in Parramatta, New South Wales, for a very long time, but now in 1929, as the local newspaper, the *Cumberland Argus and Fruitgrowers Advocate* quaintly pointed out, *'In physical vigour, he is younger than many who haven't lived nearly as long.'* Indeed, the sixty-four-year-old had handled countless cases in both the Parramatta Police Court and the Small Debts Court, so it was with long-practised composure that he listened to the particulars his latest prospective client was providing for the submission of a claim to the latter.

"I came to New South Wales from Queensland last year and began working for Thomas Waters, the manager of Waterside Estates of Kenthurst as a permanent farmhand and ploughman on the tenth of November," the man said.

Kemp scribbled a note on his notepad. *'10ᵗʰ November 1928'* and underlined it. He knew something of Waters. The man had been before the courts in the past, although he couldn't remember the details offhand, but it would be in the court records and he would look it up later.

His client, William Smith, was dressed in a blue pin-striped suit and presented a neat and trim appearance as he sat opposite him on the other side of Kemp's polished mahogany desk. The heliotrope tie toned smoothly with the suit, and the outfit was nicely set off by a fashionable white silk shirt with a soft collar.

Kemp studied the man closely but discreetly as he spoke. It was something he was adept at because he'd learned long ago that looking directly into the eyes, although informative, wasn't the only way to gauge a person's sincerity and was in some cases counter-productive, creating a mental barrier and making a nervous client feel uneasy under the scrutiny. Small changes in other facial features, an unnatural fidgeting and unnecessary movement of the hands, and the changes in tone of a person's voice could also help significantly in assessing the degree of truthfulness in the statement being articulated by the appellant. From these and other small signals, he could often appraise the extent of probable success in the courtroom and advise the client whether or not he was prepared to proceed with the action, because even if a client had been honest in the quest for reparation in some matter, his or her demeanour in the dock of the Small Debts Court was capable of influencing a Magistrates verdict one way or the other.

This was a perplexing case, however, and presented a problem in Kemp's usually accurate mental assessment process. Smith's features exhibited an outwardly calm disposition. There were seamed lines on his face that spoke of years of exposure, possibly toiling under the harshest of the elements, and hard manual labour was written plainly on the hands that seemed a little too large for his otherwise slim and light framed body. There was also more than a suggestion of raw power in the thick wrists that peeped out from the ends of the blue serge coat sleeves, but his voice disclosed a weakness in his ostensibly masculine carriage. It was much too high, almost feminine, and implied a nervous intensity which Kemp felt would not sit well with a moderately perceptive Magistrate.

After Smith had completed the description of his complaint against Thomas Waters he sat back in his chair and waited in passive silence while Kemp scribbled notes on his notepad, and when the solicitor had finished his scrawl he threw his pencil down on the pad.

"It sounds like a straightforward enough case, Mister Smith, and I *am* prepared to represent you in court, - on one condition." He contemplated Smith for a moment as if considering his next words carefully before he continued. "You must tell *me* the whole truth if we are to have the greatest prospect of success in your claim."

Smith's eyes widened, apparently in surprise at Kemp's inference that his version of the events leading up to this accusation of an injustice against him by Waters had been incomplete. "But I *have* told you everything, Mister Kemp," he said. "I don't believe I've left anything out…"

Kemp smiled. "…You've certainly provided me with a detailed and clear-cut account of your complaint, Mister Smith," he said, "and I believe what you have told me *so far* is factual, but you are holding something back from me about *yourself*, - are you not?"

Smith's shoulders seemed to sag slightly and he gazed back at Kemp, but his eyes seemed out of focus and far away as if his mind was in another place. "Is it really necessary to know anything about *me* for the possibility of success of this litigation, Mister Kemp?" he said. "After all, you said it sounded like a straightforward enough case and I have no criminal convictions of any kind to confess to…"

"…The case itself is straightforward, Mister Smith," Kemp said, "but straightforward cases sometimes don't work out as expected if the defendant increases his chances of gaining the sympathy of the court by exposing some aspect of his accuser's past that the accuser hadn't thought worthy of revealing to his counsel."

"Very well Mister Kemp," Smith said at length. "I *do* have something about myself that I should tell you, but before I do I must ask for your confidence and your integrity in this matter as I don't want my personal affairs to become common knowledge. My hopes for future employment may rest entirely on your diplomacy."

Kemp was intrigued, but as always, he presented an unruffled outward appearance. "You can rest assured, Mister Smith," he said. "There is nothing about your personal life that I am at liberty to divulge to *anyone* and if it is not pertinent to the validity and accomplishment of your claim it will remain in confidence between the two of us."

Smith leaned forward in his chair as if the walls had ears. "This is difficult for me to speak about Mister Kemp, but," he hesitated and looked down at his hands, which Kemp noticed were now clenched together, probably to stop them from shaking. "My appearance is *not* entirely what it seems," he said in a quiet trembling voice. "You see, although I have been living my life as William Smith since I was a teenager, I believe I am, - I," he hesitated, took a deep breath, and straightened his shoulders. "I am at least, - partly, - a *woman.*

"Partly a woman?" Kemp's voice rose slightly as his mind absorbed the unexpected information. "Are you saying that you are a *hermaphrodite,* Mister Smith?"

Smith nodded, but he seemed uncertain and his eyes were downcast. "I, - I think that is what I am, but I'm not, - sure of it, Mister Kemp. It's possible I was named Wilhelmina by my mother, although she mostly called me Billie. My mother seemed to think there was something not quite right with me when I was little, so I'm *really* not sure who or *what* I am." The tears began to form in his eyes. "I have lived most of my life far from the capital cities and I have never been examined by any specialist in that field, so I don't know."

"I understand Mr, - er, Miss Smith." Kemp frowned. "Do you mind if I continue to call you Mister Smith; it will simplify things…?"

His client managed a thin smile through his tears. "…I'd prefer that you do, Mister Kemp."

"Well then," Kemp said gently. "I'm not sure that this can be kept off the court record. In truth, my early opinion is that it *must* come out in court at some stage and you can be left in no doubt whatsoever, Mister Smith, when it does, it will be used to attempt to assassinate your character, - possibly with the most dreadful consequences on your prospects of success."

Smith looked at him with anxiety written on his small oval face. "But I've done nothing wrong, Mister Kemp. I've never been in trouble with the police, never drank alcohol and I've never smoked a pipe or cigarettes in my life…."

Kemp nodded. "…I *do* appreciate your point of view, Mister Smith, - and it is certainly not illegal for a woman to dress like a man

151

under the Westminster Law system that governs us." He paused before adding as if it had been an afterthought, "…although I'm not sure if that reasoning applies to a hermaphrodite as well. You see, it *is* almost certainly an offence for a man to dress as a woman unless in a theatrical production or something similar. That is not a form of discrimination as it would be obvious to any reasonable person that there is no valid reason for a man to don women's clothes, but it is indeed sometimes practical for a woman to assume a mode of dress that is suitable for the function being undertaken, such as when doing manual labour in factories and the fields."

"I have been doing such manual work all my life, Mister Kemp," Smith said, daubing his eyes with a small handkerchief. "Would that allow me some leeway to plead my case against Waters without the loss of my good character in the process?"

Kemp shook his head. "Perhaps not; the regulations don't distinguish between particular tasks, and even if it is simply a woman's personal choice, essentially, she hasn't broken the law." He sighed and shook his head in a minor display of frustration. "But, unfortunately, there *are* some women who have taken advantage of this concession to the practicality of work requirements or personal choice and used it for their own nefarious purposes. When the world read a few weeks ago of the romantic and shameless frauds of *'Captain Barker'*, the woman in England who *'married'* another poor unsuspecting woman and swaggered with supreme insolence through several affairs, there was a feeling of revulsion against such an astonishing subversion of nature."

"Smith looked shocked. "She *married* another woman?" he said.

Kemp nodded again. "Yes, I'm afraid so, but she was caught and is being dealt the Westminster justice that is due to her, - *not* because she dressed as a man, but because she has fallen foul of the law, including common theft and lying under oath so that she could realise her unholy vows without hindrance. The public sentiment was initially divided, even here in Australia; some declared that it was her affair alone and that she was entitled to live her life however she wanted to and that the unfortunate 'wife' must have been either profoundly stupid or extremely gullible to fall for such a hoax. It was also speculated that the wife was compliant in the deceit and therefore was equally guilty, but as I said, Barker has been convicted for *other* reasons and many people who looked on her with some admiration as a somewhat romantic and quixotic figure have turned against her and have not forgiven her for it. The publicity over the Captain Barker affair has also prompted the Australian press to revisit that tired old account of the unsavoury character, Edward De Lacy Evans, something they do on *'no news'* days about once every five years or so. De Lacy left his home in Ireland to travel to Australia in 1856, He eventually moved to the central Victorian city of Sandhurst, which is now known as Bendigo."

Smith nodded. "I know Bendigo well," he said.

Kemp went on. "De Lacy worked in various occupations in Bendigo, including those of carter, miner, blacksmith and ploughman over many years. He made international news in 1879 when he suddenly went completely insane and was taken by force to the Bendigo Hospital because he was deemed to be dangerous to others, but when told to take a bath, he refused and promptly absconded from the premises. The following day he was arrested at his home and brought to the Police Court where the Magistrates agreed with the medical assessment that he was suffering from 'softening of the brain' and ordered him to be compulsorily committed to the Kew Lunatic Asylum near Melbourne. There he was held down and his clothes removed so that he could be bathed and it was revealed he too had been born a woman. It was then very quickly established that he was a woman by the name of Ellen Tremaye. She was even worse than Barker, having married *three* different women during her twenty years of masquerading as a man."

The look on Smith's face reassured Kemp that his client was a far different prospect to the disreputable wretches he'd just spoken about and he hastened to make the distinction clear. "The feeling of revulsion that lingers with the public over the Barker case may harm your case by simple association, even though the two are very different in the eyes of the law."

"Thank you, Mister Kemp," Smith said; he looked relieved.

Kemp gazed at his client thoughtfully before continuing. "Do you still wish to proceed with your suit against Mister Waters under the circumstances that it may reveal your secret to the world?" he said at last.

Smith paused and his shoulders shook as if he'd only just realised at that moment that the impending decision would most certainly be a huge turning point in his life. "I *must* proceed with this claim, Mister Kemp," he said. "I have fallen on tough times again and I need the money that I am owed simply to survive." He hesitated. "In any case, I have always done a fair day's work for the wages I earn and it is my right to have it. If my story has to be told to the world to achieve justice then so be it. I shall face it like a..."

"...like a man?" Kemp said, an ironic smile turning up the corners of his mouth.

"No, Mister Kemp," Smith smiled too, but the sadness remained in his eyes. "Not just like any man; like the kind of man I've been used to *being*, and working alongside; a tough, honest, hard-working man of the bush."

"Very well then, Mister Smith." Kemp took a gold watch from the fob pocket of his waistcoat and glanced at it. "I have no more appointments for today and it is still early. It will be an opportune time for you to provide me with some details of your past life so that I can better understand your situation for the prosecution of your case, - but only if you feel that *you* want to talk about it, and of course, should you agree to tell me your story, it will be completely off the record."

Smith sighed and nodded, and Kemp sensed a kind of release of pent up emotions in his high-pitched voice. "I haven't been able to talk about my past to many people…" He paused and Kemp thought he'd decided not to go on, but he shrugged his thin shoulders and continued. "…Well, to a very few special people before now Mister Kemp, but I will provide you with as little or as much information as you wish to hear."

He sounded apologetic and Sholto Kemp leant back in his chair and folded his hands over his ample midriff. "Take as long as you like, Mister Smith," he said. "I'm sure it will be an interesting story."

10 The Waif

I was a thin little waif, with a small oval face and close-cropped brown hair. I was short for my thirteen years of age and was yet to display any outward signs of impending womanhood if indeed that is what I was to become. *'Perhaps Billie will never be a real woman,'* I'd overheard my mother say. *'I can't put my finger on it, but something's not quite right with that child.'* That was over two years before when I was about eleven, and I'd never had the chance to question my mother as to what she'd meant by it because she'd died quite suddenly not long after the remark was made.

One day I crossed the Yarra River and walked slowly along Clarendon Street towards the South Melbourne Markets, hoping that the painful welts on my legs wouldn't be noticeable to any passers-by, for there were plenty of people out and about at that time on a Saturday morning in Melbourne, all, no doubt, hoping to secure their produce for the week ahead at bargain prices. I turned into Coventry Street and the aroma of freshly baked bread and pastries made my mouth water and my empty stomach rumble, for I'd gone without anything to eat since the morning before. I walked past a patisserie, where people queued patiently, waiting to receive their share of the new batch of croissants that had just been taken warm from the oven, and then I passed between the rows of stalls where fruit and vegetable sellers perched high above their mountainous displays, but I kept going, for I was heading for the waste bins out in the laneway at the back of the main sheds that backed on to the St. Kilda railway line.

I knew there would be several other people scavenging for scraps out there too, the dregs of Melbourne humanity, down on their luck and with rags hanging off their backs. The pickings would be better later in the day after the markets closed, of course, but the number of people jostling for the best of the discarded produce then would be so great that someone of my small stature would have had no chance of competing with them and indeed my very safety would have been at risk; it was better to move in now when things were quieter. The outer, damaged leaves of the cabbages and the unsaleable tomatoes and potatoes, bruised in the often rough journey to the market along outer Melbourne's unsealed roads, were better than nothing and still made a tasty broth despite their unwholesome appearance.

Survival was the major challenge I'd constantly faced in the last year or so as my father's mental and physical state steadily worsened. I'd come home from school on a Friday afternoon to the dingy rooms we occupied in a tenement building in the Docklands area, rented at one

155

shilling a week from the Melbourne Harbour Authority. He wasn't home so I sat at the small table and started on my homework. I was quite a talented student and was popular with my teachers, - or perhaps, thinking back on it now, they knew something was terribly wrong at home and felt remorseful and helpless for not intervening. Anyway, whatever the case, they made sure I had the necessary books and pencils and instead of scolding me, gave me extra tuition the next day if I'd failed to turn up for school, or couldn't produce the previous day's homework. I appreciated their kindness and thoughtfulness, and it spurred me on to try all the harder to learn everything I could because I knew that education and hard work were the only means I'd ever be able to draw on to bring my father and me out of the depths of poverty that he'd dragged us into.

He'd been drunk again when he arrived home later that evening and he'd taken the belt to the back of my legs, accusing me of hiding food from him and drinking his beer. *'Why would I do that?'* I thought miserably, *'I can't stand the smell of it on his breath when he comes close to my face to threaten me with more punishment.'*

My father had always had the propensity for inflicting violence on those who incurred his wrath, however unintentionally they'd fallen foul of his temper. He was a big domineering man, while my mother had been short and slim as I have turned out to be, and I'd witnessed his outbursts with wide-eyed terror from the relatively safe vantage point behind my mother's ragged, shapeless skirts as she strove to protect me, her only child, from harm. That had often resulted in my mother taking the subsequent beating herself, which she did with a whimper, but without further complaint. *'Now don't you go telling anybody at school about this, Billie,'* she'd say. *'It will only make it worse for me if you do. Promise me you won't say anything to the teachers that will get your dad arrested; promise me, Billie my love.'*

I'd been at school when my mother's unhappy life ended abruptly and I'd suspected from that time onwards that the poor woman had endured one beating too many at the hands of her brutal husband, - my father. The Coroner could find no conclusive evidence with which to lay any charges against him, however, and the openly grieving man was given the benefit of any doubt that had been cast in the minds of the investigating police. *'Perhaps if their inquiries had gone so far as to explore the motives of the Smith family in leaving the United States of America in 1907, three years before the tragic event, to live in squalor in the docklands of Melbourne in the south-east corner of Australia, the investigation may have uncovered other reasons to pique the interest of authorities,'* I remember thinking.

A commotion at the edge of one of the fruit and vegetable stalls attracted my attention and I turned to look curiously in the direction it came from. It was not unusual for arguments to break out between stall vendors or between vendors and customers who thought they'd been overcharged or underweighted on the scales, but this was slightly different. The wails of anguish that rang across the concourse were not the result of such a disagreement over injured honour, but of a more direct physical altercation of the kind of which I was used to being on the receiving end.

A young boy, bigger than I was, but possibly about my age, was being escorted from behind a stall by a burly Mediterranean looking man in a dark blue striped apron over white shirt and trousers who, with his thumb and forefinger pinching the squirming young fellow's ear, muttered to the gathering audience about the serious consequences of the young thief pilfering a sixpence from the money-box on the payment desk behind his back. The boy's comical sideways stagger as he was dragged along incited laughter amongst the spectators and even I managed a weak smile despite feeling his pain. I was well used to physical punishment for little justification, but it seemed to me that in this case the boy had been caught in the act of doing something he shouldn't have. A deft kick to the youth's backside immediately after his ear was released completed his ejection from the premises where he'd evidently been employed and he scurried away amongst the crowd of onlookers, no doubt to rue the dishonesty that had just led to his swelling ear and instant dismissal.

The Mediterranean man looked about him with a sullen expression on his swarthy face as he wiped his hands on his apron; *'probably a gesture to illustrate the finality of his decision to terminate the youth's employment rather than any suggestion of possible contamination of his fingers due to contact with the young thief's ear,'* I thought wryly,

The man's eyes roamed about the amused spectators and finally settled on *me* and I cringed under his stern gaze. "Hey you, leetle boy. Do you want a good job for today, leetle boy? Pay good wage all right. You small, but seem to have an honest face. You can count the money, no?"

My mind raced. *'He thinks I'm a boy.'*

He looked around at the milling crowd in front of his stall. "No time to waste; customers waiting; you want a job today, leetle boy? You come now." the man said again more urgently.

I walked quickly over and faced him, although my head was only level with his chest. "Yes sir, - I do *want* job, - and I *can* count," I said,

157

trying hard to change the tone of my soft girlish voice to one more suited to what I thought my new identity should sound like.

The man looked at me strangely for a moment and then shrugged his broad shoulders. "Okay then, you got job for today. What name you got boy?"

I started to mumble, "Wilhem..." but then I quickly gathered my wits. "er, - Billie it is sir."

The man's swarthy face broke into a wide grin. "You no call me sir, young Bill. You call me boss, - or Luigi. I'm Luigi Pavetto, okay?"

I grinned too, my confidence soaring, and threw him a mock salute. "Yes *boss*," I said.

Luigi pointed to the payments desk. "You sit there," he said. "I fill the bags and yell the price. You take the money and give the correct change, okay?"

I worked as if my life depended on it. When there were no customers to take money from, I followed Luigi's example without even being asked and polished the apples and pears in the open boxes with a clean rag. With that done I refilled half-empty boxes from the supplies that were brought in by Luigi's son, Armand, throughout the morning from the wagon parked outside in the side lane.

When the deep-throated bell rang to mark the close of trade for the day and the repacking and dismantling of the stall had been completed I sat on a packing case, exhausted but enthralled, my face feeling hot and flushed with the excitement of it all.

Luigi sat opposite me and laughed. "Good takings today. Hey, you very good worker, Bill," he said, wiping his brow with a rag. "I pick you straight away for good worker." He must have immediately thought about the earlier incident for a moment because he grimaced. "I not always right though, but, more often than not," he said, "You got good job if you want, Bill. Where you live, eh, - close by maybe? Early start always, this job."

My mind was racing, remembering that I'd probably get a beating from my angry father when I went home for being away so long. "I'm an orphan, boss," I lied. "I don't have a permanent home to go to." Lying became easier as I went along through my early life.

Luigi's son, Armand, a big, strapping, black-haired teenager with the same Mediterranean complexion as his father, had been listening to our conversation as he loaded empty boxes on to a trolley. "What about the outhouse shed at the back of the house, Dad," he said. "Bill could stay there for a while until he gets better digs." He looked at me hopefully. "It's pretty comfortable, Bill," he added. "It's got a good bed and its own bathroom and toilet attached."

158

Luigi grinned at me. "Armand's impressed with your work too, young Bill," he said. "It's hard to find good workers these days, especially with the new labour laws for fruit and vegetable union workers. Mama Rosa will feed you up so you're big and strong like Armand here and you can wear Armand's old clothes he's grown out of."

I could see by the earnest, expectant look in his big dark eyes that he was desperate for me to join them and I felt as if I was, - *needed,* for perhaps the first time since my mother had died. "Thanks, boss," I said, with a tired grin. "I'd like that."

It was a full three months before I worked up the courage to pay a visit to the dockside tenement where I'd spent the past five years of my young life, even though it was only a couple of miles from the Pavetto's home in South Melbourne. I'd not undertaken the journey through any feeling of affection for my father, or sentiment of nostalgia, but rather as a sense of obligation. He was, after all, the only relative I knew of in the world and, despite the risk of bringing down his wrath on me for deserting him if he happened to be drunk, I wanted to interrogate him about my past and find out whether there were other relatives I could contact in America; whether I'd been registered at birth as a boy or a girl and whether my name was William or Wilhelmina. There were so many questions I needed answers to and I knew that I had somewhere to quickly escape to if the situation became dangerous. I had misgivings, however, as I approached the desolate building and saw from a distance that the third-floor window to the dingy room was closed and curtained, and my sense of dread increased significantly when I trudged up the stairs and found the locked and boarded up entrance door.

The caretaker was of little help; he was new to the job and regarded me with the indifference of someone who regarded any question put to him as an imposition on his valuable time. "Don't know, lad," he said. "The man was a hopeless drunkard. He walked out one day; muttered to a neighbour he had to go look for some woman called, Wilhelmina. He never came back; owed five shillings on his rent, so we sold his belongings to pay his debt. He could've drowned down the docks, I reckon. He headed in that direction." The last statement was made with a shrug of his shoulders as he turned and walked away, a clear indication that our conversation was at an end and he had nothing further to contribute.

I stood there for several minutes as I tried to take in the fact that I really *was* an orphan now. *'So that's it,'* I thought. *'He had to go and look for a woman called Wilhelmina.'* Was it *me* my father was searching for or was it just a coincidence that he had a friend called Wilhelmina? It was a fairly common woman's name at that time and I'd never heard my father call me anything other than Billie. I turned away from that awful part of my life and retraced my steps to join my new family at the markets without looking back.

* * * *

It was the most difficult decision of my young life thus far when I said goodbye to Luigi and Rosa Pavetto. They were both distraught when I broke the news and they pleaded with me to stay, but I'd been adamant that I felt I was too much of a burden on them and I only moderated their grief a little by promising to write to them whenever possible. I did keep that promise, although not as often as I should have, as I realised much later. Armand had already enlisted in the army and had gone off to fight for Australia in the 'Great War', as many young men of his age were doing at the time. Luigi had fallen into bad health and had relinquished his contract on the market stall he'd leased from the South Melbourne Council. In any case, much of the farm produce across Australia had either been requisitioned by the army or was in short supply because so many working farmhands had enlisted, leaving the fields fallow. They were not supposed to do that, because the crops still needed to be grown to feed the nation, but who could blame the strong young men who wanted to participate in the war for their country's sake.

I knew in my heart that it was providential I'd made the break at that particular time too. The stress of the daily pretence of posing as a boy had become a little too much for me and at sixteen I supposed that my appearance might change enough in the next year or two to make the deception even more difficult to maintain in the future, - you know, growing breasts and such, - although there had been no signs of anything like that happening so far. I'd developed a strong bond with Armand and we'd worked close to each other for much of the time at the markets, but I'd caught him looking at me strangely several times as if he sensed something was amiss. *'Perhaps my female scent is getting stronger as I get older,'* I thought. I remembered the whispered conversations with my young, giggling girlfriends in the corner of the school playground. *'Oh, there's that Johnny B... Ugh, he's been running around all day and he smells just like a boy.'* And he did; Johnny was a big masculine sort of boy and he'd begun to radiate a distinctive male scent when he exerted himself on the playground, and despite my consensus with my little friends in scorning Johnny's *'smell'* in the schoolyard, I had to admit that as I'd gotten older Armand's male scent after a hard day at the market had excited me in a way that I'd never felt before. I remember thinking, *'I'm sure that's the way it's meant to be between men and women, and I'm certain Armand has already realised that my scent is different to his.'* I couldn't have continued to mislead him for much longer, - and I didn't want him to find out that I was not the sociable and sometimes cheeky young boy he thought I was, for I realised that he would have been confused by his feelings of 'mateship' towards me and he wouldn't have understood why I'd *had* to deceive him. He would then probably have hated me for it, but when I did reconnect with him several years ago it was a different matter, at least for him anyway. I'd perfected my deception to the point where I was confident I'd eliminated all external traces of my femininity, - even my female scent had been replaced with the smell of leather and rawhide, - and although I had intended to confess to Armand and hope that he'd understand and forgive me enough to let me be a part of his life again, it wasn't to be, for circumstances had intervened and it was too late for me to realise my impossible dream.

Mama Rosa had noticed little changes too, more so than either of the men had I think, and she sat me down one day when we were alone and pleaded with me gently to tell her what was happening to her little boy. I was so scared that she'd have Luigi throw me out of their home that I burst into tears as I told her about my early life, but I needn't have worried, because she took me in her arms and cradled me as if she was the mother that I'd never had the chance to get to know. When my tears had subsided she told me that no matter what physical struggles a person had to endure in their life it was what was in their heart that mattered. Everyone is different in one little way or another, she said, and we must try to do the best we can with whatever burden God asks us to carry on our shoulders.

I'd taken the train from Melbourne's Spencer Street Station and disembarked at the small Victorian town of Bendigo, which you mentioned earlier. At that time it was the first major stop on the Western Railway line about a hundred miles north-west of Melbourne. On first glance, it seemed a well-to-do sort of place with many old ornate buildings in the town centre, but I knew I had to be careful with my savings and so I took the first wide side street I saw, looking for a cheap boarding house. It was a good move for, no more than two hundred yards along the street I came upon a run-down two-storey hotel with a sign on the wrought iron fence that said *'Cheap rooms for rent'*. I made my way up the three wide stone steps, opened the door at the top and found myself in a dim, windowless, musty smelling parlour. A loud bell above the door had announced my arrival and so I waited in front of a large desk for someone to make an appearance. It was several minutes before a door at the far end of the parlour was thrown open, letting the light from a window somewhere beyond it into the parlour, but that light was immediately blocked by a shabbily dressed woman who wobbled her large frame through the opening. When she saw me she stopped, scowled, and took a cigarette from the corner of her mouth. "What is it you want? I've got no money so you'll be sore pressed to get any charity here. Away with you now before I lose my temper, - dragging an old lady down the stairs for nothing, do you mind." The last part of her rant was accompanied by a wheezing cough that left her gasping for breath.

I stared at her in silence until the tirade was over and then I slowly advanced further into the light. "I'm not looking for charity, Mam," I said. "I've just arrived here from Melbourne and I want to rent a room from you. I - I saw your sign out there, - on the railing." I pointed over my shoulder at the closed door.

The woman looked surprised for a moment. "Ah, do you now lass?" she said between puffs on her cigarette. She still scowled as she looked me up and down. "You look awful young to be renting on your own. And have you got any money to pay for the room then, - or are you expecting to get tick until you find work? I suppose you've come to *work* here and you're not here for the clean Bendigo air."

I shook my head. "I've got money, Mam. I'm not looking for credit, and yes, - I am here to find work," I said.

The woman's scowl softened slightly. "Ah, yes, well that's a different story. It'll be two shillings a week, - in advance. Clean sheets every Monday. Only one gentleman friend at a time, mind; I've got my reputation to think of, you know. There's a washbasin in each room and two communal bathrooms, one upstairs and one downstairs." She stopped and wheezed again before adding in a more gentle tone, "If you take one of the upstairs rooms you'll have a bathroom to yourself because the other rooms up there are empty. You'll have to keep it clean though because I can't get up the stairs like I used to."

I was elated. It had been a lot easier than I'd thought it would be and I felt that my host probably wasn't as fearsome as she made herself out to be. I also had the sudden feeling that she knew I needed some privacy in my life, although how she could have known that was beyond me at the time. "Okay Mam, I'll take it," I said.

The woman sat down heavily on a chair behind the desk. "What's your name lass?" she said.

Without thinking I said, "It's Bill, mam." I quickly corrected myself. "…er, - Wilhelmina, mam. Wilhelmina Smith." I said.

My host seemed unperturbed. "Wilhelmina, eh; that's an awfully long name for a wee mite like yourself to be carting around. I suppose your friends call you Billie, do they?"

I nodded and heaved a sigh of relief, thinking at the time, *'This pretence is not getting any easier, no matter which way I portray myself.'*

She pulled open a drawer and scooped the two shillings that I'd placed on the desk in front of her into a tin money box. "Okay Billie," she said. "I'm Mrs Jennings. Mister Jennings is long gone to the big brewery in the sky and I'm sure he's making better liquor up there than the stuff that finished him off down here." Her ample bosom heaved as she giggled at her own joke, and then she wrote something in a ledger, passed a key across the desk and threw a glance at the door she'd entered the parlour by earlier. "Up the stairs there; I've given you the bedroom at the back. It's got the best view and it's next to the bathroom. If you don't mind I'll just sit here for a wee while. I'm fair worn out now; I've been up and down the stairs *twice* today."

I took the key and began to walk towards the door. "Thanks, Mrs Jennings," I said. "I'll be right."

She spoke to my back. "It's none of my business, Billie, but what kind of work are you looking for?"

I turned and faced her again. "Anything I can get, Mrs Jennings," I said. "…maybe some kind of housework, - cleaning and scrubbing, - that kind of thing."

Mrs Jennings stared at me in silence for a moment. "You've probably come to the wrong place for that kind of work, lass," she said eventually. "Bendigo isn't what it used to be a few years ago. When the gold mining was at its peak there were forty thousand people here. They sank the shafts to a thousand feet and were still finding gold, but the groundwater came in and beat them in the end. The pumps couldn't keep up. There were a lot of wealthy people hiring servants and cooks and the like, pretending to be as good as the Melbourne socialites, but it's not like that now. We've been in a big decline for the last twenty years."

I shrugged my thin shoulders in resignation. "I can do outdoors work if I have to, Mrs Jennings. I don't mind toiling under heavy loads…"

Mrs Jennings' next words chilled me to the core. "…Yes, I can see you're beginning to develop into a strong looking wee thing. I thought you were a *boy* when you first came in until I heard you speak, but it would've been better for you getting work around here if you *had* been born a boy."

I locked the door to the communal bathroom that was now to be mine alone for the foreseeable future and stood in front of a cracked mirror that hung askew on the wall, pulling the heavy woollen shirt I'd worn on the cold Melbourne morning over my head. I looked at my half-naked body. The last couple of years had toughened my small frame. Rosa's food had been good and the hard work at the South Melbourne Markets had filled me out, but there was still no visual sign of breasts developing on my smooth chest. The toned look of my pectoral muscles and my upper body, in general, would have done Johnny B- from my schooldays proud. I bathed, and for the first time in two years pulled on a dress that I had bought just before I left Melbourne. It felt strange, but I knew I had to try to reclaim my female identity once more before the change became too familiar to me and it was too late to turn back.

I thought of my mother, the small, battered woman from whom I'd inherited my short stature, and my mind went back to the words that had affected me so much and probably would do so for the remainder of my life.

'Perhaps Wilhelmina will never be a real woman,' I'd overheard my mother say. *'I can't put my finger on it, but something's not quite right with that child.'*

* * * *

I set out the very next morning on my mission to find work. It was a cool, windy autumn day in Bendigo and people hurried past me, some with hands thrust deep in the pockets of their fur-lined jackets and others with woollen scarves encircling their necks as they went about their business. I felt strangely uncomfortable as the breeze gusted and my skirt flapped against my bare legs. *'I must persevere with wearing these clothes,'* I thought, *'even though it will be difficult to get used to it all again'.*

I'd been in Bendigo for three weeks and I still hadn't secured *any* kind of work. I was becoming desperate; my savings were diminishing quickly and it seemed to me that no one wanted to employ a young girl under any circumstances, but particularly one who had the temerity to doorknock every fashionable house in the high end of town asking to be given any job whatsoever, be it heavy gardening or scullery work. I realised in the end by the doubtful looks I received from the head housekeepers and chief gardeners who interviewed me

164

that my determination and resolve was being misinterpreted as the scheming and devious behaviour of someone who was most likely a young criminal from Melbourne; someone who was not to be trusted in their master's homes by the conscientious and mostly long-time domestic servants of the wealthy citizens of Bendigo. In fact, my final attempt to secure a position almost ended in disaster. I'd knocked on the door of a very large house and it was answered by a balding, pot-bellied butler dressed in faded black livery. I'd put my case to him although I cringed under the piercing, bloodshot eyes that seemed to strip me naked as he looked me up and down.

He leered at me. "You'll do *anything*, to get some kind of work you say? All right then, come on in and I'll see what I can do for you, but you'll have to be nice to me." He reached out and began to stroke my hair with one hand as he gripped my arm with the other, but my years of heavy work with Luigi had hardened my muscles and I ripped his hand away and punched him in the gut with all of my considerable strength. He doubled over and gasped and I ran, not stopping until I'd rounded the corner at the end of the street.

I went back to my room and threw myself on the bed, still shaking from the experience, and I shed many tears, but they were not tears of self-pity as one might have expected a vulnerable young girl who'd narrowly escaped such coarse treatment to have shed. No, they were the tears of a *strong* young person who was frustrated with the realisation that there was no hope of escaping from the classification society had categorised me under. The expectation was that I'd conform meekly to the social order without complaint and with no redress for any exploitation of my lowly position in life, but I was not prepared to succumb to that evaluation of my worth; I was stronger than that. I rose from my bed, took off the dress I'd worn in my encounter with the lewd butler, and put it in the bottom drawer of the bedside table, far out of my sight and my conscience. It was with a feeling of guilty satisfaction then that I buttoned up the grey flannel shirt and tweed trousers and pulled on the heavy, blucher boots that I'd been used to wearing for the previous two years, for it was, to my mind, a kind of symbolic casting off of the shackles of conformity.

Mrs Jennings wasn't to be seen as I crept down the stairs and made my way out into the street. It probably wouldn't have mattered to her anyway as I found out later, but she was one of the few people who *had* seen me dressed as a girl in recent years and I was conscious that the transformation from Wilhelmina to William, or Billie to Bill might have affected even *her* sensitivities.

I found it comparatively easy to secure a job on a dairy farm after I resumed my male persona. The work was hard, much harder even than the effort I'd had to put in at the South Melbourne Markets, but I was determined to succeed and I toiled willingly under the physical discomforts of the arduous work, for I knew it was the only way I could survive. There were many times when, after working in the frozen mornings, I had to force my fingers open, so stiff and contracted had they become with the many hours spent milking cows, and I formed a plan to travel further north to New South Wales as soon as I had saved enough money to tide me over until I could find another position.

As time went on and I travelled from one place to another, I found it easier to keep my personal situation secret. People didn't get to know me very well and generally just accepted me as a quiet and unpretentious little man who wanted to keep to himself, but whenever I *did* feel that someone suspected there was more than a hint of doubt about my gender, I did the only thing I could; I simply moved on. And so, Mister Kemp, here I am after living as a man for the last fifteen years of my life and my mother's words are still there in my mind to haunt me. *'Perhaps Wilhelmina will never be a real woman. I can't put my finger on it, but something's not quite right with that child.'*

11 The Claim

The following is taken from Bill's letter left in his box of possessions and addressed to me.

Mary Jane McConnell.

It was mid-July when I was summoned to Sholto Kemp's rooms again and he got straight to the point of my visit. "I have a note from the Clerk of the Parramatta Court," the solicitor told me. "Your case has been non-suited because Thomas Waters has been declared a bankrupt. That means you cannot recover the debt from him."

The shocked expression on my face must have told him of my disappointment, as he quickly continued. "All is not lost, though. Waters transferred his property and accounts over to his wife, Mrs Matilda Waters, before his bankruptcy application, obviously in a bid to avoid payment, but that may be to your advantage as I believe the Magistrate may view that action as a partial admission of culpability."

"So I now have to claim from Mrs Waters, I suppose?" I said.

Kemp nodded. "Waters is really not very smart. Since you worked for both of them his wife will be held responsible for their joint outstanding debts in the normal course of events, but there is one other thing you should know which may influence your decision on whether you want me to proceed." He paused, shook his head slowly, and picked up a document from his desk. "It was what I suspected would happen and what I warned you about. Thomas Waters visited me and gave me a copy of a report he has made to the police..." He adjusted his reading glasses and read the text of the document. '*...that I believe that my former employee, although a hard, reliable worker at ploughing and other heavy tasks, is a woman.*' He looked at me over the rims of his glasses, but I didn't comment. "Sergeant Roberts of Parramatta Police Station has been given the assignment of investigating the accusation," he continued. "I know Sergeant Roberts well. He's a good man and would know that it is not an offence for a woman to put on men's clothing for work. His investigation would only be carried out to ensure that no other law has been broken."

"I still want to go through with the claim, Mister Kemp," I said. "I've had time to think about the consequences of the possible revelation to the world at large that I am either a woman in disguise or some strange creature who is neither man nor woman and who should be on display in a circus freak show." I was adamant and my voice rose in helpless anguish as I contemplated the unfairness of it all. "I didn't have any choice in how God made me; I have done nothing wrong and

I want justice to prevail at whatever the damage it sustains to my private affairs."

"I admire your courage, Mister Smith," Kemp said, calm and smiling despite my outburst. "I agree with your sentiments; you certainly have done nothing wrong and have been merely a victim of circumstances beyond your control, but we must now come up with a strategy that will dispel any doubt in the *Magistrate's* mind as to your good and wholesome character, and at the same time manoeuvre him away from the stereotypical image that *all* guiltless people who've had to make that same choice now have to bear because of the likes of Captain Barker and Edward De Lacy's criminal abuses."

My face lit up immediately. "Are you saying that there are *some* other genuine people like me who are just trying to live out their lives in peace without resorting to sordid false marriages and affairs?" I asked.

"Oh yes, certainly," Kemp assured me. "Don't think for one minute that you're alone, - and I don't believe that any fair person would think you're *some strange creature who should be on display in a circus freak show.* I'm sure there are many instances of people burdened by similar complexities in their lives who are simply going about their business as you have been, - and there are some celebrated cases of women who've bucked the system, so to speak, and have been admired and even acclaimed because of it. Take the case of 'Jockey Jack' for example."

I frowned and shook my head. "I haven't heard of him, Mister Kemp," I said.

Kemp smiled. "There you are, Mister Smith; you've assumed that I'm talking about a man just because Jack is a man's name. Jockey Jack is actually a woman whose real name is May McDonald," he said. "She lives in Albury on the New South Wales side of its border with Victoria, and quite a few legends have grown up around her, mainly because she's a bit of a storyteller when her beginnings as a so-called *man-woman* are called into question." Kemp held up another document he'd taken from the folder on his desk. "She'd always loved riding horses and became a child jockey in her early teens, she's told people usually, fooling every official and trainer alike at the racecourses she frequented into believing that she was a boy, - and she's claimed the racing stewards only found out she was a girl when she had a fall at the Warrnambool Races and was taken to the jockeys' room to be examined. That sudden embarrassing exposure, shocking as it must have been to everyone concerned, didn't deter her though, and indeed only served to make her bolder. She then began openly dressing as a man in public about twenty years ago in 1908, when she was perhaps twenty years old. She was such a good jockey, however, and so much in demand by country trainers that race stewards turned a blind eye and she was allowed to ride at provincial racetracks across Victoria long after she'd become well-known to be a woman. She went to North-East Victoria in early 1910 and worked horses on a Greta property and raced at Greta, Moyhu and Corryong. In 1916, when she was new to the Albury district, and people *there* realised she was a woman who rode against men in horse races, she gave journalists interviews that appeared in several newspapers." Kemp looked at my astonished face and smiled again. "I suppose you must be wondering how I have come to have so much information about the woman."

I nodded. "Yes, Mister Kemp; it did cross my mind," I said. "Do you have an interest in horse racing?"

Kemp shook his head. "No, I don't, but May McDonald never mentioned in any of the interviews she gave to the journalists that she'd twice gone to jail for theft, in 1910 and 1915. It was a fascinating case that piqued my interest. The first time she came to *my* notice as a solicitor was when she was mentioned in the *Border Morning Mail* as a man in December 1910. She'd been charged under the name of *Jack* McDonald at Corryong Court with stealing a bridle and halter and was jailed for three months at Beechworth Prison. She was sent there by train but it was forced, due to unforeseen delays, to stop overnight at Wangaratta." He smiled and nodded to himself as he recalled the report of the incident. "It could have been most unfortunate for her because the local constable was also the Wangaratta Racecourse stipendiary steward and he recognised her as the formidable May McDonald, of 'Jockey Jack' renown. Luckily he was sympathetic to her cause and made sure she had the necessary privacy that her femininity required."

"It sounds like she wouldn't have been too worried about being caught out by the Wangaratta police anyway since she'd already been racing as a woman jockey," I said. "She seems to have flaunted it without a care in the world. I wonder where she came from and what induced *her* to decide to live her life as a man. Is it possible she and I share the same, ah, - *physical characteristics?*"

Kemp shrugged. "She's given so many different versions of her childhood background, depending on which reporter she's talking to and possibly what mischievous mood she's in that where and when May McDonald was born is uncertain, but the report on her exposure at the Warnambool races mentioned no dissimilarity between her physical appearance and that of any other woman, as far as I know."

169

"Appearances can be deceptive, Mister Kemp," I said, trying to conceal the flush of embarrassment I felt at having to discuss my physiology. "The difference between a woman and a hermaphrodite may not be readily apparent in such a cursory and accidental examination by racecourse medical staff untrained in that particular area of expertise. You see..." I hesitated, unsure about how to explain to this stranger, - a kind and considerate professional, but still a stranger, - my reason for such a statement. "...my masculinity is hidden, but it's there nevertheless."

"I suppose that must be true enough," Kemp said, matching my colouring. "I certainly have no familiarity within that field either, but I'm sure you are aware that women were not at that time, - and still aren't, - allowed to ride in races against men, so it may have been merely those circumstances and her competitive nature that drove her to rebel against what she saw as an injustice towards women on the racing tracks."

I nodded, partly regaining my composure. "I am well aware that it's long been considered amongst the horse-racing fraternity that it's too dangerous for women, as well as for the male riders around them, to compete against each other. There are special conditions under which the women jockeys can ride against each other, known quite scornfully amongst the males as *'Powder Puff Derbies'*, and they're only put on as novelty events at picnic meetings in the bush towns. I didn't compete in any of them, of course."

Kemp picked up his reading glasses again. "The Tallangatta Court report of January 16, 1915, during which May was accused of stealing money from a man at the Laurel Hotel at Mitta Mitta stated,-

'It may be recalled that Miss McDonald made her debut at a race meeting in Tallangatta in 1911, in circumstances which caused the countryside to wonder. The spectacle of a man-woman parading about in their midst created a sensation which is still talked about locally. The accused, who appeared in court in masculine garb, was attired in a neatly-fitting suit, with lounge hat. She showed her feminine side, however, by frequently bursting into tears during the proceedings.'

Kemp looked over the rims of his spectacles. "This time she was jailed in Beechworth again, for a month, but it was after she was released that she went to live near Albury, working as a horse-breaker and trainer. The townspeople got on well with her, especially after her frank interviews with the press and, they either didn't know or took no notice of her past transgressions, as country folk are inclined to do. They accepted her for what she was, an excellent rider and trainer, but the Police Superintendent for the Border District, William Childs, got to know of her and stated publicly that she was an embarrassment to her gender. He demanded that she dress like a lady and told her there had been complaints about her wearing men's clothes, including a waistcoat and watch chain. May told him that *she* herself hadn't had any complaints, she wasn't going anywhere, and…" He paused and smiled at me. "This is interesting; she said *she wouldn't change her clothes as they were part of the attire she needed to wear to look after her horses.* It was a perfectly stated defence of her stance on the matter. She knew her rights and made the Superintendent look a bit insensitive and pompous in the opinion of many of the residents of Albury, and it had the consequence of endearing her even more to her neighbours. She was even seen by some as a symbol of the enduring heroine of the Australian bush."

I must have looked stunned. "She was taking a huge risk in telling the Superintendent of Police where to go though, wasn't she?" I said in a hushed voice.

Kemp nodded. "Quite true; it *was* a big risk. Superintendent Childs wasn't someone to meddle with either. As a detective he'd introduced the fingerprints system into NSW in 1903, and he's recently become the state's Chief Commissioner, but at the time May took a gamble that she had the support of the people she lived amongst and worked with, - and it paid off. Nothing came of any anticipated police action over 'Jockey Jack' and May McDonald is still happily settled down in Albury doing what she loves best, breaking in, training and riding racehorses."

I sighed, astonished at May's determination to carry on her life the way she wanted to, but well aware that *I* wasn't capable of taking the same path. "I don't think I'd ever take on the constabulary, Mister Kemp," I said, "but when this is over I'd like to go back to Queensland and try to put a new life together, maybe doing the same as May McDonald, training and riding horses, but I'd have to go to a place well out of the way, like Innisfail or Cairns, where people wouldn't have heard of this case and if they had, wouldn't know of my involvement in it. I like it up north and the people are like the Albury locals, - very accepting of someone who might be, - *slightly* different." I immediately thought of my introduction to Innisfail and bit my lip. *'There are a couple of crazy Italians up there blowing up the rocky hillside with dynamite. Pavetto's one of them, - reckon they're going to put cane in next year, - probably blow themselves up more likely; good riddance to them too. That'd be two less olive skins in the district to take over our land.'*

171

"Well *most* of them are accepting of someone different," I corrected myself, "but I'm sure I'll always have to be careful to only trust those who have proved themselves to me to be genuine friends, - perhaps for the rest of my life."

Kemp regarded me thoughtfully and I was surprised at the warmth evident in the voice of such an outwardly professional man "I hope we can achieve the result you need to be able to live your dream, Mister Smith," he said, and I knew then by his gentlemanly manner that I'd made the right choice in trusting him, not only with my case against Waters but with the handling of the secret I'd carried with me through most of the adult years of my life.

* * * *

It was a week later that Sholto Kemp's secretary ushered me into his office again. I was certainly happier than I'd been when I ventured there for my first appointment with him and I still felt quite confident he'd do his best to achieve the outcome I hoped for. I'd deliberated over our previous conversation many times during that week and I came to the conclusion in the end that in my quest for justice I'd stumbled on a solicitor of abundant intellect and shrewdness. I was certain he'd deliberately told me about May McDonald and her achievement in exploiting the sympathy of the common people to overcome the prejudices of powerful, but bigoted individuals in authority, quite deliberately to set me at ease. It was probably a ruse he'd used many times before; provide an example of what had been achieved by someone else under similar circumstances, and let it sink in before guiding a client towards accepting whatever bold scheme he'd come up with to help win the case.

I was very much interested to hear what that scheme might be. "You said we need to adopt a strategy that will dispel any doubt in the Magistrate's mind as to my good character, Mister Kemp," I said once the preliminary greetings had been completed. "Do you have something in mind?"

"I've thought about this very carefully and I *do* have a plan, but I need you to be brave, - as brave as May McDonald's alter-ego, 'Jockey Jack' has been, - if you want to achieve the goal you've set for yourself," he said.

'As brave as Jockey Jack?' I thought. "Go on, please." I drew in a deep breath, waiting for his reply.

"I want to ensure that your personal story is leaked to the press," Kemp said.

172

My startled look was probably not unexpected and he held up his hand in an appeasing gesture. "As I told you before; you'll be in a much better position to influence the deliberations of the Magistrate if you're seen to have the sympathy of the general public on your side."

I must have looked at him a bit pensively for he continued in a persuasive tone. "Oh, it's not so uncommon to try to influence a Stipendiary Magistrate in that sense; they're not Judges you see; they're voluntary Court officials who reflect the will of the people on the delivery of justice over minor disputes between two parties and, - despite the anticipated extended coverage of your case by the press due to the sensitive question of your gender, - by law, this *is* still nothing more than a minor dispute over non-payment of wages. Captain Barker's antics have alienated many of the common people to individuals who appear to flout the people's perception of what is right and decent, and so we must get the message across to the public before the hearing, that yours is an entirely different situation to hers. We must show them, - through the Magistrate, - that this case deserves to be treated in the context of a simple monetary dispute and not about whether *you* are a man or woman or anything in between. I have reliable contacts in the *'Sydney Sun'* and *'Truth'* newspapers and I can ensure that your story is published without your name being mentioned. I promise you it will be done with the greatest sensitivity."

"I understand, Mr Kemp," I said, "but what if the journalist asks me questions that will make my identity obvious?"

"I would never ask you to *lie*, Mister Smith," Kemp said with a mischievous smile, "but there *are* ways to answer such questions without committing yourself if you are careful about how you put the words; leave things unsaid and just try to guide them towards what you want them to think."

I smiled back at him but I'm certain my words conveyed my true feelings. "I'm well aware of *that* strategy, Mister Kemp," I said. "I've been using it to get myself out of challenging situations for many years."

* * * *

"I'm very happy with the article, Mister Kemp," I said. "I'm sure you were aware that I had some reservations when you first proposed the concept, but the journalist was very agreeable and treated me with the greatest respect." I smiled across the desk at the man in whose experience and methods I'd come to trust. "I never once made any admission to being either a woman or a man at any point in the

173

interview, - I only hinted that I'd been brought up in my early childhood as a girl, - but the journalist had already made up his mind in any case, that being the sole reason for his visit and his estimation of the public's interest in the article. He did attribute several sentences to me that I didn't quote, but that was for exciting compassion in his readers for my plight, and I can't blame him for using what he called, *'journalistic licence'* in my favour."

Sholto Kemp picked up the copy of the *Sydney Truth* newspaper and slipped on his reading glasses. "It's a pity the article only made page thirteen though; the *Sydney Sun* had the same story on page two," he said wryly.

The Sydney Truth 18th August 1929
'I CAN'T GO BACK TO MY SEX!'
'Truth' Discovers 'Man-woman' Who Fiercely defends Right to Masquerade
AUSTRALIA'S MOST ROMANTIC FIGURE

Consider, in this present century of emancipation and equal chance for the sexes: a girl donning youth's clothing at a young age, and now, at the age of 29, fiercely declaiming the right to sink her feminine identity forever in the battle to live and succeed!

Discovered by 'Truth,' this girl is not presented to Australia as a cockshy for derision and ridicule. The usual impersonator is, prima facie, a fraud, and often a coarse insult to the decencies, but the world will read this story with a generous impulse in favour of the lonely little figure whom it illustrates.

Is there any insult to convention in the masquerade of this Sydney resident who has given her vivid story to the world through 'Truth'? If there is, then the rebuffs of fate to a dauntless-minded child may be said to have squared the account with convention.

The tale brings to the city a breath of high adventure, as brave as it is appealing, but for the reason that excusable inquisitiveness would bring a host of spectators and annoying attention, the name of the young woman who lives at the moment as a man, and has lived in this way for so long, will not be given. Police Sergeant Roberts, of Parramatta station, could disclose it, only he most certainly won't, for the reason that the woman has thrown herself on the mercy of the law and the motive for the impersonation was transparently honest. It is no offence for a woman in our legal code to live as a man, though it is for a man to pose as a woman.

There will be many who read this on far-away stations and in lonely camps who, with a shock, may come to the realisation that an old-time workmate of theirs is the star of this astounding story. She has been farm labourer, railway navvy, cane-cutter, drover, orchard worker, cattle breeder, horse-breaker and wallaby shooter in Western Queensland. Through how many bleak, forgotten camps has she drifted with her secret?

Come with a 'Truth' representative who interviewed her as she toiled at the plough in a field near Eastwood last week.

Behind her team in grey flannel she walked, sleeved short, in tweed trousers; around her neck a silk handkerchief, blucher boots on. A small, rather slim figure, this. An intense, deep-tanned face, hands big and arms brown and muscular. Years of continuous outdoor toil have given this 'man-woman' finely developed shoulders. Her hair, close-cropped, is showing an occasional grey streak, buffets of the world on a young frame.

Listen to her nervous intensity, after the meeting:

'You must not photograph me! I have done nothing wrong, and nothing that I am ashamed of. If you photograph me you will reveal my sex to many of the people I have worked for and worked with and, besides, it will not do me any good when I seek a job in the future. I believe in giving a man a fair day's work for my money and I have never had a complaint from a boss as to my work. I can assure you, the way of a woman who has been brought up as a man and who cannot do women's work is not easy'

As you listen to her, sympathy with a clean battler for the decent things of life wins you over completely. There is nothing in this humble toiler of the earth to evoke derision, and as you go back and find from her the philosophies and accomplishments of the worker who has sacrificed her sex, and says never again will she take on the clothing of her kind, you gladly find approval to smother the first feeling of censure against her.

In Queensland, the far North-West, Northern Territory, Victoria, South Australia, N.S.W. and New Zealand she has worked her way, and, having mixed it with characters as crude as they were noble, as diverse as they were colourful, she emerged with her secret close-held. The girl speaks of her camp experiences with the relish of a sundowner remembering old courtesies on his weird pilgrimages. She has formed friendships which are based on something more than philandering in slender-pillared indoor gardens, and. because of her situation, she must be the most astonishing woman in Australia today from the point of view of experience. But never, so she told 'Truth,' has she smoked or drunk when the campfire circle drew in at night, and the husky fellows

175

with her must often have chivvied their chum on his rectitude in these matters.

Really, it was a strange concession to a forgotten birthright that this girl refused to go the limit most others in similar circumstances would have gone, but her abstinence in not smoking or drinking is a tribute to a clean, forthright character. She said that she has camped out for months on end without a tent, and has lived in the wilds of Western Queensland with no other whites within fifty miles.

She was born in the United States of America, she said and came to Melbourne with her parents at the age of seven. Her mother died shortly afterwards in somewhat mysterious circumstances, and her father took to drink and treated her brutally, so brutally, indeed, that she left him.

Consider this mite at that crisis in her baby life. No one would have wanted to employ a homeless child under the circumstances, where her very determined spirit would have been an argument against her. Pluck of that description is easily misunderstood by the average person, so into boy's clothes she got, and then she found it comparatively easy to secure a job in the kind of manual labour that is normally reserved for men.

Can you picture the strange misery of the child? Misgivings of a thousand disturbing varieties must have assailed her in those early days of her make-believe. Added to her mental troubles there were the physical discomforts of her arduous work. Did the thought of reverting to her own feminine ways ever recur to the girl? She will readily admit that it did often. But then, as she answers you, a spark of unusual intensity comes into her eyes and she speaks to the caller with an almost fierce rush of challenging question and answer.

'How could I? How could I? I could not do women's housework. I had lived with men mainly, and I could not cook much or look after a house. 1 had either to continue as a man or go on the streets as a woman! Why, any decent woman would have done as I did if she had to. I always went straight. I have done no harm to anyone, and have earned my own living, and earned it fairly!'

One of the accomplishments of this daring female is her ability on horseback. When working on stations in Queensland and western N.S.W. she was rarely out of the saddle except to sleep, and she learned to ride exceptionally well, so that one of her jobs on several stations was to break in young horses. It was her undoubted ability in this regard that earned her the title of 'The Jockey' on one station.

Finding work scarce in Queensland last summer she came overland on her pony to Sydney. She is particularly proud of her pony.

She bred him herself on her farm and has trained him to allow no one but herself to catch him or to ride him. He is a magnificent little animal, and very fast.

She worked on several orchards In Central Cumberland, in the Parramatta district, and one employer refused to pay her wages. She instituted court proceedings against this man and intends leaving for Queensland immediately the case is settled.

'What sort of a worker is your employee?' the journalist asked the pretender's current boss, who incidentally, has no idea that his employee is a female.

'He is the best worker I have had for years, a very reserved little chap, but he's worth two of the last man I had,' he declared.

That is the story of Sydney's 'man-woman' and the sadness and intensity that abounds in it rings true, and offers insult to no one. One hopes that the girl will be left to pursue her own destiny, queer to the verge of impossible though it seems at first sight. She is a character that could flame across the leaves of a best-seller, exuding philosophic quips gleaned from her remarkable pathway in life. But she prefers to remain unknown.

To the one or two who now know of her true personality, she is a living challenge to convention, which would probably in her childhood days have consigned her to an industrial school for girls had she never sacrificed. It were far better that a human being should revolt against the tyranny of convention and find expression for the will to succeed than submit humbly and forever despair of realising a legitimate ambition.

This girl on her pony rides down through the pages of romance and unfolding nationhood. Somehow she seems to typify the spirit of Australia, debonair, self-sufficient and challenging. To unmask her would seem a gratuitous insult to a brave battler. It brings a breath of high enterprise into the arid great city, the knowledge of that stripling, living, footing it with husky men, battling spiritedly to success.

"It turned out to be a wonderful idea of yours, Mister Kemp," I said as he laid the newspaper back on the top of the desk.

Kemp took off his reading glasses and proceeded to polish the lenses with a handkerchief he'd pulled from the lapel pocket of his jacket. "Ah yes, the story *has* been well handled by the press, Mister Smith; a well-executed effort I think, and it captured the ambience that I wanted to convey perfectly?" he said, his voice husky with restrained elation. "And your personal contribution to the accomplishment of the ploy was indeed significant; it was bravely conducted by you, considering the stress it must have put you under."

I shook my head. "There was no real stress involved in feeding them the story they wanted to hear without giving away my innermost feelings," I said, "after all, as I said to you last time we met, I've had to use that very same strategy to get myself out of awkward situations many times in my past life."

"I understand, Mister Smith, and perhaps the stress is all on my part," Kemp said. "There *is* always the chance that an honest client will bring a perfectly good case undone due to unwarranted personal feelings of being guilty of unconscionable conduct and I simply want you to continue to believe in my approach to this case so that we can remedy the injustice the Waters' have brought upon you."

I nodded. "I may have been guilty of misleading people for many years, Mister Kemp," I said, "but that was not a cunning performance I put on when I spoke to the reporter about my past life. It came sincerely from my heart."

Kemp nodded and smiled too. "I'm in no doubt about your sincerity, Mister Smith, and I believe we are ready for the hearing on 28th August, ten days from now. It will be heard in the Small Debts Court in front of Mister Flynn S.M. The Waters' have engaged the services of Mister Earnest D. Roper, instructed by H. R. Andrews and Company."

12 The Magistrate's Decision

With the introductions and preliminary business completed, the Stipendiary Magistrate, Walter Flynn, had taken a short break from the bench while he attended to some private matter and Sholto Kemp relaxed in his chair, looking across the polished wooden floor of the courtroom at his young, but formidable adversary, Ernest D. Roper.

Known as David, Roper was 29 years old, the same age as Kemp's client, William Smith, but from a vastly different background. He was a product of the University of Sydney, where he'd received many prizes for his mathematical abilities. His Bachelor of Arts degree included triple Honours: a Class I Honours in both Mathematics and Logic and Mental Philosophy and a Class II Honours in English, and in 1925 he'd achieved Class II Honours in his Bachelor of Laws degree. Later that year Roper was called to the New South Wales Bar and practised out of Chancery Chambers in Phillip Street, Sydney.

Roper sat deep in conversation with Matilda Waters, the defendant. Next to her was her husband, Thomas, who'd been the initial respondent until his bankruptcy plea had disqualified him from the proceedings. Sholto looked at the man with contempt. *'Thomas Waters is an unimposing man who's been in more trouble than Judas Iscariot at the Last Supper, over the previous few years,'* he thought grimly.

He turned his attention back to the file that lay in front of him, taking the opportunity to read the brief notes that he'd prepared.

William Smith v. Matilda Waters
to be heard before Mister Flynn, S.M.
at the Parramatta Police Court
on 28 August 1929 at 9.00 am.

William Smith alleges that Matilda Waters of Waterside Estates at Kenthurst refuses to pay his wages.

The said William Smith has instituted court proceedings claiming £39/13s/3d from Matilda Waters.

A cross-claim has been filed by Matilda Waters, in which £45/8s/6d has been claimed from William Smith for 126 meals supplied, thirty-one weeks of horse feed for agistment of Smith's horse, and other expenses incurred by her during Smith's tenure at Watersides Estates farm.

Terms of Employment

William Smith is suing under the Orchard and Vineyard Workers Award for work wages earned but withheld from March 10 to May 3, 1929. He commenced working for Matilda Waters at Kenthurst on November 10, 1928, and an arrangement was made between them whereby Waters was to pay £3/12s/6d a week, provide Smith's pony with feed, and allow Smith a dozen eggs weekly.

Smith worked for nine weeks at the agreed rate of pay and kept a record of the payments made. On January 12, 1929, when there was a drought that affected the operations of the estate, a new arrangement was entered into whereby Smith would receive £2/10s/-d a week until the drought ended.

From March 10, 1929, when the drought broke, it was arranged that Smith would be paid £4/4s/-d a week. Smith claims that he never received the four guineas at any time.

Cheque Returned

Smith states that he had applied on many occasions to Matilda Waters for payment and once was given a cheque drawn on the Bank of Australasia, Pitt-street, Sydney, for £10 by Matilda Waters' husband, Thomas Waters, who is the Manager of Waterside Estates.

The cheque bounced, and it was returned to Waters.

Smith states that Thomas Waters failed to keep appointments arranged between the two and that on one occasion a wait of two or three hours failed to see Waters arrive.

Kemp closed the file as the Magistrate returned to the bench and the hearing resumed. William Smith took the stand wearing a navy blue coat and waistcoat, and dark trousers with a light pencil stripe. The coat which, like the waistcoat, was unbuttoned, seemed too long for his small stature, drawing even more attention to his girlish appearance than his clean-cut features had already suggested, Kemp thought, but he smiled at him encouragingly and then turned to face the interested spectators in the gallery, many of whom were members of the press who sat poised on the edge of their seats with stubs of pencils hovering over their dog-eared notebooks.

"Mister Smith, I'd like you to tell the court about the 126 meals you are alleged to have been supplied with by Mrs Waters," Kemp said, still facing the gallery.

"The only meal provided for me was the last Christmas dinner. Apart from that I resided in a tent at the foot of Waters' property and prepared my own meals most of the time." Smith said. *'His voice, though not essentially a woman's, would probably be noticeable among a group of farm labourers,'* Kemp thought.

"*Most* of the time, Mister Smith?" he said. "Would you provide the court with further details about that, please?"

"Yes, I will sir," Smith said. "Matilda Waters sent meals down on a couple of occasions, but they were so cold and unappetising that they had to be thrown to the dog."

180

Kemp continued his line of questioning until he was sure that the Magistrate had heard enough of his client's testimony to understand that it was a reliable and honest account of the situation in which Smith had found himself. "No further questions, your Worship," he said.

Rising to cross-examine him, David Roper made no attempt to dispute the version of events that Smith had provided, and Kemp winced as he realised that the scenario he'd suspected would take place was about to unfold without any time-wasting procrastination.

"What's your name?" Roper asked.

Smith replied in a clear voice. "It's William Smith."

Roper persisted. "Is that your *real* name?"

Sholto Kemp shook his head in irritation. Smith didn't seem to be intimidated by Roper's stern tone at this stage, but he knew well his adversary's reputation for bulldog-like tenacity and he began to worry.

"That *is* my real name," Smith said.

Kemp interjected, addressing the Magistrate. "Has this anything to do with the case your Worship?"

Roper looked at Kemp and then at the Magistrate, who frowned, seemingly annoyed by Kemp's interruption.

"It may have a lot to do with it," Roper said stiffly.

Magistrate Flynn agreed. "If that is an objection, Mister Kemp, it is denied," he said.

Roper turned again to the plaintiff. "I ask you again. What's your *real* name?"

His client was still defiant, Kemp noted. "My real name is William Smith," he said again.

Roper then changed his approach. "In what name were you registered at the time of your birth?"

Smith began to appear a little flustered. "I don't know; my mother died when I was too young to question her about it. She called me Billie, so I was registered as William Smith, I suppose," he said in an irritable, but subdued tone of voice. He glanced at Kemp and his eyes seemed to say, *'I'm doing my best. Is it good enough?'*

Kemp smiled at him approvingly. *'I would never ask you to lie, Mister Smith, but there are ways to answer such questions without committing yourself if you are careful about how you put the words; leave things unsaid and just try to guide them towards what you want them to think.'*

Roper became more direct in his line of questioning. "Billy could be a boy's or a girl's name, Mister Smith. As a matter of fact, you were born a girl, were you not?"

Kemp rose to his feet again. "I object to that. These questions are being asked for the purpose of aggravating the witness. What has this got to do with the case?" he said, his voice rising.

The Magistrate was unimpressed by his outburst. "It has this to do with it, Mister Kemp," he said tersely. "The claim is made under an award. That award is for male persons. If the plaintiff is a woman, how can she claim under the male award?"

Kemp could see the futility of his argument, but he persisted doggedly. "The Waters' employed the plaintiff as a male, and agreed to pay the male wage. That should be considered to be a legally binding contract, your Worship."

The Magistrate hesitated for a moment as he deliberated Kemp's argument. "I *will* allow the questions to be asked," he said with an air of finality. "I too want to know the answer to the defending Counsel's question."

Roper smiled politely at Kemp and then continued his verbal assault on the plaintiff with renewed vigour. "You're a girl, are you not?"

Smith's demeanour had subtly changed during Roper's barrage of questions, from one of defiance to cautious justification. "I have suspected for a very short time past that I'm a *hermaphrodite*. As far as I know, that's possibly what I am," he said

Roper's eyes lit up at his confession. "Ah, I see, - you say you *think* you are a hermaphrodite, but you've been masquerading as a man. Please remind me what constitutes the term, - *hermaphrodite, Mister William Smith.*"

Kemp was worried. He could see that his client was faltering under the pressure of Roper's interrogation and it was not looking good for the outcome of the case. Smith looked stunned.

"Well it's, - a person who is, ah, - not quite a man and not quite a woman, I suppose," Smith said.

"You *suppose*?" Roper's tone was indignant. "You *suppose*, Mister Smith, - or should I address you as Miss Smith? Have you ever encountered any other *hermaphrodites* in your life, Mister Smith?"

Kemp again jumped to his feet. "This has nothing to do with the case, your Worship," he fumed. "The defendant's legal Counsel is determined to humiliate the plaintiff without getting to the point of the reason we are here."

The Magistrate disagreed, reiterating his previous decision on the matter. "Sit down Mister Kemp," he said irritably; "the defendant is entitled to know whether the plaintiff is a male or a female."

Kemp reluctantly sat down and Roper again addressed Smith, going completely on the offensive. "I put it to you that you have known all along that you're a woman and have sought to gain an unfair advantage by deceiving Mrs Waters."

Smith shook his head. "No," he said, his voice becoming more wavering. "I don't believe I'm a complete woman and I've never tried to gain an unfair advantage over anyone, - as far as I'm aware."

Roper changed tack again. "Did you not represent that you were a woman to reporters?"

Smith looked over at Kemp. "No, I didn't," he said cautiously.

Roper looked unconvinced. "But you did supply the *'Sydney Truth'* reporters with a lot of information about yourself that inferred you *knew* you were a woman?"

Smith shook his head again. "Only as an article of adventure; they wanted a story and I gave it to them."

Roper continued in the same vein. "Did you not supply the information to the reporters as to your sex?"

Smith was adamant. "No, I did not," he said. "They decided that for themselves."

"Is it not a fact that you are a woman?"

"No."

"Is it a fact that you are not a man?"

"I'm neither; that's why I said I *suppose* I'm a hermaphrodite."

David Roper looked over at Kemp and smiled, perhaps sensing that he'd gained the upper hand over him, at least in this part of the proceedings.

The questioning continued about the payment of certain money and Sholto Kemp looked around the press gallery. Some of the reporters were busily jotting down notes while others were gathering up briefcases. The interesting part of the hearing was over for them, - at least for today, and the rest of the day's minutes would occupy no more than a single statement in the next day's news.

His attention was brought back to the bench when Roper asked for a non-suit. "There is no proof," he said to Magistrate Flynn, "that the plaintiff comes within the terms of any award."

Kemp disagreed. "It's the *'Orchard and Vineyard Workers Award'* we're claiming under," he said tersely.

The Magistrate shook his head. "No Mister Kemp; if you are claiming under that award, you are claiming at the rate for *male* employees. You take a risk that way, Mister Kemp. If your client is indeed a woman then she can't claim under the male award. Are you certain that's the way you want to go?"

183

"My client has been working as a general farm and orchard hand," Kemp said. "He has done the ploughing and all the heavy work that a male worker would do. It is grossly unfair that counsel for Matilda Waters has brought my client's *apparent* gender into public attention in this instance; in fact, *that* seems to be the only basis for any plea of non-culpability in the matter of the non-payment of the wage that was agreed upon between them..."

David Roper cut in. "...It is not the *only* issue, your Worship," he said, "but it is an important one to consider since the *'Orchard and Vineyard Workers Award'* not only applies solely to *male* workers, but it applies only to certain irrigation areas, of which Watersides Estate is not included."

"Ah," the Magistrate said. "In that case, it could come down to the simple agreement between the two parties as to what wages were to be paid. I'm still concerned about how this would be viewed by the unions concerned since there is a shortage of jobs in the agricultural sector and the situation seems to be getting worse each day. I'm going to adjourn until I have secured some expert opinion about the ramifications of employing someone who *may* be a woman to do what has been traditionally considered a man's work."

He turned to Sholto Kemp. "In the meantime Mister Kemp, I think your client may have to seek medical advice to reach some conclusion on the associated question, - the question of your client's true gender. He, or she, as the case may be, seems to be confused as to exactly what a hermaphrodite is, - and I have to admit that I am too since I've had no prior knowledge of this kind of, ah, - occurrence in any past cases that I've presided over."

* * * *

"Well, you've made the front page of the *'Cumberland Argus and Fruit Growers Advocate'* anyway, Mister Smith," Sholto Kemp said.

Smith smiled at him across the desk. "I don't want any more publicity than *that*, Mister Kemp," he said. He picked up the newspaper and read the headline again.

IS WILLIAM SMITH A WOMAN?
STRANGE CASE OF CLAIM FOR WAGES
"Smith" Denies Disclosing Sex to Press
MAGISTRATE SUGGESTS EXPERT MEDICAL EVIDENCE

"Obviously they had no interest in the progress of your claim," Kemp said. "The thrill in the reporting is simply as to the question of whether you are a man or a woman."

Smith glanced at the text again. "Yes, you're right there, and I hope this will be over soon with no other adjournments after this one so that I can forget about it and get on with my life, Mister Kemp," he said.

Kemp looked at him in a kind-hearted way and his voice was full of sympathy. "It *will* be over soon," he said. "The next hearing is scheduled for September 11th so we've got almost two weeks to go over everything again. In the meantime, keep your chin up, Mister Smith; remember what you said to me when we first met? *'If my story is given to the world then so be it. I shall face it like a tough, honest, hard-working man of the bush.'* I think you'll find that the interest of the general public has waned now with the newspaper's focus firmly on the current financial situation in the world that's on everyone's lips."

* * * *

Early in 1929, the Australian National-Country Party coalition Federal Government made major expenditure cuts, causing a sudden and unexpected decline in project funding that led to considerable unemployment across the nation. It also proposed to cut award wages and dismantle the commonwealth Arbitration system as an emergency measure. The uproar over its industrial reform policies triggered widespread industrial unrest and in October the Federal Government was unseated by the Labor Party. The news of the crash of New York's Wall Street Stock Market on Black Thursday, October 24th and the pandemonium that followed in the five days after, had barely sunk in with ordinary people in Sydney's western suburbs when, after various delays, the case of William Smith v. Matilda Waters was reconvened on November 12th.

* * * *

'Cumberland Argus and Fruit Growers Advocate'
14th November 1929
WILLIAM SMITH IS A WOMAN
Claim for Wages as Farm Labourer
MEDICAL EVIDENCE OF MUSCULAR DEVELOPMENT
The man-woman case is over. William Smith is a woman. And her claim for wages as a farm labourer was successful.

185

*By the father of her present employer, Smith was described as a
competent worker who seems to understand every phase of farm work.*

*The husband of the woman Smith was suing admitted having
recently been committed for trial on two charges of false pretences.*

The counter-claim against Smith was unsuccessful.

*The man-woman case, which has been 'hanging fire' for some
time, was concluded at the Parramatta Small Debts Court yesterday.
William Smith claimed nine weeks' wages as a farm labourer from
Matilda Waters, of Kenthurst. In addition to the wages...*

Sholto Kemp looked at his client over the rims of his reading
glasses and grinned. It wasn't often he'd had as much satisfaction from
the outcome of a small claim as he'd had with this one. "Waters was a
bit too scheming for his own good in the end. He got on the wrong side
of the Magistrate right from the very start of the day's proceedings by
lying to him," he said, his grin broadening.

Smith smiled too, but with more restraint. "Yes, I'm happy with
the outcome; the Magistrate seemed fair-minded and explained the
reasons for his judgement very clearly," he said, "but I don't quite get
your point about Thomas Waters. *We* knew he was a liar, but how did
the Magistrate come to the same conclusion so quickly?"

"The protracted delay in resuming the hearing obviously didn't
suit his Defence Counsel, David Roper, who is much in demand on
other cases and Waters sought out the services of Mister John
Andrews," Kemp said. "John, whom I know quite well, knew of his
pending trial and was reluctant to represent either Waters or his wife,
Matilda, and by the time he'd spoken to me about the case over the
phone he'd already decided not to take it on." He tossed the copy of the
newspaper onto his desk. "Read the paragraph I've underlined," he
said.

Smith picked up the newspaper.

*...When the case was called yesterday Mister Waters asked the
Magistrate if he would allow it to stand over until two o'clock. He
explained that his solicitor, Mister Andrews, was engaged in another
Court. He agreed to pay the costs of the day if an adjournment until
some other day could be granted.*

*Mister Kemp, who appeared for Smith, intervened, telling the
Magistrate that Mister Andrews had told him over the phone that he
was not coming up, at all.*

*Waters then conceded that what Mister Kemp said was true.
'That's quite right. I've had to get another solicitor, who can't be here
before two o'clock,' he said.*

The Magistrate was unimpressed. 'I don't think your application is bona fide, Mister Waters,' he said quite bluntly 'You tried to deceive me. You told me that Mister Andrews would be here at two o'clock. I'll go on with the case without an adjournment.'

Waters said, 'In that case I'll have to consent to a judgment.'

The Magistrate wouldn't allow it: 'You can't consent,' he said. 'You're not the defendant.'

Mrs Waters was called in and she decided to go on with the case...

Smith looked up and frowned as he passed the copy of the *'Cumberland Argus and Fruit Growers Advocate'* back across the table. "That was an outright lie to the Magistrate about Mister Andrews being absent on another case, one of many lies Waters has told over the past few months. How could he possibly think he could get away with it?" he said.

"He was clutching at straws by then," Kemp said. "He'd lost control of the situation and didn't trust his wife to be clever enough to lie as capably as he believed *he* could. Yes, it was certainly the turning point of the case in our favour and he would have been much better off leaving the defence to his wife, Matilda and staying out of the limelight, considering his shady past was likely to be uncovered, but he was so arrogant he thought he could weasel his way out of any scrutiny of his past transgressions."

Smith shook his head. "He met more than his match in you, Mister Kemp."

Kemp picked up the newspaper again, suppressing his pleasure at the thought of how fittingly the case had played out. "Waters was so incensed by the Magistrate's decision to deny him his opportunity to speak that he got around it by getting his wife to call him as a witness," he said. "That was a big mistake. The newspaper report reflected his words.

...Mrs. Waters, who did not give evidence herself, called her husband as a witness.

Waters stated that he was acting as his wife's agent when he engaged Smith. 'She was to do general work in the orchard and on the farm. There was no provision about her keep,' he said.

Waters stated that Smith was paid her wages in full. 'Her horse was there for twenty-seven weeks,' he said, 'and it was fed the whole of that time. For three weeks she had two horses there, and for one week she had three horses. They all had to be hand-fed.'

Waters added that he made no contract in regard to Smith's meals...'

"The Magistrate didn't believe any of it," Kemp said. "He could see that Waters was struggling to remember his prepared statement, and when I asked him to provide written evidence he'd paid you, he produced a record book in which your signature appeared nine times, although the date in each case had been filled in by him."

"Yes that's right," Smith said a bit self-consciously. "I signed Waters' book nine times for nine weeks' wages when he asked me to do it because he said it was the usual practice in the industry and saved time in accounting. I signed first for £20/10s/- and then wrote my signature eight more times opposite a blank space. I was a bit too trusting there I suppose," he said, screwing up his nose, "but I had no idea what kind of a man I was dealing with in Thomas Waters."

Kemp nodded. "You *were* too trusting as you say, but it worked in your favour in the end." He continued reading aloud.

'...*Further cross-examined, Waters said that on one occasion he had given Smith a cheque for £10. In regard to the fact that the cheque was dishonoured when Smith presented it, he explained that it was a company cheque and that the secretary of the company, Mister Mavers, had neglected to sign it. That, he concluded, was the reason it was dishonoured...*'

"Another lie," Smith said, his face showing his exasperation. "It was a personal cheque and he told me that it must have been a mistake by the bank."

Kemp nodded. "When I questioned him about that he admitted that the credit balance of the Waterside Estates, Ltd., on which the cheque was drawn, was only 3/9d."

"So it was going to bounce anyway, whether or not it was a personal or company cheque," Smith said.

Kemp continued reading.

'...*Do you say that Smith is trying to put one over you; trying to claim wages that have already been paid?*'

Waters answered, 'Yes I do.'

'*If your story is true,' Mister Kemp said, 'you were paying the plaintiff money when he owed you money?*'

Waters replied, 'Yes, that's right.'

Mister Kemp's questioning continued. 'You're saying the plaintiff is dishonest?'

Waters replied, 'I should think so.'

Smith could hardly contain himself. "It's no wonder the Magistrate didn't believe he'd be paying me when he says I owed him money. Who would ever do that?"

"Yes, it's difficult to believe he'd try to put that one across," Kemp said. He shook his head and carried on from where he'd left off.

'...You've been in a fair amount of trouble yourself, haven't you, Mister Waters?'

Waters seemed uncomfortable by this turn of events. 'Yes, I've had some trouble,' he conceded.

Mister Kemp probed further. 'Two years ago you were convicted of obtaining £250 by means of false pretences from a man named Mobbs at Glenorie?'

Waters answered, 'Yes.'

Mister Kemp drove home his advantage. 'You were sentenced to six months, and the sentence was suspended. Isn't that true?'

Waters looked guilty. 'Not that I know of,' he said. 'I was released on bond to repay the money.'

Mister Kemp continued to press him. 'Your two sureties for the bond money at the time were a conveyancer named Ward and a solicitor named Phillips. Is that correct?'

Waters replied, 'Yes,' but this reporter sensed that his self-assurance and arrogance had all but disappeared. He was certainly a different man to the one who'd entered the courtroom with a swagger that morning.

Mister Kemp must have sensed that too. 'And at the time of your examination in bankruptcy, both your sureties were in gaol?' he said.

Waters was becoming rattled. 'Yes, that's true' he said, but his gaze was directed downwards towards the floor of the dock and his reply was muffled.

Mister Kemp wasn't finished. 'Weren't you committed for trial a couple of days ago on two more charges of false pretences?'

Waters raised his head momentarily and looked Mister Kemp in the eye, perhaps thinking for a moment that he'd be able to gain a reprieve from his worsening predicament. 'Yes, but I have a complete answer to that,' he said.

Mister Kemp ignored his attempt to justify his rebuttal of the new charges brought against him; 'Hasn't this man Mavers, the secretary of your company, also been committed for trial on the same charges?' he said.

Waters again became subdued. 'Yes,' he said in what this reporter recognised to be a rather timid tone of capitulation.

Mister Kemp changed tack again. 'You had no fault to find with the plaintiff's work, Mister Waters, did you?'

Waters shook his head. 'No; I never saw much of it,' he said. 'My wife oversaw the work he, - she did.'

Mister Kemp continued in the same vein. 'But you rang up my office and said, and I quote; 'She's a woman; she's a woman', didn't you?'

Waters raised his head again in what this reporter took to be a momentary spark of defiance; 'I didn't know she was a woman. I thought it was justification for my argument against paying her a man's wage...'

Mr Kemp smiled scornfully at the defendant in what this reporter identified as a sign of his contempt for the man and then he turned and addressed the Magistrate, Mister Flynn. 'I put it to you that the figures in Waters' book were a wicked forgery. He is a bankrupt, an inveterate swindler, and now has been committed for trial for false pretences; is there anything he hasn't done in the way of dishonesty? I further put it to your Worship that the Waters' are guilty of not paying the wages agreed to between them and the plaintiff and as specified previously in the plaintiff's submission to the court.'

Smith smiled, but his face still showed tension. "You certainly summed it up very well, Mister Kemp," he said, "and the Judge agreed with your appraisal..."

"...As I've said before, Mister Smith, Stipendiary Magistrates are *not* Judges; they're voluntary Court officials who reflect the will of the people on the delivery of justice over minor disputes between two parties," Kemp said. "They don't have to be satisfied beyond *all* reasonable doubt, as they would have to be in a criminal case. Mister Flynn actually said that in his summing up of his decision."

'On the whole, I am satisfied that Smith worked for the period she states. Considering all the facts, I am reasonably satisfied, - not satisfied beyond all reasonable doubt, as I would have to be in a criminal case, - that the plaintiff has established her claim, and I give a verdict for the amount claimed, £31/11s/3d with £1/5s/3d costs.'

Sholto Kemp stopped reading and placed the newspaper on the desk. He looked at his client thoughtfully before he spoke again. "Well then, Mister Smith, that concludes our professional contract," he said. "You've been awarded costs, so there's no need for you to worry about that; my secretary will take care of it. If there is anything further I can do for you please don't hesitate to contact me. In the meantime, it has been a pleasure to work for you on your claim and I wish you every success in the future."

Smith smiled, but he looked weary, Kemp thought. The whole business had obviously been a little too much for him and he would no doubt be happy that it was over. Kemp shook hands with his client across the table and then Smith made to get up, but there was still something left unsaid and he sat down again quickly. "Now that our professional contract is over, I'd like to thank you for the compassionate way in which you've handled what must have been a strange set of circumstances for you to come to terms with. I suppose you haven't come across anyone quite like me before," he said.

"That much is true," Kemp said. "Mister...," he hesitated, "would you mind if I call you by your first name?"

"I'd like that Mister Kemp. My name is *Wilhelmina.*" Smith pronounced the name with such passion that Kemp was visibly moved.

"It's a beautiful name, Wilhelmina," he said, his voice husky. "You must call me Sholto and yes, I must admit that I haven't come across anyone quite like you before in either my professional or personal life, but that doesn't mean that I would treat you with any less respect or esteem than I would any other person. We are all equal in the eyes of the Lord, you know." He frowned. "I must say, however, that I have been a little perplexed by your demeanour since the resolution of your claim. You haven't reacted to your momentous win in the way that I would have expected of someone who has reclaimed the equivalent of several months' wages at the adult men's award rate."

"Oh, I can assure you that I am very happy with the outcome of my claim," Wilhelmina said, "but it is the *other* revelation that has been a bit of a shock to me."

"The result of the medical examination?"

"Yes Sholto, - the doctors' diagnosis has been a little overwhelming to digest, to say the least."

Kemp clasped his hands under his chin. "I understand, Wilhelmina," he said, "but your willingness to undergo the medical examination helped your case immensely."

"It was difficult for me to submit to such a thorough and intimate physical inspection and the questions asked of me were just as challenging to answer," Wilhelmina said, "but both Doctor Waugh and his associate, Professor Windayer, were very professional and I understood that the questioning was necessary to determine not just my physical state, but my mental state too. To be perfectly honest, - I was just as interested in finding out the truth of the matter as the Magistrate was."

The first Witness was Doctor Waugh. He said that he had examined Smith and found her physically to be of the female sex. 'On questioning her,' the doctor said, 'I found that she did not function as a woman. Her muscular development is such that she was able to carry out the laborious duties of a man as well as a man could. Professor

Windayer also examined Smith at my request, and he has passed a similar opinion as to sex and also as to Smith's ability to perform the duties of a man.'

The Magistrate; 'Would you say that her muscular development was as great as in a man of similar age and weight?'

Dr Waugh; 'I should say so, on account of her having already done those duties.'

The Magistrate; 'Would muscular work of that character prevent the organs of the female from functioning?'

Dr Waugh; 'It would tend to do so.'

The Magistrate; 'You won't say it would do so absolutely?'

Dr Waugh; 'No, I couldn't say absolutely.'

The Magistrate; 'There is no doubt whatever about her sex?'

Dr Waugh; 'No, none at all.'

The Magistrate; 'It is not correct that she is a hermaphrodite?'

Dr Waugh; 'No, although she had the impression that she was. Professor Windayer suggested that she could possibly be considered to be, what has been termed, a Pseudo-hermaphrodite.'

The Magistrate; 'Thank you, Doctor Waugh. If you state that she didn't know she was a woman then I don't think we need to pursue this any further.'

"A possible Pseudo-hermaphrodite?" Wilhelmina said. "Who would have thought there was even a term for such a condition as mine?"

Kemp agreed. "I've never heard that term used before either, but medicine is not my field and I'm sure Professor Windayer knows what he's talking about."

Wilhelmina frowned. "I *still* don't fully understand what it means, but I do know now that there are many people who have been born with the same condition and I'm not some kind of an oddity who should be ashamed of my body." She looked away and sighed as her mother's words came flooding back into her mind.

'Perhaps Billie will never be a real woman. I can't put my finger on it, but something's not quite right with that child.'

She turned back to the solicitor and smiled sadly. "The doctors agreed that I would never be able to conceive a child, because of my *'unusual'* female internal organs, but that doesn't matter to me anyway."

"Then why are you looking so depressed? I've told you about 'Jockey Jack' and his alter-ego, May McDonald. She is still happily settled down in Albury doing what *she* loves best, breaking in, training and riding racehorses. Why can't *you* do the same?"

Wilhelmina shook her head. "I'm a different type of person to what you have described May McDonald as being, Sholto. I admire her courage in taking on the constabulary and anyone else who gets in the way of her ambitions, but I don't think I'd be capable of being so resolute in the face of all the public attention *she* receives." She smiled again, but the sadness remained in her eyes. "I told you that when this was over I'd like to go back to Queensland and try to put a new life together, maybe doing the same as May McDonald, training and riding horses, which is my passion too, but as you know, I can't legally do that as a woman, - if I'm to accept that the doctors are correct in their diagnosis and that's what I am."

"No, as we agreed before, theoretically it's banned," Kemp said, "and if you're not willing to fight the system as May McDonald has done, then you have little choice but to find another means of making a living as a woman, perhaps as a domestic servant or something like that."

Wilhelmina Smith stared at him for a moment as she gathered her thoughts and then she straightened her shoulders and shook her head in a gesture of defiance. "As I told you once before, Sholto, I may have been guilty of misleading people for many years, but that was not a cunning performance I put on when I spoke to the reporter from the '*Sydney Truth*' about my past life. It came sincerely from my heart and I simply can't go back to doing domestic or other types of work that females traditionally are supposed to do. I *will* find a place far, far away from here, where people will surely not have heard of me or read about this legal action and will accept me on face value for the contribution I can make to their horse racing and training business without poring over and analysing my personal life."

Sholto Kemp pushed his chair back, stood up and held out his hand. "I wish you the very best of luck in whatever you decide to do, Wilhelmina and I sincerely hope you have a happy and prosperous life ahead."

Wilhelmina took his hand and smiled. "Thank you for being so kind, Sholto," she said. "Perhaps you are the last person in my life who will ever have known me as a woman and I can assure you that if it is necessary for my happiness and prosperity I will continue to live under false pretences for the rest of my life."

* * * *

Wilhelmina Smith left the Parramatta District in New South Wales shortly after she received the proceeds of her successful court action in December 1929. It was the beginning of the Great Depression and many people, both men and women, had taken to the roads across Australia seeking any kind of work in their efforts to simply survive. Wilhelmina would not have looked out of place alongside her fellow travellers; in fact, she was better prepared for the rigours of the bush tracks than many of her companions, some of whom were failed financial planners who had lost their own money and that of their clients in the recent crash of the Stock Market. In her Bill Smith alias, she drifted west, found work on some of the wheat farms in the New South Wales hinterland where she'd worked previously, and eventually crossed the border once more into Queensland and worked on cattle stations west of the Darling Downs. She travelled further north through Cunnamulla and Charleville and into the Channel Country she knew so well, a wilderness that was far outside the limit of the inquisitive Sydney newspaper journalists and their scandal-hungry readership. Little did she know that the worldwide financial collapse had taken such a toll on the national consciousness that her own small financial courtroom win and the consequent exposure to public scrutiny of her personal issues had already been consigned to the very bottom drawer of the newspaper archives.

Conclusion

As I said at the beginning of this story, - …around the same time that I, Mary Jane McConnell, squawked my way into the light of day, Wilhelmina Smith slid unobtrusively into Cairns. She arrived with several packhorses, a pony that she rode and very little else. Wilhelmina fitted the category of the post-depression drifter perfectly. Nobody knew or cared where she came from. She was a slight, but tough-looking little individual with a thin, sun-bronzed face that peeped out at the world from underneath a much weathered wide-brimmed felt hat… and so that almost finalises my account of the tragic and often misunderstood life of Wilhelmina 'Bill' Smith.

I am proud of my nursing colleagues at the Herberton hospital; they were wonderful to Wilhelmina. Every nurse had found out almost immediately that the person who'd been admitted as 'Bill Smith' was a *female*, or so it appeared, but it wasn't discussed amongst us or with the domestic staff at any time. We were all professionals and Herberton wasn't a big town, so we knew word would have got around pretty quickly if anyone had breached our rule of the inviolability of the privacy of our patients. They didn't.

Smith was, and still is the most common English language surname and Wilhelmina was also a popular female first name at the turn of the twentieth century, possibly due to the worldwide popularity of the young Queen Wilhelmina of the Netherlands, who'd acceded to the Dutch throne in 1890 at ten years of age.

The failure to find any relatives and the lack of a birth certificate led to many theories about *our* Wilhelmina's origins. Some people formed the belief that she was born in Western Australia and was brought up in an orphanage in Perth. Others thought she'd been born in a Sydney hospital in 1886. That particular theory would have placed her in her late sixties or early seventies when she was still riding in horse races, a feat that was not impossible, but highly unlikely. It was what the hospital administrators accepted, however, and remains on her record, as far as I know, to this day. You might ask why I didn't set the record straight about Wilhelmina's origins at the time when these theories were doing the rounds, but the fact is I hadn't opened the box of newspaper clippings and her handwritten notes at that stage. I knew of course from our discussions that she'd been born around the turn of the twentieth century, but that wouldn't have been enough to persuade the hospital administrators that their notions were incorrect and I felt it was better left alone.

The terms Hermaphrodite and Pseudo-hermaphrodite are not used now and are considered either misleading or offensive to some people. The term Intersex, which was first coined as far back as 1923, is currently used, but even that has its limitations in describing the multitude of diverse combinations of physical variances that exist amongst people with this condition. I'd like to tell you about an interesting booklet that is available from the National Library of Australia. It focusses on a subject called;

Complete Androgen Insensitivity Syndrome (CAIS)
Published by the Department of Endocrinology and Diabetes
Royal Children's Hospital, Flemington Road
Parkville, Victoria 3052, Australia
© Garry L. Warne 1997
Sponsored by the National Library of Australia
ISBN 0 9587416 1 1

The foreword to this enlightening document tells us;

Some medical conditions are easy to talk about and some are more challenging. A condition like Androgen Insensitivity Syndrome (AIS), which affects the development of the genital and reproductive system, raises some very uncomfortable issues about gender identity that are difficult to put into words. How is it that a woman can be born without a womb and with testes? For generations, women with AIS, and their parents, have struggled to understand this apparent contradiction. Many would have had no idea that there were others with the same condition unless the condition had been 'in the family'. Even then, discussion about a subject relating to genital development and sexual feelings may have been taboo.

We are now in an age when sexual matters are openly discussed in the media. This freedom is presenting opportunities for the community at large to be given some information about the existence and nature of AIS. The community will become more understanding and accepting of unusual medical conditions when they are better informed about them and the problems they cause. The same applies to women with AIS. It is a difficult condition to accept, but women will be helped if they have access to both good information about it and adequate opportunities to discuss the complex feelings that are bound to arise as this information is being absorbed.

This book has been prepared to provide women with AIS, and their families, with accurate medical information about this condition and guidance on how to find help.

I don't know whether Wilhelmina (Bill) Smith was afflicted with CAIS or not. I suspect she'd eventually formed her own impression that

196

the 'expert' doctors who'd diagnosed her as a Pseudo-hermaphrodite in 1929 were speculating. They were baffled by her condition and were being pressed for an answer by the Magistrate, - an answer that simply wasn't available to them at that time.

Professor Windayer suggested that she could possibly be considered to be, what has been termed, a Pseudo-hermaphrodite.

Whatever the case may be, Wilhelmina sought to gain nothing from her decision to hide the true nature of her femininity except the equality in living and working conditions that don't exist even now, half a century on from her death, and anyone who still holds the view that she purposely lived her life under false pretences to gain an unfair advantage over the men she worked alongside, or to gain notoriety by emulating the romantic and shameless frauds of *'Captain Barker'*, the woman in England who *'married'* another woman, must be possessed of a hard and cold heart indeed.

Any such idea that hers was an undemanding and effortless path to follow will be immediately rebuffed if a moment is taken to reflect on what Wilhelmina would have had to endure in her life to live as a man. She would have surely had a daily battle with innuendo, suspicion and mockery, - and that doesn't even come close to the conflict she would have had to endure in her mind. The practical and sanitary needs of a woman living amongst men would have been a continual stress on her too, although perhaps she would not have had the additional strain of having a monthly cycle to consider. She was still able to rise above all of the demands that weighed upon her and today should be rightly regarded as one of Australia's great pioneering women, but Wilhelmina was no 'rebel with a cause' and even if she didn't have CAIS; she was still a victim of circumstances largely beyond her control.

In 2005, both Australian and overseas contributors raised money to place an appropriate memorial on her unmarked grave at the Herberton Cemetery in Queensland. The Herberton Lions Club Inc. coordinated the erection of a fitting tribute to this remarkable woman with a splendid headstone for her final resting place in the Herberton cemetery where she is now interred under the name of Wilhelmina "Bill" Smith.

Wilhelmina, rest in peace.
Mary Jane McConnell

Other books by Laurence Joseph Murphy

Annie Bags
The Lady in Rags

ISBN 978-0-9923046-1-4

Annie Bags; The Lady in Rags is also available as an Ebook
ISBN 978-0-9923046-0-7

Annie Ferdinand was born into a noble family in Prussia in 1851. Her mother died when she was very young, a loss that affected both her and her father significantly. She travelled to London, England with him and there, met and fell in love with a well-bred Englishman, but her happiness was short-lived, for he vanished suddenly from her life. She set out to find him, knowing that her very existence depended upon looking into his eyes and seeing his love for her reflected in them. This is the story of her search, its awful conclusion and the reason for her becoming known around the Northern Queensland goldfields of Australia as the legendary *Annie Bags*.

Ghost Warrior
Jimmy Morrill

ISBN 978-0-9923046-2-1

Ghost Warrior, - Jimmy Morrill
is also available as an Ebook.
ISBN 978-0-9923046-3-8

The barque Peruvian was lost in a gale off the east coast of Australia in February 1846. When it was found wrecked on the Great Barrier Reef several months later there was evidence that some of the passengers and crew may have constructed a raft and abandoned ship. Nothing further was heard, however, and it was assumed all on board had perished.

A shipping agent based in Sydney in the Colony of New South Wales, Clem Ross, had contracted a young sailor James Murrells, (also known as Jimmy Morrill) for the voyage, and he became obsessed with the possibility that Jimmy and perhaps others may have survived. Seventeen years later a man claiming to be a sailor from the Peruvian made contact with shepherds at an outstation on the Burdekin River near Cleveland Bay in North Queensland telling the astonished men that he had been living with an Australian Aboriginal tribe. The man was Jimmy Morrill and this is his story.

The Sound of Liberty

ISBN 978-0-9923046-5-2

The Sound of Liberty
is also available as an Ebook.

Felix Reitano arrived in Sydney, Australia from Naples, Italy in 1896 as a young teenager. He quickly learned to speak English after a chance meeting with an equally young aristocrat from England. Felix travelled to Queensland, first to the sugar cane town of Mossman and then to Halifax, a small cane farming settlement about 100km north of Townsville. In Halifax, he met and fell in love with a Scottish lass, Sarah Livingstone.

Sarah's journey to Australia at the age of nineteen, having grown up in a small poverty-stricken village in Scotland with limited knowledge to prepare her for what lay ahead, was also truly remarkable and was only matched in true pioneering spirit by the man she married.

Felix and Sarah's story would have been similar to that of many pioneering families and therefore tremendously admirable, but not independently productive in the retelling. What set them apart, however, was their unusual (at that time) inter-racial marriage and the unique complications they were confronted with due to the rise of Mussolini's Fascism and the effects of Italy's entry into the Second World War on the side of the Axis powers.

www.ingramcontent.com/pod-product-compliance
Lightning Source LLC
Chambersburg PA
CBHW070300120726
47910CB00007B/2320